# Tiger Found
## *A Jack and Ginger Mystery*

## STEVEN GALE

iUniverse, Inc.
New York Bloomington

# Tiger Found

## A Jack and Ginger Mystery

*This is a work of fiction. All of the characters, names, incidents, organizations, and dialogue in this novel are either the products of the author's imagination or are used fictitiously.*

*iUniverse books may be ordered through booksellers or by contacting:*

*iUniverse*
*1663 Liberty Drive*
*Bloomington, IN 47403*
*www.iuniverse.com*
*1-800-Authors (1-800-288-4677)*

*ISBN: 978-1-4401-0617-0 (pbk)*
*ISBN: 978-1-4401-0619-4 (cloth)*
*ISBN: 978-1-4401-0618-7 (ebk)*

*Library of Congress Control Number: 2008941182*

*Printed in the United States of America*

*iUniverse rev. date: 11/20/2008*

# ACKNOWLEDGEMENTS

We are indebted to a number of people who helped us with the writing of *Tiger Found* as it grew and evolved as a novel. We would like to thank: Karen Frank, Anna McAlistair, Mike Jones, and especially Ron Star for their helpful legal research into various of the more subtle aspects of our story; Charles O'Reilly for introducing us to the mystery genre where characterization dominates plot as the primary driver and for continuously sending us supportive evidence to urge us on; Kristoff Kohlhagen for so graciously sharing his inner knowledge of Charleston with us; Cris Dovich and David Tufts for their insights into South Beach, Miami and to Cris for letting us in on the world of hotel concierges; and Charles Cornwall, Lynn Gibson, and especially Jennifer Fisher for their important editorial suggestions that contributed greatly to the narrative flow of our story. And a special thanks to Jason Houston for bringing both Doctore Majorana and his fictional nephew Franco's dialect to life both for Cy and for our readers. And a great thanks is due Stephanie Rinehart Poteet for her tireless work on our behalf: reading, typing, copying, and mailing manuscripts, and for her enthusiasm about our novel.

We owe a special gratitude to fellow William and Mary alumni Mary Beth Bracken and Clyde Culp who so enthusiastically donated not only very gracious sums to The College of William and Mary Alumni Society, but also their names to two of the characters in the following story.

We dedicate this book to our parents
and their grandchildren.

# *PROLOGUE*

## *August 26, 1965*

### Milwaukee, Wisconsin

Either that shadow's following me or the beers are playing tricks on my mind. He laughed to himself. Not much light on the deserted street. The cars driving out of town from the game had dwindled down to a sporadic two or three at a time. And the lights from the parking garage and the stadium itself had long been dimmed. Only the lights from the tavern created any shadows on the deserted street.

Then he remembered the watchful stranger in the corner of the tavern. Brooding over his one drink. Never quite staring at him, but seemingly always watching him out of the corner of his eye. He had looked vaguely familiar. Couldn't place him, but sure he'd seen him somewhere before. He felt a chill despite the humid August night.

No! There, something moved again! Between the two houses across the dark street. He reached out to a post to steady himself. Slipped his hand into his pocket to feel the comfort of the knife blade. Think. Only three minutes to catch the last bus home. Forget it. It's just the beer. He stepped forward. "Damn," he involuntarily cursed out loud, "I left the kid's souvenir from the game on the bar."

He stopped, turned back to the warm glow of Al's Tavern. No more sign of the shadow as he reversed direction. It had been the beer, after all.

As he reentered the bar, Al looked up, grinned. "Just can't stay away? Don't you think the beers at the game and the two here with your brauts were enough?"

"Fuck you, Al. I left the kid's stuff on the bar and I've barely got time to catch the last bus."

"Shit," Al responded. "I thought just this once you'd got something for me!" He winked at Robby at the other end of the bar.

"Sure, Al. In your dreams. By the way, what happened to the dark guy in the corner?"

"No idea," Al said. "Never saw him before. Finished his drink and left just before you did."

"OK if I go out the back door?"

"Sure. See ya again Thursday night?"

He waved a yes as he stepped out back into the alley. He immediately had second thoughts. The double-row towers of stadium lights three blocks away were now completely dark. In the murkiness of the deserted alley, crates and boxes loomed above him. Shadows no longer posed a problem---there were none. His only thought was catching the bus.

He took four quick steps, stumbled, and stopped dead. Something moved. Behind him. It was no shadow. He reached for his knife, and, in his haste, dropped the package. Groping for the bag, he saw a figure silhouetted against the street light above the buildings behind the tavern. Advancing toward him. Even through the beer, the bus and the kid's dropped bag faded in importance. He ran through the alley toward the lights of the street ahead.

He cut the distance in half as footsteps pounded behind him. Fifty yards ahead he heard the bus coming. He pulled the knife from his pocket as he angled toward the street center. Suddenly he tripped and sprawled face down. He felt himself jerked to his feet. Strong hands gripped his shoulder from behind. And then......nothing.

# Chapter 1

## December 20, 2007

### Berkeley, California

Leafing through the mail in her office in the Physics Department on the Cal campus, Professor Mary Beth Bracken was startled to see an envelope from Cy Fapp postmarked two days earlier in Charleston. Her trembling fingers clumsily tore it open. A folded note dropped to the floor as she hurriedly started reading the letter.

> *November 26, 2007*
>
> *My dear Mary Beth,*
>
> *If you are reading this letter, then much of what we have discussed over the past weeks has been very helpful. More importantly, I now know your skepticism to have been unwarranted. And, of course, it shows once and for all that you were always right. We are---or now, more correctly, were---in the same profession all along! Less importantly, you will never see me again.........but let me explain...*

1

After reading the entire letter through for the second time, she picked up the note that had fallen to the floor and read it. She stared out the window overlooking the campus, her eye naturally going to the clock on the face of the Campanile. Finally, she picked up the phone and called Cy's old number. Cy's partner Jack answered on the third ring.

"Hello, Fapp's Private Detective Agency."

"Jack, are you and Ginger both there? This is Mary Beth Bracken. In Berkeley."

"Yes. Hi Mary Beth, this is Ginger. We have you on speaker here in the office. What's up?"

"I don't quite know how to tell you this, but I've just heard from your boss."

"Cy? You heard from Cy? Where is he? Is he OK?"

"Sort of. You guys say he disappeared on November 27th, right?"

"That's right."

"Well he wrote me a letter the night before that, explaining where he was going and how." She looked down at the postmark. "It was mailed from Charleston a month later...two days ago in fact, and I just got it here today."

"Where is he?" Jack and Ginger asked simultaneously.

"Well it seems that the suspicions he had been subtly sharing with me over his last month may have been right. It seems that either you guys have the most sophisticated, clever serial killer in history out there in South Carolina, or, against all rational logic, Cy's investigations into parallel universes and the disappearance of a well known Italian physicist in 1938 have paid off in unimagined dividends."

Ginger glanced at Jack and wondered out loud, "And to think, this all started out so innocuously, with Bailey Lee bursting in on Cy and me that Friday morning.Could that *really* have been only two months ago?"

Jack leaned back. "And it was only five weeks before that we started looking for Cindy Boisseau. Who could have known."

# Chapter 2

**Charleston, South Carolina: Two months earlier**

It was impossible for Bailey Lee Ellis to enter a room without her very presence demanding complete and immediate attention from everyone. Cy saw Ginger's eyebrows shoot up. "Nice outfit, Bailey Lee," he commented.

As Bailey Lee swooped down once to air kiss his cheek, her voice faltered. "Now now, Cy. There's no time for our usual taunts. Carter is missing. I need your help."

Ginger rose and held out her hand. "Bailey Lee, we haven't met. I'm Ginger Grayson, Cy's newest partner. Have a seat. I'm sure Cy's about to offer you some sweet tea or coffee. What can we get you?"

Cy shot Ginger a withering look and reluctantly pushed a donut through the clutter on his desk toward Bailey Lee. "I knew it had to be something urgent to get us out here during your lunch hour with no notice. So, when did you last see Carter?"

Surveying the room with obvious distaste, she turned smiling to Ginger, barely hiding her skepticism that the pretty young woman with the long blonde hair standing before her

4

could possibly be a private eye. To Bailey Lee's trained eye, Ginger was the kind of young woman to be careful with--- clearly not from Charleston, but dressed nicely to accent her medium build and attractive features. She was tall, maybe 5'8," probably around 30. And clearly bright. Her brown eyes boring into Bailey Lee's gave the impression of never missing a single detail. "You stay right where you are, darling. This old leather couch is good enough for me. I've already had croissants and tea at Charleston Place." She settled in, enveloping herself in her vivid indigo shawl, as if to protect herself from Cy's environment. Her silver gray hair coiled elaborately atop her head helped to elongate her rather round face. Her Grecian nose and strong chin made her look, despite the gray hair, at least a decade less than her 60-plus years. And she knew it.

"So," Bailey Lee observed, "this is where Cy Fapp, the famous Charleston sleuth, works his missing person magic. I must say I expected something a bit more...well, a bit more *grand.*"

She looked around again. She'd known Cy since he was a young boy and knew better than to let his general appearance, sloppy dress, unkempt graying brown hair under his old worn out baseball cap, and ill manners unsettle her. Let alone mislead her about his abilities. Many a Charlestonian had learned the hard way not to underestimate Cy. He might be a pain to deal with, but he was sharp, focused, tough, and relentless.

"It's hardly magic," Cy retorted grumpily, his characteristically wrinkled long sleeved shirt matching his disheveled hair. "More like fact finding. And I'd say, in that regard, we're off to a very slow start this morning."

"Sorry," Bailey Lee replied, clearly feeling unfairly reprimanded. "The simple fact is, Carter's gone and I don't know where."

"When did you last see her?" Cy asked.

"Dinner last night."

"Where?"

"In the dining room."

"At your home?"

"Of course."

"What did she do after dinner?"

"The usual for her Thursday nights. She left to give her ghost tour. I must say I think it's a silly waste of her time. But she enjoys it."

"What time did she leave?" Cy asked, clearly exasperated at Bailey Lee's inability to stay on the subject.

"8:30."

"When did she come home?"

"She didn't."

"How do you know she didn't?" Cy asked, now visibly annoyed.

"She didn't call me or come kiss me goodnight before going over to the carriage house."

"When does she usually come home?"

"She's usually home by midnight."

"Has she always come home before?"

"Not always, but when she doesn't, she always, always calls to say she won't be home."

"Always?"

"Always," Bailey answered. "And Cy, I'm her mother. You've known us both since she was a little girl and I just know something's wrong. Something's very wrong."

"What'd the police tell you?"

"I talked to Dan. He said the Missing Persons people aren't convinced there's been any foul play. But they want me to call if I hear anything at all. He was so officious. And after all I've done for him and his brother! He's *your* former partner. Can't you talk to him?"

"Bailey Lee," Ginger interrupted. "Was Carter unhappy about anything last night? Did she seem distracted? Upset about anything?"

"Oh, Ginger," Bailey Lee said. "Sorry. You obviously didn't know my little girl. She's always happy. She's never been unhappy. Last night she was as bubbly as ever. If there was anything different, it was that she seemed in a hurry to get off to her tour."

"Bailey Lee," Cy interjected. "You said Ginger '*didn't*' rather than '*doesn't*' know Carter. Do you have reason to believe Carter is dead?"

"Dead?" Bailey Lee almost screamed. "No! *No!* I just know there's something very wrong. There's no way Carter just didn't come home. Cy, please help me."

Before the air even stopped swirling around Bailey Lee's departure, Ginger looked in amusement from her spot on the couch up at Cy who was still sitting behind his desk. His frumpy appearance and slumped posture did not disguise how much larger he was than his junior partner.

"Boy, how many more like her do you have around?" she asked.

"Plenty," Cy said, lighting up a cigarette in obvious relief. "I thought three years investigating in Charleston and you'd be used to 'em by now."

"I obviously don't run in her circles," Ginger laughed while looking out the window. "And in Virginia they're a touch more subtle."

"Well," Cy said, blowing out a long, satisfying plume of smoke, "Keep learning---it's part of your job."

Ginger, trying unsuccessfully to hide her distaste at Cy's smoke, asked, "Were you serious about taking on this case?"

"Deadly."

"Well, she's certainly not my picture of the distraught mother," Ginger said. "Looks like she just stepped out of the salon. Every hair sprayed into place. And her make-up, my God, she even took time to curl her eyelashes and tone her blush to match that designer outfit. Glad she didn't accept my offer of tea---she'd have expected crust-less chicken salad sandwiches with it. I doubt she could bear up under the wrong mayonnaise."

"Feel better?" Cy said.

"My point is she seems more like a tight-assed Charleston matron looking for attention than a mother distraught over her daughter's disappearance."

"I've known Bailey Lee and Carter Ellis for thirty-five years. Ever since Carter was a little baby. Bailey Lee doesn't seek attention. She attracts it. She's always been disdainful of my line of work. I've never seen her like this...something's happened. She wouldn't normally be caught dead in my office."

"OK," Ginger said. "OK, start with what you know. Is there a current boyfriend? Girlfriend? A recently jilted lover? Where's the father? Which ghost tour does she work for? Who is her boss? Where was Robert E. Lee's ghost last night?"

"Very funny!" Cy snapped at her. "When's Jack due? He was going to give us the post mortem on the Pinckney and Williams cases. I'd rather get it all done at once when he's here."

"Jack left me a message that he had to run an errand. He can't get here 'till late this afternoon. But I have a couple of questions in the meantime. How do you know the Ellises?" Ginger asked.

"Dammit. This'd be better with the three of us."

Getting no reaction from his partner, Cy shrugged and went on. "Bailey Lee and my mom were close friends. They met at Garden Club teas---since you mention it---and then worked for years harassing homeowners and preserving Charleston from their perches on the Historical Society."

"And the lovely Carter?"

"When I headed out to UVA in '74, she was a seven-year-old girl that I'd babysat from time to time. When I came back in '78, she was a little brat of eleven. We lost touch then, until she was a young woman ten or eleven years later. Mostly social since then, shared each other's troubles, complaints."

Ginger raised an eyebrow.

"No," Cy said. "No romance ever between us if that's what you're hinting. More like the little sister I never had."

"She and her mom as close as Momma claims?" Ginger asked.

"Well, that's always been odd," Cy said. "Bailey Lee has always gushed about their closeness. But since she was a little girl, and, as recently as last week, Carter always made it clear to me that she resented, was repelled by, and, in fact, almost disliked her mother. It's as if they lived together in parallel worlds."

"Then why did she stay here in her mom's carriage house of all places?"

"Family systems are funny. Simply moving away from a family problem doesn't necessarily make someone a happy person or solve the problem. There's an odd dependence, a love-hate relationship, a need to keep trying to please."

"Maybe she stays around for Momma's money?" Ginger asked.

"Well, there's that."

"Carter doesn't quite sound like the happy, bubbly person that Momma describes her to be."

"Happy?" Cy said, stubbing out his cigarette in the ash tray. "Carter Ellis hasn't had a single happy day in her life."

# Chapter 3

## *September 5, 2007*

### Charleston, South Carolina

About five weeks earlier, just after Labor Day, Jack and Cy had first been approached by a Mrs. Rose Boisseau in Cy's office. She wanted them to look into the disappearance of her daughter Cindy.

"Tell us about the rabbits again, Mrs. Boisseau," Jack said, about an hour into the conversation.

"Sorry." Cy said shaking his head at his partner. "Jack's our resident movie buff, Mrs. Boisseau. And sometimes he gets a little carried away. How long has she had the rabbits?"

Mrs. Boisseau looked disapprovingly at Jack. He was tall, thin, had short black hair, dark brown, almost black, eyes, and his boyish appearance hid the fact that he'd seen his 40<sup>th</sup> birthday several years earlier.

Jack had been Cy's first partner. Undergraduate degree in Economics from Washington and Lee and a Masters in Criminology from Georgetown. Before graduate school, he'd spent six years in the Army. Infantry officer, Captain. A military brat himself. A decade after Cy had started the agency, Jack had been recommended to him as the perfect private detective to add to his practice by both a police captain and a private detective Cy had known and respected for decades. Of course, characteristically, Cy hadn't known he either wanted or needed a partner at that time.

In the end, Jack had turned out to be the perfect colleague. Bright, hardworking, and a perfect complement to Cy's introverted nature. Good cop, bad cop. Mr. Inside, Mr. Outside. According to Cy's female sources, he even complemented Cy in physical appearance, handsome versus rugged tough guy. A point that Cy had never gotten around to conceding.

The combination of his dark good looks, obvious intelligence, and odd sense of humor always had the effect for some reason of either immediately disarming or just as immediately annoying female clients. Never anything in between. Mrs. Boisseau's body language made it immediately clear into which camp she fell.

"Cindy's had rabbits ever since she was a little girl. There were always one or two and, in fact, Jo Jo is still at home with me. As far as I know, she just had the lop-eared one here at school. Einstein."

Neither Jack nor Cy filled the silence.

Mrs. Boisseau flattened her skirt against her thighs. She was a petite woman in her late '40's, with hawkish features, and gestures to match. She peered out at them, looking from one to the other, and ran her fingers through her short hair, dyed blond to disguise the increased graying. Sighing, she finally went on. "That's one of the things that makes me sure something's happened to her. No matter what the police say."

"Are you sure there weren't two rabbits?" Jack said. "Or three?"

"What does that have to do with my daughter's disappearance?" she snapped, not bothering to hide her annoyance with Jack.

"Look...." Cy started.

Jack cut him off. "We don't know what's important and what's not important. You're here to hire us to find your daughter and *we're* here because we like to help people, and we're good at it."

"And, of course, there's the money," she added pointedly.

Jack watched his partner, enjoying Cy's discomfort at being put in the position of being the good cop. After a career as one of Charleston's finest, Cy's had never been comfortable stepping out of character to be nice, even to clients. But Jack and Ginger had always found it the most productive way to get hidden information out of reluctant witnesses. Even clients.

"Look," Cy said. "You're right, of course. But, let's back up a second. The rabbits may or may not be important. If there was more than the one, Cindy may have taken one with her. If Einstein is the only one, she may be planning to come back for him. If it was an abduction, the abductor might have the other rabbit. If there *is* another rabbit"

"Sorry," she said. "To the best of my knowledge there was only Einstein. Talk to her roommates, they might know."

"OK," Cy said. "Let's go there. Go to the roommates again and then let's talk about her boyfriends."

"Before we go there," Jack said, "where is Mr. Boisseau?"

"He and I are separated."

"Since when?" Jack said.

"Almost a year and a half."

"Getting a divorce?"

"Is that relevant?" she asked.

Jack sighed theatrically. "Until we know more, anything can be relevant."

"He filed five weeks ago."

"Two weeks before Cindy disappeared?"

"Gosh, both a movie buff and a math whiz," she said sarcastically.

Cy ignored her comment. "Where is Mr. Boisseau now?"

"At work in Columbia."

"South America or South Carolina?" Jack asked.

"South Carolina." She sighed, running both hands through her hair.

"Why isn't he here?" Cy asked.

"Look, this is about Cindy. Not about Jim and me. We've agreed to end the marriage. This is a sensitive time in a bad relationship. Jim thinks private detectives are a waste of time anyway."

"And you don't?" Jack asked.

"I'm frustrated with the police. I think something has happened to her and I can afford your help....wait a minute. Neither Jim nor I have done anything to Cindy if that's what you're implying."

"We're only asking questions," Cy said. "We have no idea what's happened to your daughter, if anything."

"Is she a happy person?" Jack asked.

"She's always been the happy, cheerful type. Cindy had the typical teenager's rebellion against her father. She always had lots of friends and pets. She's a really happy, social person. Even after her brother left home, she was upset. But then she bounced back to her old self."

"What about the divorce?" Jack asked.

"Same thing. She was worried for me at first but then she seemed OK again."

"Let's go over our list and see if there is anyone else we need to talk to," Cy said.

"I did what you asked," she said, pointing to the papers on the table. "It's all in the list I wrote up last night."

Jack frowned. "Only one boyfriend in over a year at the college?"

"No," she said. "There were more. I just don't know their names."

She looked up. Filled up the silence with, "I don't know how many, though."

Cy looked thoughtful. "You said Cindy's brother left."

"Yes. Jim, Jr., walked out on us six years ago when he was twenty. None of us has heard from him since."

"Would Cindy have told you if she was in touch with him?" Jack asked.

"Well, of course, she would...." Mrs. Boisseau started to cry. "No, she wouldn't have."

# Chapter 4

## *September 6, 2007*

Jack and Cy looked up as Ginger entered the office, laden with bags for their lunch. She placed the bags down carefully among the clutter on the desk and dragged a chair over to join her colleagues.

Jack opened one of the bags and peered in. "How fitting. Rabbit food for lunch."

Ginger glanced at Cy. "What's he talking about?"

"Oh," Cy said, "a possible, minor lead in the case we're going to discuss."

"If you guys want 'greasy spoon,' get it yourself," Ginger said. "I'm not lighting Cy's cigarettes for him and I'm not baking chicken fried steak for you guys."

"Humph," grumbled Jack. "I'll eat the sandwich but the sprouts are yours."

"All right, children," Cy interrupted. "Let's get to work. Ginger, we need to catch you up. But first, where are we on all our loose ends?"

"Nothing is pending," she answered. "But it does look like they're going to call Jack to the stand on the Watkins case. The cops are harassing me on whether we turned over all the evidence in the Harrington case."

"So," Jack said. "Ginger, can you handle them alone or do you need help?"

Ginger glared at Jack in the ensuing silence. Over the past several months, she knew her relationship with Jack, especially in front of Cy, had become edgy. Cy was unalterably opposed to any romance in his practice. But, despite her best intentions, she had become attracted to her partner. And she was pretty sure the feeling was mutual. But now, like a couple of clueless high school kids who don't know how to broach the subject, they sniped at each other whenever they were in public. And avoided being alone together at almost all cost.

"There are no loose ends I know about," Jack finally said, glancing at Ginger. "As you know, the Miller case turned out to be our standard run-away. The only problem there is collecting our bill."

"OK." Cy said. "As I finish grazing through my alfalfa, Ging, I'll catch you up. A case came up yesterday. Jack and I interviewed the mother. Jack, jump in here if I leave anything out."

Cy slid Ginger a photo of a cute, but not pretty, petite young woman with long dirty blonde hair, a button nose, and green eyes, and summarized: "Cindy Boisseau, age 19. Sophomore, College of Charleston, 5'3", 105 pounds, non-virgin. Two roommates, indeterminate amount of bunnies, at least one...."

Jack interrupted, "....Einstein," as Cy finished, "...boyfriend."

"What?" Ginger said. "I'm lost. Who's Einstein, the bunny or the boyfriend?"

"The bunny," Cy answered. "Certainly not the boyfriend. Where was I? Oh yeah. Disappeared three weeks ago. One roommate called Mrs. Boisseau, the mother, and, at the mother's insistence, the police. It's the first instance her roommates claim of her not returning without at least calling by 2 p.m. the next afternoon. No evidence of foul play. Parents separated a year and a half. Going through a divorce. Older brother bailed six years ago. Hasn't been heard from since. Missing Persons followed up on Cindy for a week, no leads. Mother thinks police dropped the ball and she came to us. The father dislikes private eyes. May not even know she contacted us."

"Any reason not to take this case?" Ginger said.

"The father hates PI's," Cy said. "The parents are in the middle of a divorce---it could get messy. But if Mrs. Boisseau is right and the police are at a dead end, then I think we should take it."

"I'll talk to Dan and see if he knows where Missing Persons is on this," Ginger said.

"Maybe one of us should talk to Missing Persons instead of to Dan?" Jack said.

Cy was clearly annoyed. "Everyone in Charleston knows that even though Dan is a homicide cop, he's my former partner and is a conduit between us and Missing Persons. It's worked for us for years. Why the sudden skepticism?"

Jack glanced at Ginger. "Nothing. I thought it might make sense to diversify our sources---but let's go on."

Jack's uncharacteristic shot at Dan jarred Cy. Set him to thinking back over old ground. Something was connecting to this case. An elusive thought stirred in his brain, and suddenly it all came rushing back.

It was the Riley case. Fall of '93. Cy's last case on the force. He and Dan had been looking for any trace of the kid for a week. Day and night. Dan, back then, young slim, outgoing. He was the personable partner, in stark opposition to his grumpy, rumpled, stocky alter ego. But in this case, opposites worked perfectly. The two had become a very effective team, becoming close friends in the bargain.

Susan Riley had last been seen at a party on campus. There'd been problems with her before. She'd run away twice in high school. Disappeared twice with boyfriends from college for a week or so at a time. The captain told them to drop it. Made it clear that there were other, higher priority cases that needed their focus. He was insistent that Riley was a standard repeat runaway case. He swore the girl would show up in a week. Insinuated that Cy and Dan were neglecting two other homicide cases that had strong leads at the expense of this wild goose chase.

But Cy and Dan felt strongly that something was different about this. It hadn't felt like a standard runaway this time. For one thing, the missing girl was no longer a student. She'd graduated the year before. Then there'd been the fight at the party. And the day before they'd learned that she'd had a fight at work. Her boss said she'd been failing increasingly on the job. For a week she'd been coming in later and later. And, coupled with that, she had become more and more distracted. On her last day, he said she simply refused to do her job. She became argumentative and insolent. When she started a shouting match with him in front of the other employees, he'd had no alternative but to fire her. By the next night, she was gone. And Cy and Dan had been assigned the case.

But after a week with no further progress, they succumbed to the captain's pressure to table the case. They got back to work on the "more important" cases. But it had never been in Cy's nature to just let something go. He couldn't. He convinced Dan that, given what her current boyfriends had told them, they still had a chance to find the girl and prevent a tragedy. So, he and Dan went back at it. After hours, on their own time.

Sure enough, the more they pushed, the more inconsistent everybody's stories became. It turned out that she'd been seen with an older man, not only at the party, but before as well. It took them three days to discover that there were actually two men that she had been seeing. One was an owner of a King Street Liquor store. The other was the number two man at the Park Commission, Jack Stacey. Both came up dead ends. But the more they pushed on these two men, the more the internal pressure to drop the case ratcheted up. It simply didn't smell right.

And, of course, both Cy and Dan were too stubborn, or too stupid, to let it go. Between the two of them, they set up a rotating surveillance on the two men and Susan Riley's apartment. One night, Stacey showed up at the apartment on Dan's watch. He called and rousted Cy who'd been watching the seventh game of the Blue Jays, Phillies Series. What was to become a horrible evening was burned deep into his memory. He missed Joe Carter's walk-off homer by minutes. Funny what you remember forever.

Cy got there in time for the two of them to follow Stacey from the apartment out to a small house on Folly Beach.

Once parked, Stacey left the car's trunk open and hurried into the house. Only moments later, he emerged from the back of the house, slowly dragging what looked like a large rolled up rug. Cy and Dan got out of their car and pulled their guns.

When Dan called out his name, Stacey dropped what he was carrying and sprinted back into the house.

Dan motioned for Cy to go right, while he headed for the back door. Cy, gun in his right hand, had used his flashlight to edge open the rolled-up package. He recoiled as a bruised and battered, detached arm rolled out. The delicate wrist and painted nails were those of a young woman. There was blood everywhere. It was an old rug, rolled up to carry parts of a dismembered corpse.

At that point, shots rang out from the other side of the porch, and Cy sprinted to the nearest wall. He had hunched down for cover, and sidled along the house toward the direction of the shots. He had called out for Dan, but had gotten no response.

At last, he'd heard a moan from the porch and a scrambling sound from inside the house. Cy saw Dan struggle up from the porch only to collapse in a heap at the bottom of the stairs. As Cy rushed to his partner, he heard Stacey's car start up. Dan was weak but conscious. He mumbled something. Cy called for back up and went after Stacey. From where he knelt over Dan, Cy had seen Stacey's car careen through the yard to the beach.

He had given chase, frantically calling for backup and help for his fallen partner. It had been a wild ride --- through vacant lots, along the water, and, for one stretch, actually on the hard-packed sand of Folly Beach. He had had a bad moment when Stacey had gone into an uncontrolled skid, sideswiping a motorcycle and sliding sideways into an empty shopping center parking lot. The car had stopped momentarily and then had come roaring out of the lot, straight at Cy. The details of the rest of the chase had long receded from his memory.

Except, of course, for the end.

Stacey had driven into a residential neighborhood just off the beach. It hadn't taken Cy long to find him, but even then, he had arrived too late. Lights, gunshots, and screaming had led him to a house. He had rushed into the back of the home, and there he'd found Stacey lying on the floor, bleeding from at least two bullet wounds. A young black man was standing over him, gun in hand, and a little girl, clad in a pink nightgown, lay across the room, bleeding from a gaping gunshot wound.

Dan had lived. The little girl and Jack Stacey hadn't. Evidence of at least three grisly murders had been found in the house at Folly Beach. Susan Riley had been the most recent victim, only hours before Cy and Dan had arrived on the scene.

Cy and Dan had argued for weeks afterward. Cy had had it with bureaucrats and regulations that prevented good cops from doing their jobs. Dan was vehement that only the department gave them the leverage and authority to get the job done. As far as Dan was concerned, private eyes just got in the way.

In the end, Dan had been unable to talk Cy out of resigning from the department, and Cy had been unable to talk Dan out of staying. Each was convinced that his friend was wrong about how they could be most effective at stopping missing persons from becoming permanent tragedies. Yet even though they had gone their separate ways, after fifteen years together on the force, their respect for one another had remained. Possibly increased. Dan continued to be one of Cy's few friends. And their working relationship was well-known throughout the community.

Cy shook his head to clear it and suddenly realized that his two colleagues were staring at him. He looked back and forth between Jack and Ginger. "Is everything OK here? Can we go on?"

"Yeah," Jack said, looking a little puzzled.

"You just seemed lost in thought and we didn't want to disturb you," Ginger smiled. "I figured you were either planning a gourmet dinner for the three of us, or you were well into solving Cindy's disappearance."

"OK," Cy said, obviously a little embarrassed. "Let's get on with it. Ginger, I'd like you to talk to the roommates, and Jack, how 'bout you follow up on Tommy Harper, the one known boyfriend. Also see if you can find anything on Jim, Jr. I'll go to Columbia and talk to dear old dad and stop by the college and see Cal on the way."

Cal Abrams was the head of security for the College of Charleston.

"Do you want me to take Cal since you have to drive to Columbia?" Jack asked.

"Nope, I've got it."

"Maybe I could help Ging with the two roommates," Jack suggested.

"Gosh," Ginger said. "Thanks. Nice try, but I think I can handle two coeds without you."

"OK, guys," Cy said. "C'mon. Let's meet at the Blind Tiger at 6:30 tonight. Ginger, how about taking Barnum with you?"

"Good idea," she said. "Having the dog along usually disarms young girls. And," she added with a laugh, "in this case, we get the added benefit of getting a read on Einstein under pressure."

As she turned off Pitt Street with Barnum hanging out the passenger side window, Ginger pulled into the first parking spot she saw. A bit of a walk would do them both some good. Ginger loved going through these college neighborhoods, with the mix of students, professors, and merchants. She couldn't help thinking back on her own undergraduate days at Boulder. She unconsciously wrinkled her nose as she remembered the snow. She certainly didn't miss the snow.

Bikes were chained to black iron gates, and rolled newspapers, still in their plastic sheaths, littered the walkways leading to enormous old homes, many now subdivided into student apartments. The patchy lawns and overgrown hedges hinted at student occupation even before she saw the telltale banks of free-standing metal mail boxes on porches. Nearby, a young man in a black tank top and jeans worked feverishly on a bright orange Chevy; the car's hood and trunk yawned open as he juggled various tools. Second- and third-hand cars competed for space with new Lexus and BMWs.

Unlike Boulder, she noted that the well-preserved historic homes alternated with the down-at-the-heel student dwellings. Ginger stopped almost directly across the street from 40 Bull. On her side of the street stood a well-kept, single family home. She peered through its green wrought iron fence and willowy hedge to a lovely 3-story pale yellow home with a lower porch and two levels of piazzas. A charming circular fountain anchored the miniscule carpet of lawn. Even though no water cascaded over the winsome bronze boy playing a flute at its center, the sculpture at least promised eventual refreshment.

In contrast, the house across the street where the girls lived looked dilapidated and neglected. Ribbons of paint peeled from the old wood siding and shutters hung askew, their once green paint faded to grey. Barnum impatiently pulled her across the street and nosed the trees in front of the home. As they walked up the warped steps, she noticed that someone had at least tried to brighten the porch with pots of various colored impatiens on several small tables. She knocked on the door. No response. Knocking again, she heard something stir inside. Barnum busied himself enthusiastically, running around the porch nose-down, as if stale beer was a whole new sensory experience.

A sleepy-eyed red head, average figure, puffy, ordinary looking face, wearing an emerald green tank top and short shorts unlatched the door, saw Barnum, and stepped back startled. "Can I help you?"

"I'm looking for Ashley or Ann," Ginger said.

"I'm Ann," said the redhead.

"My name is Ginger Grayson. I'm a private investigator hired by Mrs. Boisseau to find Cindy."

"Do I have to talk to you?" Ann said.

"I'm not the police. Mrs. Boisseau said you and Ashley were very worried about Cindy and would want to help. No, you don't *have* to be cooperative. But you can. Is Ashley at home? Can I maybe talk to her?"

"I'm sorry. Of course we'd like to help. Come on in. Is that your dog?"

"No, it's my boss' Lab."

"I had a chocolate Lab just like him when I was a little girl. They're great dogs."

As Ann opened the door further, Barnum bounded excitedly ahead of Ginger into the house.

Ginger entered the living room. "Is Ashley here?"

"What time is it?"

"About two."

"She's not in class now. I'll try her on her cell. Wait – maybe that's her coming up the steps."

Barnum excitedly rushed back outside, almost knocking down a diminutive, peroxide blonde dressed all in black. It was almost like she was auditioning for the part of the punk girlfriend, complete with spiked hair and nose ring.

"Oh, this dog is so cute," she exclaimed. "Ann, did you find him somewhere? Do we get to keep him?"

"No," Ginger interrupted. "I'm afraid he's my boss's dog. Hi," holding out her hand to the girl. "I'm Ginger Grayson and this is Barnum. I was just explaining to Ann that Mrs. Boisseau has hired our firm to look into Cindy's disappearance. Are you Ashley?"

"Yes," she said, shaking Ginger's hand. "But I already told the police everything I know a month ago. Do we have to go through all of that again? Hey, do you have a warrant to be in our house?"

"Police need warrants to come in without your permission. We're private investigators, and Ann has already invited us in."

"The police never did anything, and Ginger thinks maybe we know something," Ann added uncertainly.

"Well," Ashley said. "As long as I don't have to talk to any of the Boisseaus again."

Ginger decided to let that hang in the air for now. She asked, "Can we go into the kitchen to talk?"

"That's fitting," Ashley grimaced. "Like that's the last place you'd ever find Cindy."

They settled themselves on rickety stools around the cracked linoleum counter and

Ginger took out her notebook. "What is Cindy like? You live with her --- you two probably know her better than anyone."

Ann looked at Ashley and decided to answer first. "I've known her since we roomed together our freshman year. Ashley lived down the hall. We all decided to get a house together this year."

"She's fun," Ashley said. "She's happy. She likes to party. She's not too serious about her classes, but she seems smart enough to get by."

"And, she loves Charleston," Ann said. "She was always coming up with fun things for us to do. She met some neat Air Force officers who used to invite us to their 'after hours' club at their place on King Street."

"And," added Ashley, "she made sure we went on all the art walks in the French Quarter. Great free booze and food. With even some fun art work."

"Sounds like Cindy enjoyed a good party," Ginger replied. "Can you tell me a little about her family."

"Her parents are jerks," Ashley said. "They're getting a divorce, and they put her in the middle of their problems. Cindy blames herself, and, even though she doesn't like her mother, she feels obligated to be there for her."

"And Cindy and her father?"

"They weren't speaking," Ashley said.

"Is there something there?"

"What do you mean?"

"You said she didn't speak to her father. That she blamed herself for her parents' divorce. Is there something between Cindy and her dad that might be important?"

"Cindy would never talk about her dad," Ashley said.

"Are there any brothers or sisters?"

Simultaneously the two girls blurted out contradictory answers. "There's a brother." "No."

Pausing, Ginger looked at Ashley. "Why did you say 'no'?"

"I told you I want nothing to do with the Boisseaus," Ashley answered tersely. "To Mr. and Mrs. Boisseau, he doesn't exist anymore, and," glaring at Ann, "we promised Cindy we'd never tell anybody about her brother. She was embarrassed about her whole family, and especially that her brother never contacted her after he left. We promised to respect her privacy about her family."

"Look," Ginger said. "We've agreed to try to find Cindy. I'm assuming you two would like her found. I don't know yet what information is relevant and what isn't. But withholding information from me could cause enough time to go by that Cindy might come to some harm. Or do the two of you think she already has?"

"You mean, like, murdered?" Ann said.

Ginger decided the question was rhetorical. In her two years of investigating, a better opportunity to be quiet had rarely come up.

Ashley finally broke the silence. "What else are we supposed to think? She wouldn't leave that fucking rabbit alone with us for three days let alone three weeks."

Ann frowned. "Cindy could meet a guy she liked and sometimes not come home the next day or the next. But she always left word with us by one or two the next afternoon of where she was and when she was coming back and what to do with..."

"Fucking Einstein," Ashley finished her sentence for her.

"What was the longest time she stayed away?" Ginger asked.

"Two nights," Ann said.

"Was it always guys?"

"Yes," they both replied.

"Always the same guy?"

"No," they both said, laughing.

The mood had suddenly shifted from one of antagonism to one of girl talk. Camaraderie.

"Well," Ginger thought out loud, "I guess when Cindy and her mom talked, all they talked about was Mrs. Boisseau. Her mom told us there was only one boyfriend she knew by name."

"Yeah, Cindy was pretty wild," Ashley said.

"Or at least more successful than us," Ann added.

"Maybe I'm out of touch with the singles scene in Charleston these days," Ginger said. "How many boyfriends were there?"

"Answer a question for us first," Ashley said. "How on earth did you get to be a private eye?"

"Ever since I was a little girl, I wanted to be an FBI agent. I majored in pre-law, criminology. I got side-tracked in Boulder by a boyfriend who was a graduate student there. After college, my Aunt got me a job as a paralegal here in Charleston. She was dating my future boss, Cy. She introduced us, and I saw the chance to do what I always wanted to do. Help people. And Cy and Jack, his partner, needed some help. So Cy grudgingly agreed to try me out. That was three years ago, and here we are."

"Well," Ann said conspiratorially, "and, how many boyfriends do *you* have, Ginger?"

All three started laughing as Ginger began to answer and then stopped. Her cell phone buzzed. She glanced down to see a text message to call Jack. "Not urgent but maybe important. Please call."

She looked up. "Sorry, I have to call my partner?"

She stepped into the hall to call Jack. No answer. She frowned and stepped back into the kitchen.

In his Columbia office, Jim Boisseau sputtered as he was forced to repeat himself. "Goddammit, how did you get into my office?"

Cy, not having been offered a seat and not expecting to, looked up at the taller man. "Boyish charm, a knight's errand explained, and a cup of Starbuck's for the assistant. Gets me in every time. I'm the knight in shining armor trying to find your daughter."

"Do you have a warrant?" Boisseau said. "A badge?"

"Whoa!!" Cy said. "Time out. I'm trying to find your daughter. I'm one of the good guys. No need to be hostile. Can I get you a cup of decaf?"

Boisseau held his hand up, palm out, as he headed back to his desk. He had to walk around the edge of the desk to keep his ample belly clear of the mahogany. He was the size of an ex-linebacker. Gone slightly to seed. Practically a stereotype of a former Clemson football player, now playing at executive. Sharp features, receded hairline. All but bald. Maybe handsome at one time, but certainly no longer. "Let me see your ID, buddy."

Cy handed him a card with his left hand, and held out his right.

"You're a fucking private eye," Boisseau sneered as he pointedly ignored Cy's attempted hand shake. "'Fapp and Sons.' Are you one of the boys, or are you Fapp?"

"I'm Fapp."

"In my experience, PIs aren't worth crap, Fapp. Don't tell me the Charleston police came up with you in desperation."

"If we can get through the preliminaries, we'll be done with this very quickly. I know you're busy. When did you last see your daughter?"

"I don't remember and I don't have to answer your questions. I'd like you to leave my office, now."

"Look, we're off on the wrong foot here. We're trying to find your daughter. I assume you want her found. Am I right?"

"Look, gumshoe. Or is it Dick? There's no mystery to solve here. The little slut ran off with one of her fifty or sixty boyfriends or girlfriends and she's having a great time on my dollar at some beach somewhere. Probably with the little punk piece of ass she lives with. If you want my advice, follow her little black leathered roommate for a week and you'll find her."

"Thanks for the tip," Cy said. "We'll get right on that as delicately as you suggest. Can you please tell me about your relationship with your daughter."

"My relationship with Cindy is none of your fucking business."

"So there's absolutely nothing at all you can tell us about your daughter's whereabouts or when you last saw her that can help us?"

"Nothing that can help you and nothing that I haven't told the police. Get out now!!" He jabbed at the intercom and yelled, "Dorothy, get security in here. Now!!"

"No problem," Cy said to Boisseau. May as well keep pushing. No way this guy winds up helping intentionally. And I can't do any more harm than I already have. "Only a couple more questions. Can you tell me about your relationship with your son?"

"Get out."

"Your wife?"

"Wait a minute. Did that bitch hire you? Has she gone out and hired a private dick to poke around in our affairs?"

"Have the police ever had to intervene in your obviously heartwarming relationships with your family members?"

At this, Boisseau moved menacingly toward Cy just as a large uniformed figure stepped through the doorway behind him. Cy deftly sidestepped Boisseau's clumsy attempt at a shove.

"If that's your best shot, I can see why you need a security guard."

"Sam, get this asshole out of here."

The guard stepped between the two and smiled so Boisseau couldn't see him. "Cy, what have you gotten yourself into now?"

"Chief," Cy said, laughing as he recognized him. "Why on Earth did you give up your cushy highway patrol job to start guarding overweight, neurotic executives? Why and when?"

"Sam, you know this guy?" Boisseau asked, retreating again to the safety of the desk. "Get him out of here. Then come back and we'll discuss whether or not to press charges."

"Come on, Cy. Let's go," Chief said as he took his arm.

"That's fine," Cy said. "We're done here anyway. I only had one more question, anyway.

He turned back toward the desk. "Mr. Boisseau, which of your quotes would you like for me to use as your greeting to Cindy when I find her?"

"Goddammit, Sam, get him out of here."

Cy winked at Dorothy as he put his arm around Sam and headed down the corridor.

"Chief, I've missed you. Has it really been three years since you and I found the Wilkinson girl in Hilton Head?"

Seeing Dorothy's failed attempt to stifle a smile over Cy's shoulder, Chief replied in a stage whisper. "I see you're making the same warm, cuddly impression on everybody as always. How do you do it?"

"Just the same old boyish charm," Cy answered. "It works every time."

"Sorry about that," Ginger started when she got back in the kitchen. "Why don't we just start then with a list of Cindy's current boyfriends?"

Ashley and Ann exchanged glances. "The truth is," Ashley said, "just like we told the police, we don't know each one. Cindy had this arrangement. Well, we all did, but Cindy most often, of locking the TV room when she was entertaining guys."

"Guys?" Ginger asked, looking back and forth between the two girls.

"Not that way," Ashley said. "Whenever any of us wanted to be alone with a guy, we locked the others out of the TV room."

"So," Ann added, "a lot of times we never met her friends." She looked over at Ginger. "...I mean friend... until the next morning. If at all."

"How many guys are we talking about over the last six months?" Ginger asked. A long silence now ensued while Ashley and Ann engaged in an obviously unfamiliar activity. Their body language suggested that long periods of quiet thought were unusual.

"This is way too hard," Ann said.

"OK then," Ginger said, "while we're sitting here talking, why don't you jot down any names you can think of---her current and former boyfriends. Numbers, too. If someone wanted to harm Cindy, I find it hard to believe it wouldn't be someone you knew."

"Well," Ann said. "It could have been someone she picked up in a bar."

"Did she hang out in bars and pick up guys indiscriminately?" Ginger asked, visibly surprised.

"Not when we were together," Ashley replied. "But she went out alone at least once a week."

"Which bars?"

"I don't know. All of them I guess. Vickery's, Wet Willies, Blind Tiger, Big John's, Wild Wing Cafe, the Vendue Roof Top."

"And she came home once a week with a strange guy you two would meet?" Ginger asked, clearly astonished.

"No, not when she stayed at their place," Ann said, eyes downcast.

"Wait a minute, Ann," Ginger interrupted. "Didn't you say she never stayed anywhere without letting you know where she was and when she was coming home?"

"Yes," Ann said.

"Do you keep phone numbers around – or on scraps of paper?"

"We have lots of scraps of paper with numbers over in the phone drawer," Ashley said, pointing across the room.

"How 'bout before I leave," Ginger suggested, "the three of us go through those scraps of paper and come up with a list of places Cindy stayed?" She looked thoughtfully around the room. "Did Cindy do drugs?"

Ann and Ashley glanced surreptitiously at each other in silence.

"A little. No *real* drugs," Ann finally added.

"What about coke? Crack?"

"Is there any way we can get in trouble here?" Ann asked. "Are we going to get Cindy in trouble?"

"If you two abducted Cindy," Ginger paused and looked at each separately before going on, "helped someone abduct her, or are withholding information from the authorities about Cindy's abduction, you can get in trouble. But no one in Cy's agency, or in Missing Persons for that matter, cares about your personal habits. All we care about is finding Cindy. Was Cindy a professional?"

"What do you mean by that?" Ann asked, startled.

"Was she having sex with men for money?"Ginger said.

"No way!! College sophomores here aren't doing that. We've never heard of anything like that on campus," Ann said indignantly.

Ginger, surprised at the girls' apparent naiveté, continued through their shocked silence. "No calls from strange men just leaving a call back number?"

"No, Ginger, really," Ann sputtered. "That's not who Cindy was at all. She was just a girl away from home for the first time having fun."

"OK," Ginger said. Changing to a more measured approach, she paused and then went on. "I'm relieved to hear that. Look, I'm not here to judge Cindy. That's not my job. I'm just trying to find out as quickly as possible where she is. OK?"

Both girls nodded. Now embarrassed.

"Let's go back to one more thing. Tell me about her brother."

"She has an older brother," Ann said. "Jim. He's twenty-five or twenty-six who left home about six or seven years ago and has never seen or spoken to anyone in the family since."

"As far as you two know, Cindy was never in touch with Jim, Jr.?"

The girls answered, "No!" Loudly. In unison.

"Well," Ann added uncomfortably, looking away from Ashley.

"Ashley, my only interest is in finding Cindy. When I asked if she had brothers or sisters, you immediately said 'no.' And now when I asked if she's in touch with a brother, you immediately said 'no.' Why don't you tell me about Cindy and Jim?"

"Can I talk to Ann a minute alone?" she said.

"Sure, that's fine. Any problem with me and Barnum going to Cindy's room and meeting Einstein?" Getting no objection, she headed down the hall. She quickly tried Jack again.

"Hey!" he answered. "How're the girls and the rabbits?"

"You'll love the girls. And, oh yeah, only one rabbit. Einstein. Barnum's about to detect him in his cage," she laughed. "What's up? Miss me?"

"I'm just about at my meeting with Tommy. Anything I need to know?"

"Nope. Nothin' yet. Sorry."

"OK. See you at the Blind Tiger. Bye, Ging."

Jack hung up on Ginger and entered Hasta La Pasta. He had no trouble picking Cindy's ex-boyfriend out of the handful of people scattered around the restaurant. Tommy was precisely as described. Slightly less than six feet, wiry, cleft chin, brown eyes, long, dirty blond hair, with a scraggly beard.

This was one of those perfect "hole in the wall" college joints---hefty portions, no frills and, most important, cheap prices. He guessed that Tommy was a regular. He walked over to the table looking out on King Street and held out his hand. "Excuse me, are you Tommy Harper?"

The young man looked up and took his hand wordlessly.

"Hi, I'm Jack Crisp. Thanks for agreeing to meet me here for coffee."

"Nice of you to accommodate my afternoon break," Tommy said. "Besides, this might be my only chance to meet a real private eye. I thought you guys only existed in books and movies."

"Well, we're even. You're my first physicist and I thought *they* only existed in books and movies. Besides, you can't use that line. It's already taken by Lauren Bacall in *The Big Sleep*. I think she tells Bogey that they might also be 'greasy little men snooping around hotel corridors.'"

Seeing Tommy's confusion, Jack felt sorry for him. "Private detectives, that is, not physicists." Still getting no reaction, Jack shrugged. "What will you have? I'm gonna have my regular double cappuccino."

"I'll start with bruschetta, then spaghetti carbonara with café mocha. Would you please ask Gina to remember to have them make it al dente this time?"

"Got it. Be right back with your order, sir!"

As he headed to the counter shaking his head, Jack mused to himself that *this* was going to be a lot of fun. Returning, he started right in. "As I told you on the phone, I can use your help. What do you know about Cindy's disappearance?"

"Not a thing," Tommy replied tersely.

"Well," Jack sighed. "What can you tell me about Cindy that might help me find her?"

"I know pretty much all I want to know about Cindy."

"All *I* know about Cindy is that the mother says you are the former boyfriend and that her daughter is missing."

"I said that I was willing to help you, not that I knew *how* to help you. I've told the police everything I know. You'd think by now the cops could have found her."

"Well, do you care?"

"Cindy was a really good kid. I cared about her a lot. We were really close until I cut it off."

"You're talking about her as if you think she were dead. What do you think happened to her?"

"Yeah, I think she's dead. She was a really sweet but mixed up kid. She just couldn't stop having fun with every guy she met."

"Did she sleep around when she was your girlfriend? Is that why you, as you say, cut it off?"

"Yes and yes. And that's what I told the police."

"That had to be rough. If she had been my girlfriend I'd still be angry."

"Angry enough to kill her?" Tommy asked.

Jack laughed. "Wait a minute. You're the physicist and I'm the detective here."

"So you're rubber and I'm glue," Tommy smiled at Jack insincerely, "and I'm supposed to answer my own question."

"Something like that," Jack answered, unmoved by Tommy's grade school taunt.

"Yeah," Tommy snorted. "Mad enough to kill her if I was the type. But I'm not. And I didn't."

"You've obviously thought about this. Do you know of any suspects more likely than you?"

"No."

"Do you have an alibi for that night?"

"No. But if I were the type, the chef or the waitress would be my second victim. It'd be justifiable homicide, too. As usual, no matter what I say, this damn spaghetti is over cooked all to hell! Every damn time!"

Barnum trotted ahead of Ginger into the room and frantically raced around, nose to the ground, sniffing in search of the rabbit. Within seconds, Barnum raced back in his excitement to show Ginger his discovery. "Good detective work, Barnum. I never could have found him without you." Einstein, madly cringing on the wood chips at the far end of the cage, was much less enthusiastic about the encounter.

Not surprisingly, the room was immaculate and everything was in order. Whatever state Missing Persons and her roommates had left the room in after their searches, Mrs. Boisseau had clearly straightened up according to a mother's standards. Only the things on the walls and Einstein gave any indication of the personality of the girl who lived, or had lived, in the room. A Taj Mahal poster curled off the wall, and ticket stubs from concerts were tacked to a bulletin board – Phish, Bob Dylan and Barenaked Ladies. There was also the left half of a photo pinned above the bed. Cindy with a boy's arm over her shoulder, a crowd in the background. The other half of the photo, presumably with the rest of the boy, was missing. Before leaving the room, Ginger took a last look at Einstein. The black and white ball of fur, nosing toward

Barnum, now seemed much less threatened. For his part, Barnum was visibly excited about his new friend.

"Come on, Barnum. You can come back and visit Einstein again later. Let's go."

Ginger's curiosity was now focused on the TV room. She stuck her head in and was not surprised at what she saw, but was shocked at the sheer quantity of it. At one end was a large screen TV, surrounded by stacks of CDs, tapes, DVDs, an obvious state-of-the-art stereo system with speakers seemingly on every wall, a luxurious couch with a hide-a-bed, and a bean bag chair. The walls were draped in tie-dyed hangings. Except for the posters of male rock starts, this seemed to be more a man's hangout. If it was young men you were after, this destination would sure give you an edge on the competition.

"How do you like it?" asked Ann.

Ginger, lost in thought, jumped at the sound of Ann's voice.

"You scared me," Ginger gasped. "That's quite a room! How did you all come by all that equipment? Not to mention, why?"

"All our parents, even Mr. Boisseau, agreed to give us money to furnish that room as a house warming present. I always thought it was a bit much, but Ashley and Cindy just love it. And we have yet to meet a guy who isn't blown away."

"Who picked out the equipment? The three of you?"

"Well, that's one of the things we want to talk to you about," Ann said. "Can you come back to the kitchen?"

As they reentered the kitchen, Ann called out to Ashley. "Ash, Ginger has seen the TV room and wants to know where we got the equipment."

"Well," Ashley answered, "each of our parents wanted to give us a housewarming gift. We asked to have stuff for our TV room. And, they said they would each give us a third of the expense, up to $1,000 each. But, instead, Cindy's dad showed up one Saturday with all that stuff you now see in the room. Cindy and her dad got into a shouting match that ended with her storming out of the house screaming, 'No amount of money and stuff is going to make up for what you've done to me.' Then I was stuck dealing with the asshole while he installed everything. He was such a jerk."

"Did he say or do anything to you?" Ginger asked.

"Look, the guy's an asshole," Ashley replied. "But what happened that morning has nothing to do with Cindy's disappearance."

Ginger sighed. "What does? What do you two think happened to Cindy?"

"The two of us talked," Ann answered. "We've agreed to be as helpful as we can. There were things Cindy told us that we promised never to tell anyone. But we don't think it has anything to do with what's happened to her."

Ginger became clearly exasperated. "What do you think has happened?"

"We don't agree on that. Ashley thinks she ran off to her brother and I think...I think nothing makes sense except that she's dead. Some man she met."

Ginger turned to Ashley. "OK. Now can you tell me about Jim, Jr.?"

"We don't know much," Ashley answered. "I hate like hell to help the Boisseaus bring Cindy back if she doesn't want to. What if I help you find her and she doesn't want to come back?"

"What we do for a living is find missing people. When we succeed, if there's no foul play we don't share our information with the police or force the missing person to go home. We're up front about that with all our clients, including Mrs. Boisseau."

"OK, then. Here's what we know," Ashley began. "Cindy was despondent one day. She broke down and told us that she had a brother and had run into somebody on campus who had heard he'd been killed. She's usually a really happy, nice person--- very up-beat. But she was, like, so depressed about this that we just couldn't seem to help her, even though she admitted it was just a rumor. In fact, she'd had a picture on her wall, taken of the two of them a week before he left home. Whenever anybody had asked, she'd say it was the first boy she had a crush on. She finally told us the truth."

"Had he been killed?"

Ashley paused, but finally decided to answer. "It turns out she called him repeatedly for days and got no answer. But eventually she found out he was OK."

"And?"

"That's all we know," Ashley said. "She seemed to get over her depression when she heard he was OK. But she never told us where he worked or lived."

"Did you notice she was talking to him on the phone a lot? Did he come here? Or did she meet him somewhere?"

"Cindy talked on the phone a lot," Ashley answered. "We didn't always know who she was talking to. She just seemed better. She wouldn't talk to us about him. A month later she disappeared."

"I want to go to the photograph you mentioned. Is that the picture on Cindy's wall that's been torn in half or are we talking about a different one?"

"No, no, no," Ann said. "They're totally different. The one on the wall was one of her with Tommy. After he dumped her, she tore him out."

Ashley looked sideways at Ann. "The picture of her with her brother was not there the next morning. She must have taken it with her."

"Why do you think she took it with her?"

"It is the one thing she'd take if she went to see her brother," Ann said. "It wasn't there the next day. Nobody else would have wanted to take it."

"Are both of you sure you've never seen her brother in this house?"

They both shook their heads.

"Would it have been possible for him to have gotten into and out of the house with Cindy that night, without you two knowing?"

"She just didn't come home that night," Ann said, raising her voice.

"Could her brother come in and out without your knowing?" Ginger repeated.

"I suppose so," Ann admitted.

Ginger reached down and scratched Barnum's ear thoughtfully. She finally asked, "OK, Ann, tell me what *you* think happened."

"Well, I just don't know. She went out alone just like every week, and didn't come home. It could have been some guy that none of the three of us ever knew before that night and that Ashley and I have never seen or met."

"Did she receive any calls that afternoon or evening before she left?"

"No. No messages or calls. We are clear on that and were clear with the police. She walked out the door the same way she always did when she just planned to go bar hopping alone."

"What do you mean?"

"She didn't tell us where she'd be or who with. She simply didn't have any plans."

"OK," Ginger said. "Let's go through the list. Could Tommy have done it?"

"Done what?" Ann asked. "Have killed her? Tommy is really arrogant and he had bad times with her. But we were all friends, and Ashley and I don't see how he could kill anybody." She looked over at Ashley, who was nodding in agreement. "No way Tommy could kill anybody," she added.

"The list you've been making for me---it looks like four or five guys. Any of them have a bad temper? Violent? Any you're afraid of?"

"I don't think Cindy would get herself in that situation," Ashley said. "She tended toward really sweet, nerdy guys. But one of the guys here does have a bad temper. Clyde Culp. And it's why we stopped having anything to do with him."

"That's true," Ann agreed. "We don't like Clyde. He does get angry. If you said it was one of the guys on this list, I would disagree with you. But Clyde is the only one I can imagine doing any such thing. This is all so horrible. It has to be someone we don't know. It can't be one of our friends."

"This is a waste of time," Ashley chimed in. "No one killed Cindy. She's living happily somewhere and she and her brother will never have to deal with their asshole father ever again. She doesn't even have to worry about exams next week."

"What about the Air Force officers you mentioned?"

"The police checked with them already," Ann answered. "They were away then. On a mission to Iraq or Afghanistan or some place like that."

"Some place like that." Ginger couldn't help smiling. "OK," she said. "Why don't you give me the list you have. Keep thinking of other old boyfriends, go through your phone notes, and call me if you think of anyone else. Is there anything I should have asked that I haven't?"

Both girls looked at each other, again with the we-don't-feel-comfortable-thinking body language.

"No," Ashley finally answered for both girls.

"There's one other thing I'm supposed to find out," Ginger said. "Was Einstein her only rabbit or did she have more?"

"No. Only one rabbit," Ashley said. "Einstein's it."

"OK," Ginger said. "Thanks, girls. Let's go, Barnum. Let's give Einstein some rest," she called out.

As she went to lead Barnum out, she clearly overheard Ann whispering to Ashley. "Should we.....what about the professor?"

And, she heard Ashley's answer very clearly. "No, let's not waste everybody's time with that bullshit."

# Chapter 5

## *The Blind Tiger*

That night, at the Blind Tiger, Cy looked around the bar for the waitress, saw her, caught her eye, and then turned to Jack and Ginger. "Dan's coming by in about 45 minutes to brief us on where Missing Persons is on the Boisseau case---that gives us a chance to catch up before he gets here."

Marla strutted up. "Cy and Ginger, I'll get your regulars. Jack, what's it going to be tonight?"

"Does he still have some Fat Tire back there?" Jack asked.

Marla shouted to the bartender and nodded at Jack. "Be right back."

"Which one of you two knows where Cindy is?" Cy started.

"I've got an arrogant suspect without an alibi, nothing more." Jack replied.

"Well, I need to catch you up on a bunch of things," Ginger said. "I've cleared up at least one mystery and we know a lot more about Cindy. If this is more than a mere runaway we have a slew of suspects." She looked up from her notes. "Oh yeah, and I think Barnum's in love."

"Well, spare us the suspense," Jack said. "What mystery did you solve?"

"This is not the case of the missing rabbit. There has always been and still is only one bunny. If it ever disappears there will only be one prime suspect. Barnum is 'over the moon' about this rabbit."

"I'm sure Mrs. Boisseau will be impressed with our detective work today," Jack teased.

"Let's move on to the suspects in the case we've been *paid* to solve," Cy grumbled as he tapped a cigarette on the table. This crap about not being able to smoke even in bars in Charleston was bullshit. Did they *really* expect us go stand outside every time we needed a smoke. If I wanted to live in California, I'd move there!

"OK," Ginger sighed. "By the way, Cy, did you ever check into that 'stop smoking' hypnotist I told you about?"

Cy replied gruffly, "I'm gonna quit *some* day. But as long as I can still field and hit a baseball as well as I did in college, I'm in no hurry. *Now*, what about the roommates, Ginger?"

"OK, OK," Ginger said, rolling her eyes at Jack. "What I got from the roommates and a couple of people on the block is that Cindy is a really nice kid who is, shall we say, savoring the flavors of the opposite sex now that she has the chance. Her mother was right about her not being a virgin, but no mother needs to hear the details of the sex life of a daughter like Cindy. The three girls have an entertainment room that would make a New Orleans bordello proud."

"Good thing we didn't send Jack," Cy murmured.

"Ashley's a match for him," Ginger laughed. "And if you can believe the two roommates, you could stick a meter on the front door and Charleston could solve its revenue deficit in about three months. Ann is scared to death and believes that one of Cindy's one-night stands smoked her. Ashley, the sweet little punk rocker, thinks she ran off to join her older brother."

"Was she hooking?" Cy asked. "Are there drugs involved?"

"They say no to both, although they're less convincing on the drugs. My intuition on the hooking is 'no.' Just not the right dynamic."

"Did you think either girl resented Cindy enough to be involved?" Jack asked.

"No. I can't see it."

Cy looked up as Marla approached. "Are they both leveling with you?"

"I told you---Ann is terrified. She couldn't lie to anyone. Ashley, on the other hand, is holding back. She hates the Boisseaus and there is something else about Cindy's dear old dad that she's not telling."

Ginger took a sip of her martini, gave the bartender a thumbs-up, and went on. "Either Ashley's telling the truth and Cindy's gone off with her brother, and Ashley doesn't want her found or is respectful that Cindy doesn't want to be found...or she's trying to throw us off with the brother story and she knows what really happened."

"Do either one of them think Tommy could have done it?" Jack asked.

"Neither girl thinks Tommy's involved," Ginger answered.

"On the surface he looks like a number one suspect, arrogant with a motive and no alibi. But the girls may well be right," Jack added. "My read on him is that he's a pseudo-intellectual who wouldn't hurt a fly and who thinks Cindy is just a happy but mixed-up kid."

Cy tapped his glass thoughtfully. "Tell me a little bit more about Ashley and the father."

"Seems like he came by uninvited one Saturday morning, to deliver and set up their entertainment room. Cindy left in anger after he pissed her off and something---I don't know what---happened in that room between him and Ashley."

"Something sexual?" Jack asked.

"It's the most likely explanation. She's not talking. She clearly hates the man. Whatever happened that morning turned her against the family. Did you meet with him, Cy? What's your take on the guy?"

"I like him even less than Ashley does. And," he added, "he seems to desire my company even less than Ashley does his. He had Chief strong-arm me out of his office."

"Chief?" both asked. "What was *he* doing there?"

"He's retired now and works as a security stiff for Boisseau's company."

"So you charmed Mr. Boisseau, huh?" Jack asked.

"Yeah. He's the least concerned father I've ever met in a disappearance case."

"So what's the chance he's involved?" Ginger asked.

"He's a jerk and he may have caused her to run away. It's always possible, but I don't see---even in a family that dysfunctional---this father killing his teenage daughter. It's more likely she ran away with somebody, and if she came to harm it was with one of her one-night stands, or an old boyfriend. I've dealt with parents who are disconsolate, catatonic, indifferent, and not forthcoming, but this is the first time I've had to deal with one who is hostile and aggressive. There's definitely something between those two."

They looked up as Dan approached the table with a fresh round of drinks. "Well, if it isn't 'PI' and the two dicks."

Jack winced visibly at Dan's cavalier entrance. Dan's nickname for Ginger was incredibly inappropriate and increasingly grating, he thought to himself. He looked over at Ginger. At some point they were going to have to deal with this. Jesus, he thought he'd gotten through this "how do you approach the girl" shit in high school. He looked up and suddenly realized the other three were looking at him.

Knowing he had missed something, he lamely retorted, "I'm afraid to ask what beer you got me."

"Well, never look a gift inspector in the mouth," Dan said as he put the drinks down and leaned over to kiss Ginger on the cheek as he winked at Jack.

Dan had aged much better than his former partner. He had put on very little weight, maybe five pounds at the most. He had made it a point to stay in shape since the gunshot wound the night of the Folly Beach shooting. And whereas the two friends each still had their full heads of hair, like their opposite personalities Dan's shock of black hair stood in clear opposition to Cy's silvered brown.

"Any luck with the bad guys today?" Cy asked Dan after he sat down.

"Closing in on mine, but never too busy to help my favorite posse get theirs."

"Speaking of which," Cy added, "I ran into Chief today, and he asked me to say 'hey.'"

"Chief? I haven't seen him in two or three years. What's he doing now?"

Jack responded, "Today his plate was full rousting Charleston's premier private eye out of his client's office."

Dan looked questioningly over his beer at Cy.

"It seems that Mr. Boisseau's much less enthusiastic about finding out what happened to his daughter than we are."

Dan downed the rest of his beer and wiped the foam off his mouth. "Do you want me to bring you up to date on what Missing Persons has in this case, or do you want to tell me about Chief?"

"Give us a run down on what Missing Persons' got," Cy answered.

"It's a cold trail. They don't think it's much of a mystery. They think she ran off with some guy she met at a bar that night. According to bartenders all over town, she and her two roommates have been heavy into the Charleston night scene for the last year and a half."

"Anything on that particular night?" Jack asked.

"No, she left the Blind Tiger around 11 p.m. with a complete stranger," he answered, tossing his head toward the bartender. "Sean says he'd never seen him before. Then around midnight she left Big John's bar alone."

"Any of her former boyfriends in any of the same bars that night?" Cy asked.

"Sean says she and Tommy exchanged words here before she left with the other guy. And one of her other former boyfriends, Clyde I think, was at Big John's and then again at Norman's the same time as her."

"Anybody on this list?" Ginger asked as she passed the girls' notes toward Dan.

Dan skimmed the list. "Where'd you get this?"

"The roommates," she said.

"Here's Clyde as I mentioned," Dan said as he pointed to the name on the list. "No one saw them acknowledge each other or talk in either place."

"Does anybody make Clyde or Tommy as the type who would have dragged her off?" Jack asked.

Dan looked through his notes. "They're both suspects. Either one of them might have slapped her around, but no one makes either one of them as murderers. Tommy has no alibi whatsoever and he's an arrogant little prick. Anybody in the Department who's dealt with him would like to get something on him. And Clyde is wound tighter than a cat's fur ball. But until we find a body or evidence of a crime, they're just lousy suspects."

"What about any of the others on this list?" Ginger asked.

"They all have airtight alibis. No sense in rehashing that ground."

"So, Tommy, or Clyde---in a moment of unlikely passion?" she asked. "Or who else? Any suspects we don't know about?"

"Well, there's always dear old dad," Dan smiled.

"I'll fill you in on Chief's view of Mr. Boisseau, but where's the Department on him?"

"We think he's abusive. We think he has a temper. There's sex abuse between him and Cindy in the past. His behavior toward us and now apparently toward super sleuth here is consistent with his having done something to Cindy. But, we feel it's more likely he has so much to hide in his relationships with his wife and children that he just won't cooperate. Do you all know about Jim, Jr.?"

"We know he exists," Ginger said. "We know he left home. Jack couldn't find anything on him, nosing around town. The roommates admitted Cindy had been in touch with him in the weeks before she left town, and Ashley thinks Cindy ran off to live with him."

Dan looked off into space, thinking. "That's interesting. They told Missing Persons they didn't know she had a brother. And the parents don't have a clue where he is. I brought you a copy of the phone records. They couldn't find anything interesting. Maybe you can. Frankly, if she's run off to be with her brother we don't care."

"Dan," Ginger said. "Missing Persons thinks she ran off with a barfly. I sense you don't agree. What do you think?"

"My gut tells me she's dead, but we haven't been able to turn up anything."

"Any links to anything else?" Cy asked.

"No. We could be dealing with a one-off disappearance or a serial killer. We won't know until we find a body."

"Where have you looked?" Jack asked.

"If it's a murder we don't have a clue how or where."

"Any problems if we lean on Tommy and Clyde and Pops?" Cy asked.

"Nope." Flipping through his notes, Dan looked up cheerfully as he closed his notebook. "That's all the free information---not to mention drinks---that you get from

49

Charleston's finest today. What did Chief say about Mr. Boisseau, Cy?"

"Guy's a head case. Abusive to everyone in the office. Nobody likes him. But he's a genius at operations and controls. Chief says he had some run-in with a PI over his son's disappearance and can't stand PIs. Missing Persons had an hour long interview with him, and he was going on about what idiots the police are. He hates his daughter. Curiously, he was away from the office the three days surrounding her disappearance."

"Wait a minute," Jack interrupted. "Before we pursue that, did anything pop up about Tommy's professor?"

"Whoa," Ginger said. "What *about* Tommy's professor?"

Dan looked back and forth between them. "*We've* got nothing on that. What've you got, Ginger?"

Ginger looked at Jack. "No. Jack, you tell me what you've got first."

"There were two reasons Tommy gave for breaking off with Cindy," Jack said. "One, she insisted they have unprotected sex and he wasn't willing to until she gave up her other sexual partners. And two, he began to suspect she was sleeping with his thesis advisor."

He glanced down at his notes. "Professor Easler. Why?"

"As I was leaving the house I overheard Ann ask Ashley if they should tell us about the professor, and Ashley shut her up."

Cy looked pointedly at Dan. "Well, well. Maybe we got ourselves a possible new bad guy after all."

Ginger and Jack turned off State Street and headed down Unity Alley to McCrady's restaurant. Alone. McCrady's was always Ginger's first choice whenever she had out-of-town guests who wanted good food and ambience. And tonight, of all nights, she felt like something special. One way or the other we're going to get this settled, she thought. Ambling down the old brick paved back alley to McCrady's arched entrance always put her in the Charleston spirit.

As she and Jack entered the warmth of the entryway, the maitre d', Tom, came up to greet them. The bar, with the old kegs and wine bottles slotted above it all the way up to the double level ceiling, looked inviting, but she and Jack decided to go right to their table.

"When I saw you were coming, I reserved your favorite table by the fireplace, Ginger," Tom added with a smile as he pulled a chair out for her. "I know you always want to sit facing the painting of the rooftops," he said.

Ginger nodded her thanks to Tom. "You bet. Someday I'm going to have enough money to buy one of the historic houses under one of those roofs!"

"And when you do that," Jack laughed, "I'll commission West Frazier to do a painting of the roofs as seen from your very own piazza."

"Deal," she said, punching him on the arm.

Tom took their drink order and promised to send their waiter over as soon as they were ready.

While Jack ordered, Ginger thought back on her first dinner here. Cy had brought her to McCrady's to celebrate her joining Fapp and Sons. She smiled as she remembered the day she first met Cy. Her Aunt Valerie had wanted her to meet him. Aunt Val and Cy had been dating then, what two, three years? The way she described Cy, Ginger half expected him to be brandishing a sword and riding a white horse. Former cop wanting to do good, but constrained by the rules and regulations of an increasingly confining Charleston police force, he had struck out on his own. A decade ago. Finder of missing children, wives, husbands, kidnap victims. Gallant rescuer of her lonely Aunt.

Cy had reluctantly agreed to meet her in his old office, and Ginger was shocked at first sight. A rumpled, middle aged man with a baseball cap over graying hair had growled her in when she knocked at the door. An old wood file cabinet, a beaten-up metal desk, two worn chairs. Nothing on the walls. No window. Cigarette butts overflowed two ashtrays, and a half- empty cup of coffee sat amid piles of seemingly random papers on the desk. Not at all what she'd expected from Aunt Val's description.

"Can I help you," mumbled the man behind the desk.

"I'm Ginger Grayson. Valerie's niece. I might have the wrong office. I was looking for Cy Fapp."

"Well you found him. C'mon in."

She suddenly realized that Jack had asked her a question and was looking at her, puzzled. "Oh, sorry," she mumbled. "I was just wishing I knew where Cy's line was between wanting to hear my intuition, and his thinking I'm too speculative."

"Look, Ging. Cy thinks your intuitive approach is black magic. And he doesn't think magic is a substitute for good, hard leg work. He needs to see evidence and where it leads. He thinks your gift is just that --- a gift that's a little suspect at times. But he knows you add huge value in an area where he is blind.

"There is no line. He's just Cy. And he's always gonna be just Cy---negative and surly, smoking and grumbling, but with a heart of gold. To the world, he's a curmudgeon. But it's our secret that under that grumbling exterior, he has that heart of pure gold."

"You're absolutely right," Ginger agreed. "And it's our secret weapon."

"Let everybody else think his grumpiness is *really* him. We know better and we can use that knowledge," Jack replied.

"Yeah, I suppose. But at times I'm conscious that he and I are so different. It's amazing he hired me to work with him at all. And then, I realize that's what makes him so good at what he does. He analyzes the situation and figures out what he needs. You, on the other hand, are so good at throwing yourself into new situations and asking just the right questions of people."

Jack looked up at the awkward compliment. But then looked away as he nodded and sipped his beer. "Chalk that up to one of the few positives of being a military brat. Comes from being used to moving from place to place every couple of years. But, there are lots of negatives, too, for example. I certainly don't hold back on giving my opinion!

"But getting back to your concerns about Cy's opinion of you," Jack continued. "Look, the only problem, Ging, is when you become defensive. He needs you to share all your intuition and ignore his reaction. You're useless to him if you just give up just because he doesn't seem to value your observations at first blush."

She sat thoughtfully. The use of the word "blush" distracted her. *How in the hell am I going to do this? I feel like such a dumb kid! Maybe I just grab him and kiss him right here? Why is this stuff always so hard?*

"Thanks," she finally responded. "That helps. I know he values my intuition, but seems to get especially critical when I say things in front of other people---especially in front of Dan. I'm not always right, but my viewpoint often makes the three of us rethink something."

"Precisely. Your greatest value to Cy is pushing him when you disagree."

"Yeah, but why does he have to be so disagreeable?" she laughed. "Well, not so disagreeable, but so curmudgeonly?" Holding her hand up to stop Jack from interrupting, "I know, I know. It's our little secret. But in many ways, Cy is the perfect person to be looking for disgruntled runaways."

"That and his experience have saved us from going down a lot of blind alleys. Because of his own dark side, he's been incredibly accurate in identifying which cases are most likely runaways versus foul play."

Three blocks away, a young man sitting in a corner at a neighborhood bar could feel his blood rising as he watched a girl at the bar. Vicky, his former girlfriend. Why didn't they ever learn? Insulting him by sleeping around after they were through with him. He hated that. It was always the same. Whether they decided to cut it off, or he did. Whether they stayed friends or not.

The ones who slept around just couldn't stop flaunting it around him. Meeting other guys in bars right in front of him. Like he even cared! But it was insulting, and *somebody* needed to stop them.

The guy she had been talking to had just left. He walked over to her.

"Hey, Vick."

She looked up. Her reaction was slow. The alcohol was in her eyes and in her expression. He remembered that look well. Very well.

"Hey!"

"How ya' been, Vick?"

"Super." She brushed her long brown hair out of her eyes, almost spilling what little remained of her drink. "That guy was a real jerk. I was hopin' you'd come by so he'd leave."

"You know I don't like to interrupt you. I always respected your space. You need another drink?"

"Yeah, sure," she grinned up at him. "Well, I don't know about *need*, but I'll sure take one."

He gestured to the bartender and leaned into Vicky. "Ya ever think about not hanging around here? I worry about you drinking this much around all these strange guys."

"You're such a sweetheart. *You're* not such a strange guy." And she laughed at her own joke, while she finished the new drink in one long slug. "It's getting late. You willing to give me a ride home? That'll keep me safe at least one more night, huh?"

"Sure. But I'm parked pretty far away. Why don't you sit tight while I get my car. I'll give you a ring on your cell when I'm pulling up."

In a pig's eye I'm going to be seen leaving here with you, he said to himself as he walked slowly to his car. He figured she could sit fifteen, twenty minutes without too much trouble. He'd call from a pay phone to let her know he was coming. Nothing could be on his cell. No witnesses would be able to place them leaving together, and no way they'd think he'd follow her when he'd left long before. They'd be looking for the other guy for sure. *If* anybody missed her at all!

He drove around looking for a pay phone. He called and told her it had been further than he thought. Talked her into walking up East Bay. Said he'd flash his lights as he approached her from the front.

Waited a few minutes. He pulled back onto the empty street and headed back to the bar. There she was. Up ahead. Timed his approach so that there were no witnesses around. Picked her up.

"Sorry about that, Vick. You want to stop by my place on the way?"

"Mmmm. I'd like that. It's been awhile." She leaned into him, resting her head on his shoulder, and fell asleep while he drove to his place. He listened to the familiar steady, heavy breathing that was not quite snoring. He felt the hatred welling up inside him.

It was a struggle getting her inside. She was unsteady on her feet. But he was pretty sure it was too dark for anybody to have identified her. Just another drunk girl late at night.

Once through the door, he took her in his arms and kissed her hard. She opened her eyes wide. "Ouch! That hurt!"

"You always liked it rough, Vick."

"Not *that* rough! That hurt! Don't do that." She pushed him away. "I gotta pee."

When she came out of the bathroom, he scooped her up and carried her into the bedroom. Threw her on the bed and fell next to her. She giggled and pushed him away. "You got anything to drink around here?"

"You've had enough, Vick." He put his left hand up her blouse as he kissed her neck. She turned her back and pushed up against him, spooning like she'd always liked it. He ripped off her blouse, and, before she could stop him, unhooked her bra and roughly grabbed her breasts.

"Been awhile for you, too?" she giggled.

He jerked her skirt down over her hips with his left hand, squeezing her throat with his right.

She stiffened. "Hey, stop it. You never liked it like this. You're hurting me! I can't breathe," she sobbed.

He pushed her on to her stomach, pinning her down with his body. He smashed her face into the blankets and entered her violently while she struggled beneath him.

"You were ready for a complete stranger, you whore. I wasn't good enough for you until I was the only one left tonight. I'm the last guy you'll ever taunt, you bitch!" He kept driving himself until he came and was spent, long after Vicky had stopped struggling.

He rolled over. Pulled up his jeans. He stared at the lifeless body of his former girlfriend. He felt nothing but revulsion for her. And he felt a surge of redemption and energy within him. Just as he had the other times. It was perfectly OK without sex, but he had to admit it was even better when he got to fuck them goodbye.

It was easy enough to pull the torn clothing back on her body. Good thing she was so small. He pressed her shoulders into his chest and staggered back out with her to the car. Her feet dragging behind them. Leaning into each other, drunks, just like when they had arrived. He folded her in to the front seat, went back for the weights and chains, and threw them in the back of the car.

He drove cautiously out to the marshes. No need to rush. It was always simple enough to put on his waders and float the weighted body in his arms out twenty to thirty yards in the marsh. And then just let go. None had ever floated back up. He figured he had years before that would start happening. And he knew that nobody could tie him directly to any one of them. And besides, he'd be long gone by then. Long gone.

Ginger looked thoughtfully into the center of the fire at McCrady's. "What's *Cy* running away from, Jack?"

"Good luck with that one," Jack laughed. "Given that he ducks every personal conversation, finding that out would take a real crystal ball."

The appetizers arrived and they fell into an awkward silence as Ginger picked at her tower of tuna tartare. Jack broke the silence. "Ging, why do you still let Dan treat you like that? You should call him on this 'PI' thing."

"Oh, come on, Jack. Don't act like my big brother. It's been over between Dan and me for a long time and he and I've been able to maintain a really nice friendship. If you're going to act jealous when there's no reason, it will just feed on people's rumors about you and me."

Then, suddenly changing tone, she leaned back and teased, "There *is* no reason, right?"

Jack suddenly looked over the top of his second beer into her chocolate brown eyes as a strand of her golden hair fell across her cheek, and wondered to himself why, when he knew there could never be anything between them, he just couldn't let it go. Or, failing that, on which rotation of the ferris wheel, or merry go round, he should say the hell with it and just grab for the gold ring.

"...a penny?" Ginger asked.

Jack turned crimson.

Ginger looked down into her martini, mortified. "Oh. Sorry!"

# Chapter 6

## *September 7, 2007*

Early the next morning, Cy, grumbling to himself about the tourist traffic, walked down East Bay toward the Battery on his way to meet with Professor Easler. As he neared the professor's house, he noticed a police line and quickened his pace, tossing his still lit cigarette into the gutter. An emergency vehicle and two squad cars were parked in front of the house. Catching sight of Dan up on the front porch, he started to call out to him, but stopped when he saw a smartly dressed woman making her way out the door being pulled down the steps by three little kick dogs. She asked Dan something on her way out and he nodded unhappily as she sashayed up the street toward Cy.

"Excuse me, ma'am," Cy nodded his head to the lady. "I'm here to see Professor Easler."

Clearly annoyed at the interruption, she huffed audibly and snapped back, "I see he's going to be more annoying dead than he was alive."

"Professor Easler's dead?"

"Yes, my husband died in the middle of the night and I'm off to do my mourning, such as it is, at the dog park."

"May I escort you to the dog park in your moment of grief?"

"No need. It's my time to be alone with the girls."

Dan called out to Cy. "Step on under the tape and join us. You're going to love this! As you now obviously heard, Tommy's professor turned up dead this morning."

"Murdered?"

"We don't know yet. He was found dead in his bed. The grieving widow called in at 8:30 this morning. Says she woke up at seven and he was cold as a stone."

"And the hour and a half delay?"

"Damn you're good! No wonder they pay you the big bucks! Wish we'd thought of that. Mrs. Easler says she wasn't ready to receive visitors until 8:30."

"Hmmmm..."

"Hmmmm..."

"Do you think this is related to Cindy?"

"Well," Dan replied. "I think Dr. Easler is going to be forever silent on the subject and Mrs. Easler, before remembering she had to take the *'girls'* to the park, announced, 'Other girls? Too many to count much less keep track of.' And off she went."

"How about a little matchmaking here---maybe Mr. Boisseau and Mrs. Easler want to be the founding members of the Charleston Bereavement Society."

"Would certainly fill a much-needed void."

As Ginger turned off Church Street onto Market, she saw the horse-drawn carriages lined up and waiting for their designated tour tags. She knew from friends in the carriage trade that most drivers hoped for a 1 or Reverse 1 Tag so that they could satisfy the tourists' requests to drive along the Battery, with its stately mansions and water views. But she also knew that a really good carriage driver could earn just as much in tips on the less desirable routes. In fact, she liked these other routes even better because the drivers often told seldom-heard stories of old Charleston in these neighborhoods.

As she headed to her left, up Anson Street passing by the decoy carriages, the pungent smell of horse manure reached her even before she turned into the Southern Comfort Stables. A darkly handsome man in his 30's looked over as she entered. He was putting a halter on a Belgian Draft horse which was so huge it made the man look tiny in comparison.

"Can I help you?"

"I'm looking for Clyde Culp."

"Well, you must be a detective. You've found him."

"As a matter of fact, I *am* a detective. Are you really Clyde Culp?"

"Are you *really* a detective?"

"Yes, and I'm looking for information on Cindy Boisseau."

"Are you with the police?"

"No, I'm a private investigator. Do you have a few minutes to talk?"

"No," he said, too abruptly. "I've only got five minutes." He grabbed a brush from a shelf and seemed to reconsider. "We can talk briefly I guess, if you don't mind stepping into the barn while I finish with this horse. We've got a tour coming up."

Unable to shake an uneasy feeling about Clyde, she followed him into the stable, keeping her distance from both man and horse. "I just have a couple of questions."

"OK," he said. "But you never mentioned your name. Not Dr. Shirley Watson, I presume?"

"No. I'm Ginger Grayson. I work with Cy Fapp's agency. Banter aside, where were you the night Cindy was last seen?"

"What night would that be?"

"You've already talked to the police. You know it was August 14th."

He looked up from using a pick to clean the horse's hooves. "Why don't you save us both a lot of time and read the missing persons report?"

"I read the report. I know you dated her. I know you broke up with her. I know you saw her in several bars that night. I know about your police record."

"That 'several bars' part is refreshing. Somebody says I saw her in more than one bar? I only know about Norman's."

"Somebody says they saw you at Big John's later."

"They might have, but she wasn't there when I was."

"Are you sure?"

Ginger's cell phone suddenly rang, and they both glanced at the hip pocket of her jacket as she retrieved it. She saw it was Cy. "Sorry, I have to take this. Just be a sec." She stepped outside.

"Are you guys with Tommy yet?" Cy asked.

"No," she replied, one eye on Clyde as he moved to the other side of the horse.

"Are you with Jack?"

"No, he's with the suspect."

"Oh, you can't talk? Jack's with Tommy?"

"Right," she said as she noticed uneasily that Clyde had all but disappeared on the other side of the horse. "Look, I gotta go. What'd you get?"

"You and Jack need to know that the professor died last night. Dan says maybe murdered, maybe not. See if the two of you can get to Tommy before anyone else does."

"OK. I'll try to find him." She hung up and then she jumped and startled the horse at a voice behind her. "Problemo?"

Unsettled, Ginger wheeled on Clyde. "Are you sure you didn't see Cindy at Big John's that night?"

"Was that call about Cindy?"

"It was about a different case," Ginger lied. "Are you sure you didn't see her at Big John's that night?"

"I don't remember seeing her there---and until now, I don't remember hearing anyone say she was. Did someone say she was there?"

"Does it matter?"

"Whether she was there or not, I didn't see her."

"But you did see her at Norman's?"

"Yes, and that's what I told the police."

"You didn't speak with her?"

"Nope."

"Why not? I thought you two used to be an item."

"And that's why not."

"What was she doing in the bar?"

"What Cindy always did in bars---meet guys."

"'Did?'"

"'Did' if she's been killed. 'Does' if she's still alive somewhere and hasn't changed much."

"Anyone catch her fancy that night. At Norman's? At Big John's?"

"Same as I told the police. She got real lovey-dovey with a guy in a suit who I'd never seen before at Norman's. I didn't see her at Big John's. For a detective, you've sure got a lousy memory," he winked.

She ignored him. "How did that make you feel? The guy at Norman's?"

"Aren't you going to ask me if they left together?"

"I already know you told the police they didn't. How'd it make you feel?"

"It would drive you crazy if you let Cindy's other men get to you. It was over for us almost before it started."

"That is not what I hear around town, Clyde."

"OK Ms., or is it Mrs., Watson?"

"Make it Ginger."

"OK, Ginger." Then, in a voice dripping with obvious sarcasm, he asked, "So in the version going around Charleston High Society, am I supposed to still be in love with her, or did I just never get over her?"

"Does it matter?"

"No. Look, I didn't kill Cindy. In fact, I didn't care about Cindy. Maybe you're right. Maybe I was happy to see her get dumped at Norman's that night. But, I'd gotten over it by the time I got to Big John's. She wasn't worth it. And now, Miss Detective, your time is up." Clyde started to lead the horse out to the street.

Something clicked in Ginger's mind. "Do you remember when you left Big John's?"

"No."

"Do you remember when you left Norman's?"

"No."

"How did you get to Big John's?"

"Is this a trick question? They're only two blocks apart." Clyde turned his back to her and walked away.

Ginger looked thoughtful. And said to herself, But you didn't answer my question, did you?

As she left Clyde, hurrying to get to Jack and Tommy, she admitted to herself that this had to be one of her least favorite parts of Charleston. The market was teeming with tourists in tasteless t-shirts and garish shorts even this early in the morning. "Do people ever look in the mirror before wandering out in public?" She looked around sheepishly as she realized she had spoken out loud. She was convinced that if they ever saw a photo of their ample posteriors they would swear off shorts for life. Of course, she knew it wasn't just here. People used to take pride in how they looked. Now even at the airports it looked as if most people were dressed to go out and wash their cars.

So consumed was she by her mental fashion tirade that she hadn't realized how quickly she'd made her way down Market Street. She dodged cars as she turned onto King Street, trying to remember where Jack had said he'd be looking for Tommy. Damn Jack! If only he would remember to leave his cell phone on. She quickly ducked her head into Baker's Café in case she could catch him before he found Tommy. Strike One. Next, a block further down King Street, she walked up the two flights of stairs by the Antique shop and knocked on Tommy's door. She could hear the conversation on the other side of the door immediately stop.

She knocked again and a young man in t-shirt and jeans opened the door.

"Yes?" He frowned at her.

"I'm Ginger Grayson. Are you Tommy Harper?"

"Yes. Who are you? Whaddya want?"

"It's okay, Tommy," Jack called out. "She's my partner. Go ahead and let her in."

"Good God, how many of you are there?"

Ginger pushed by him into the room, primly handed him a card, and surveyed the apartment. This was either the most meticulous graduate student she'd ever run into, or he had the best housekeeper in Charleston. "Does your housekeeper do windows?"

"I take care of this place myself. What's wrong with the windows?" He looked around.

"Well, the rumors about your great sense of humor seem to be accurate. My compliments to the little homemaker." She glanced at the table in the little breakfast alcove. She was relieved as she noted the coffee still steaming and the untouched pastries in front of Jack. She looked hard at Jack.

"I hope my interruption isn't a problem."

"Actually," Jack said, "Tommy was giving me a broad overview of his doctoral dissertation."

"On?" Ginger looked at Tommy.

"It's very theoretical."

"And obviously way beyond anything I might understand," Ginger smiled sweetly.

"Look, I got a lot to do. Are you here to talk about Cindy or get a free physics tutorial?"

"Well," Jack said, "maybe they're related."

"Come on. Let's move on," Tommy whined.

"No, seriously," Ginger pushed on. "Is it cosmology or quantum mechanics?"

"Let's get this over with. What do the two of you want?"

"Well, oddly it is related," Jack said. "Tell us some more about your suspicions about Cindy and Professor Easler."

"Aw, shit. I told you everything yesterday. I can't prove it, I don't know for sure, but I was pretty sure that the two of them had been sleeping together."

"What made you 'pretty sure?'" Jack asked.

"Look, this is crazy. He suddenly seemed to have this holier than thou attitude toward me that I'd never seen before. And Cindy was teasing me about being a student of the master---was there anything I was better at than he was? Stuff like that. I know she slept around. I know he slept around. It just fit. For all practical purposes it seemed natural to conclude it. C'mon, I don't want to talk about it."

"Did you ever talk to Cindy about it?" Jack asked.

"Yeah, and she got real coy. Asked if it would bother me."

"Did you ever talk to him about it?"

"Are you out of your fucking mind? I'm going to talk to my thesis advisor about the fact that he's sleeping with a nineteen-year-old co-ed---you think that would provide a big boost to my physics career? I don't think so."

"Were you angry at Cindy about this?"

"I told you yesterday that I was. Extremely angry at both of them."

"Angry enough to kill her?" Ginger said.

"I've answered that question at least ten times. I believe you all know I don't have an alibi. I may have had a motive. But I'm not the type."

"Nobody's ever the type," Ginger said. "On the subject of alibis, I came by last night. You weren't here. Where were you?"

Both Jack and Tommy looked at her, puzzled.

Tommy hesitated. "That's none of your business. It can't have anything to do with Cindy's disappearance. You two know the way out."

"I'm not so sure," Ginger said. "Where were you last night?"

Tommy, clearly angry, raised his voice, but answered evenly. "It's none of your fucking business, but if it's the only way to get rid of you, I was working with Professor Easler."

"Where?"

"At his house---but the subject of Cindy never came up."

"How's Mrs. Easler?"

"She'd gone to bed before I got there. What the hell are you getting at?"

"Yeah?" Jack added, looking oddly at Ginger.

Ginger gave Jack a withering look. "Was anybody else there, Tommy?"

"Not that I saw."

"When did you leave?"

"Look, are you about to tell me that Cindy's body was found at Professor Easler's this morning?"

"No. But Professor Easler's was."

"Looks like you're out in the cold without an alibi again, Tommy," Jack said, clearly surprised.

As Jack drove toward Bull Street, he turned to Ginger. "You sure threw me for a loop with *that* one!"

"I didn't have any choice. You never answer your damn cell phone and I had to blindside the jerk with the news!"

"Sorry. You handled it perfectly, though. I'd say the news was shocking and certainly unwelcome to him."

"The question is, was he shocked because he didn't know, or because he did and didn't expect *us* to, or because he was prepared to pretend to be shocked by whoever told him?"

"This kid's an arrogant rocket scientist in training, not a disciplined, cold-blooded killer. We've seen a lot of people who kill out of anger or passion, and they don't respond like he did and you know it."

"Well, he may not be a killer, cold-blooded or otherwise. But people who he's unhappy with sure are having a run of bad luck just after they see him. And conveniently, when he's alone in his room.

"Look," she continued. "The professor's dead. They don't even know if it's homicide or natural causes. And after my run-in with Clyde this morning, I make him more for the passionate killer-type we're seeking."

"OK," he said hesitantly. "Before we get to Ann and Ashley's, and while we're on the subject of throwing one for a loop, do you want to talk about last night?"

It had taken all his self control to even pay attention at Tommy's after Ginger had joined them. The second she walked in, he pictured her all but consummating their relationship last night on her steps. He could feel still feel her against him. Still smell her. They'd been like a couple of kids on their third date. Or is it on the *first date* with kids today? All this time working together, holding back, had all ended in a blind rush last night as they couldn't keep their hands off each other. But she wouldn't let him come in. Clearly she'd been ready, but she hadn't been ready. Where was she today?

"What do you mean?" She glanced sideways hoping he was watching the road. But had to quickly look forward as their eyes met and she felt the electricity. Damn! It wasn't going too fast exactly, but it was all so complicated. Not her feelings. I'm totally in to him and I've never felt surer and waited so long. And yet.......oh damn! Why is this so complicated!

"Look," Jack answered, "we can't just *not* talk about it. At night you can say 'yes' and mean 'no,' and then say 'no' and mean 'yes' like some adolescent girl, but in the end we're both adults and we know this has to go somewhere from here. After all, in broad daylight, 'yes' means 'yes' and 'no' means 'no.' Especially among consenting adults! And even more especially among professional partners."

"C'mon Jack, we each have a job to do and careers to hang on to. We both know where we are. Can we deal with it tonight? Can you wait that long?"

"Depends on the answer I'm gonna *get* tonight!"

"Hmm, I think we'll both like the answer." She wanted nothing more than to ruffle his hair and lean into his kiss. But dammit, it can wait until tonight. Somebody has to be mature about this! Dammit all! But of course, she wouldn't be flailing around like this if she *could* be more mature.

"A little anticipation won't kill you, big fella!" she added as a parting shot as he parked the car at the corner of Pitt and Bull.

"Well, we'll see what the girls have to offer this time of the morning," Jack said grumpily, heading up the steps.

Ashley, wearing a bathrobe, opened the door. "Whooooo," looking back and forth between Jack and Ginger, "...did you come back to test the movie room?"

"Very funny!" Ginger said. "This is my partner, Jack Crisp. As I said when I called, we have some follow-up questions for you and Ann."

"Partner as in he's a private eye, too, or as in, like, he's not available?"

"Oh, as of this particular moment, he's *very* available. But this call is business. You'll *both* just have to be patient!" Ginger laughed.

Ashley looked puzzled at that, but, characteristically, plunged ahead anyway. "Well I've always liked the tall, dark handsome types---especially ones with gorgeous eyes."

"OK, Ashley. We get it! Where's Ann this morning?"

"She's in the kitchen." Never taking her eyes off Ginger's amused partner. "Jack, can I get you something?"

"Black coffee'll be fine. And you should know that I make it a habit to never go out with anyone who only has one nose ring!"

As the three entered the kitchen, Ginger missed Ashley sticking her bejeweled tongue out at Jack. But Ann caught it as she looked up shyly from preparing lunch at the counter. "Hi, Ginger. You are always showing up here with interesting companions. Where's Barnum today?"

"This is Jack, Barnum's and Ginger's partner," Ashley said, pointedly positioning herself between Jack and Ann.

"I'm less loyal and less friendly than Barnum, but I'm handier when the check arrives."

"Well, we'll keep that in mind the next time we see you in a bar," Ashley said.

"OK, ladies," Ginger said. "The time has come for you to tell us a bit more about Cindy and the professor and Tommy."

As had now become their custom, the two girls simultaneously contradicted each other. "What do you mean *more*?" From one. "We don't know anything *about* them." From the other.

Used to it now, Ginger just ignored them. "Yesterday when I was leaving, you implied there was something interesting about a professor. Through Cracker Jack detecting, we've discovered you meant Professor Easler, Tommy, and Cindy."

"Cindy didn't share every detail of her life with us," Ann said sourly.

"Do you mind if I call you Cracker, Jack?" Ashley asked with a demure smirk.

"We didn't think she did," Jack said, ignoring the opportunity to be the good cop with the now clearly smitten Ashley. "We just need you to share what you know. Otherwise, we may not be able help find her."

Ashley, rejected, looked uncomfortable. "Look, she's with her brother. Nothing's happened to her. As I told Ginger yesterday, Cindy's fine."

"Have you heard from her?" Jack asked.

"No."

"If you're right, wouldn't she have let you know she was alright and asked after Einstein?"

Both girls looked down at their feet, and Ann busied herself fooling with her sandwich.

"Ann," Ginger asked, "you don't think she's safe and sound. Can you help us here?"

Ann was clearly fighting back tears. "Like I said, I think something awful...some guy in a bar. If I'm right, could she still be alive, Ginger?"

"Absolutely. That's why we took the case. We find missing people. We're not homicide cops."

"Look, you can either talk to us or talk to the police," Jack added.

"You don't make a good bully! We already talked to the police," Ashley pointed out. "The police are done with us."

"Well," Jack said, "it's gotten a little more complicated."

Both girls looked to Ginger.

"Do you think Tommy could have abducted or killed Cindy?" Ginger asked.

Both shook their heads "no."

"Was she sleeping with Easler?" Jack asked.

Ashley crossed her arms and looked annoyed at Jack.

Ann looked down. "Yes," she said quietly.

"We don't know that," Ashley practically shouted. "You're all making this sound like something it wasn't. Like we're crazy. Or worse---we don't go around telling people who we're sleeping with."

Jack and Ginger looked at each other, and Ginger nodded at him with her hands out toward the girls.

"Tommy went to Easler's house on East Bay late last night," Jack said in a flat tone, "and as far as we know, he's the last person who saw Easler alive."

"No way," Ashley blurted as both girls looked at Ginger.

"Do either of you now think Tommy could have killed Cindy? Or Dr. Easler?" Ginger said. "Or that Cindy and Tommy together could have killed the professor?"

The girls were speechless. Finally Ashley spoke up in a voice choked with tears. "Cindy wouldn't do that...couldn't do that. She wouldn't have been in town for three weeks and not let us know. Ignoring Fucking Einstein, for God's sake! And if she's been in hiding---what does that mean? It doesn't make any sense."

"In your opinion, could Tommy have done this?" Jack asked coldly.

"I just don't see how," Ann answered.

"Me neither," Ashley added. "In books and movies it's always the nice kid next door. But unless there's a side to Tommy when he's angry that we haven't seen, I don't see how."

"It's the 'unless' that will interest the police," Jack said.

"Does all this news make you afraid of Tommy?" Ginger asked.

"Oh, God," Ashley said over Ann's sobs.

Ginger's cell phone rang as she and Jack headed back to the office. She punched it.

"Hello?"

"Ginger, it's Ashley."

"Looking for Jack?" She looked over into Jack's puzzled expression and winked.

"No, Ginger, this is serious. Jack's clearly all yours. That was, like, so obvious."

"OK, Ashley," letting Jack know who it was. "What is it?"

"I feel really bad about something. When you and Barnum came over yesterday, I lied to you about Cindy taking the picture of her and Jim, Jr., with her. I couldn't tell you in front of Ann and Jack."

"Why not?"

"Because I don't want Ann to know I lied to her."

"OK, I'll buy that. But what's the truth?"

"I really thought I was helping Cindy," she said as she started to cry. "I thought she'd gone to her brother's and I didn't want the family and police to see the picture of her and Jim, Jr., on her wall. I didn't want them to know they'd been in touch. I didn't want them to start asking Ann and me questions about Jim, Jr."

"So what happened to the picture, Ashley?"

"I took it that day we called the police. I hid it. I still have it. I really thought she was safe and I was just protecting her," she cried. "Now...now, I'm just so scared."

Silence.

"Ashley?"

"I'm so sorry, Ginger."

# Chapter 7

*September 20, 2007*

## Columbia, South Carolina

As Cy drove through the quiet streets of Columbia on his way to the Boisseau's, he remembered how Valerie would always tell him, each time like it was news, about Sherman's March to the Sea. Valerie---or "Aunt Val," as Ginger always insisted---whose Charleston roots went back to the French Huguenots, spoke of William Tecumseh Sherman, like many Charlestonians, as though she'd had a personal experience with the man. She described how Charlestonians packed up their silver and jewels and paintings and sent them by wagon and carriage to Columbia to keep them out of Sherman's destructive path. Many churches sent their Baptismal and Communion silver. She always described it like it was yesterday instead of over 142 years ago.

Val's great, great grandmother had thought it foolish to pack up everything and had hidden some of her valuables in the house and instructed her slaves to bury much of the rest in the back garden. In the end her actions had saved the family fortune. For Sherman had spared Charleston, and, instead had burned much of Columbia to the ground. Along with, as luck would have it, much of Charleston's misplaced treasure.

He smiled remembering Valerie's consistent intensity whenever she spoke of "The War," catching himself just in time to pull into the Boisseau's driveway.

Rose Boisseau answered his knock almost immediately.

"Mr. Fapp," she said once they were seated, "thank you for coming to Columbia to see me. I seem less able to organize my life and do things the longer Cindy is missing."

Cy started right in. "A quick update is that, despite two weeks of looking, we have not found your daughter. And we don't know where she is. I wish I had more positive news to give you. We did find some new information that the police didn't have. My associates learned that Cindy and Jim, Jr., had been in touch, and Jack Crisp has spoken with Jim, Jr."

"How did you find him? You've seen Jim?"

"He's fine and he's extremely worried about Cindy. We're convinced he had nothing to do with her disappearance."

"No, I meant how did you find him? Where is he? How did you track him down?"

"We're detectives," Cy said, trying and failing to sound impressive. "And one of my colleagues found a clue." Regretting the sarcasm immediately. "Jim, Jr., has made it clear he didn't appreciate being found. But he is very concerned about Cindy."

"Well, of course, so am I," Mrs. Boisseau said, clearly flustered. "It's just been so long since we've seen Jim, Jr."

"We know you're very worried about both your children. You hired us to find Cindy. We weren't hired to find Jim, Jr., and in any case, one of our philosophies is that when we find an adult who does not want to be found, we respect their privacy."

Mrs. Boisseau paused to fight back tears. "I feel I've lost both my children. I'm in the middle of a divorce. I'm all alone. I don't think it's right that you won't tell me where Jim, Jr., is. I need my son. How dare you! You come to tell me you've talked to him and I can't see him. I'm paying you to help this family and all you are doing is making the situation more painful. You are worse than the police. At least they don't know anything. Where is Jim, Jr.? Where is Cindy? Where are my children?"

Cy stepped over and took her hand. "I don't think that you've lost your children, Mrs. Boisseau. You hired us to find Cindy, not to be your family counselor. Jim, Jr., is happy. He has his life together. He's got a nice home and seems content. He knows about your current situation with Mr. Boisseau, and has your phone numbers."

Cy paused, wondering if he should tell her about his meeting with her charming husband? Probably not. No point. No new information for her there.

He went on. "He and Cindy had been in touch, especially after she'd heard a rumor that he had died. He's very concerned about her. We are convinced he has no idea where Cindy is, or what happened to her. In fact, he has offered to pay our fees if it turns out to be too much for you."

Cy paused to hand her a Kleenex. "We absolutely have not given up on Cindy. We make it a practice to give periodic updates to our clients. In person. There is no need for you to take this in any way as a final outcome."

"What have you found out about Cindy?"

"There are no leads that take us to Cindy. There have been no communications to or from Cindy since the day of her disappearance. We believe we can rule out any communications with her two roommates, or any foul play by them, Jim Jr., or Jim, Sr. We are continuing to follow up leads with a number of boyfriends and people who saw her in a couple of, uh, restaurants that night. Everybody we talked to said she's a really, really nice kid. The last person you'd expect something bad to happen to. There is no evidence of foul play.

We accept the fact she is gone, but there is no trail. It is as if she vanished into thin air."

"What about the restaurants? Doesn't anybody remember seeing her that night? The night she disappeared?"

"Well, two of her former boyfriends saw her. One of them saw her with a stranger there. But she didn't leave with anybody. We're not giving up. We'll stay on the case as long as you and Jim, Jr., want us to. It's early. Sometimes people show up after a whirlwind fling."

"And sometimes they don't?"

It was a question, but he decided there was no point in answering. "We'll find Cindy for you. Is there anything else you've thought of since we last met?"

"This, this---it's the---I don't want to even say it," Mrs. Boisseau stammered through sobs. "It's the first time she hasn't sent me a birthday card."

Cy looked thoughtfully at the photo of Cindy with Jim, Jr., on the piano, but had nothing more to say.

A little over a hundred miles away as the crow flies, in downtown Charleston, Jack suddenly woke up to find Ginger still on top of him.

"Um.....Ging?" Softly. "Ging!" Louder now. "You're killin' me here. My arm's asleep."

"Hmmm," she murmured, slowly coming to. She kissed him on the forehead. "I guess chivalry *is* dead. Three nights of love making and you're *already* starting to complain!"

"Three nights? Seems like years already!"

She bit him softly on his live shoulder and rolled out of her bed, heading directly to the bathroom. "It's supposed to seem like minutes! You're...you're just hopeless," she called back over her shoulder as she closed the bathroom door.

Jack shook his arm to try get the tingling to stop. Had it really only been three days since they'd left Ashley and Ann's and started that final, mad dash? Ending up here in her bed? Well, technically, two days and, now, three nights! He rolled over and thought back to the dinner that night at Pearl. The oysters and the spices and the drinks. He couldn't stand having to keep his hands off her, and she wouldn't stop teasing. And laughing! She was driving him crazy. By the time they'd gotten in her front door, he *couldn't* stand it any longer. He couldn't help but laugh at the memory. Tearing her blouse off. Trying to pull off his shoes. Lips and tongues never leaving each other as four hands, indistinguishable as to owner, tearing off clothes and grabbing at body parts. He had no memory of entering her, only of being on top and of her saying, "Jack...Jack...don't stop...don't ever stop...please... no...yes...don't stop...oh God...Jack!" He'd always thought he'd never forget the first time, but *this* first time was clearly better than any other first time. But the details were all a blur. A blur of passion and groping and, well, everything was so wet. And so, well, so perfect. He felt himself getting aroused again, heard her brushing her teeth, and grabbed a mouthful of breath mints. Just in case.

Ginger finished up in the bathroom. She laughed to herself as she looked in the mirror. "Seems like years..." She'd make him pay for *that*. She laughed again. God! The three nights were all such a blur. Why'd she wait so long? God, that dinner at Pearl. Had it really been only three nights ago? No, two. It had to be two. Jack was right, the three nights had been a blur. He'd kept looking at her with those puppy eyes during dinner. After every oyster, he all but begged. It was so much fun, knowing where it all was going, and knowing he didn't know, and that he was clearly begging. His arms around her as they came through the door, tearing at her blouse, both of them kissing like crazy. She'd wanted to say "no" so badly just to keep the joke going, but couldn't. She looked in the mirror. Who had been on top? Her? By the time all, or at least most, of their clothes were off. She was pretty sure she'd been on top. She could still hear him moaning, hear him say,

"Damn you" when he came. Looking down at him, puzzled, and then laughing when he repeated, "Damn you for making me wait so long." God, she couldn't believe she wanted more. She grabbed the toothbrush, half-assedly running it over her teeth, and headed into the bedroom laughing.

As she jumped into the bed, she said, "Are we gonna finally talk about what to tell Cy or are we gonna fuck some more?"

# Chapter 8

**October 12, 2007**

Cy impatiently flipped through the scraps of paper on his desk while he and Ginger waited for Jack to join them to discuss their startling meeting with Bailey Lee earlier that morning. He finally looked up at Ginger. "So, where's our nimble Jack?"

"Maybe his handball game ran late today," Ginger suggested, keeping her eyes on her work. Damn, she thought to herself. Going on three weeks now and we still haven't worked up the nerve to tell Cy. Just like a couple of kids with their parents. And now the Carter case would be too urgent to distract them from their work. Damn!

"It's amazing he can fit our work in, what with his gym dates and handball matches," Cy grunted.

"You need to remind him occasionally," she chided him gently, "that you merely keep him alive to serve our ship!"

Jack slipped in through the door, pointing his finger at Ginger. "*Ben Hur*, galley slave scene!"

"Nice of you to drop by," Cy muttered.

"Sorry to be so late," Jack said embarrassed. "God, I hate driving behind tourists. Some girl was going five miles---literally---five miles an hour up South Battery, and there's no way I could get around her. I finally did and almost caused an accident with a carriage on East Bay. The car was from Delaware. Didn't even know anyone actually *lived* in Delaware!"

"Yeah, but how good a look did you get at her?" Ginger teased, quickly glancing up.

"T-shirt, cut-offs, frizzy blonde hair and not a day under ninety," Jack teased.

"Look, you kids," Cy said. "Oh, never mind.....forget it. Just catch me up on where we are."

Jack and Ginger, appropriately chastised, both quickly caught Cy up on the cases that had just been closed, and briefed him on who to call for closure.

"Well," Ginger sighed. "Then there's Cindy Boisseau. She's been gone two months now and there's still nothing. Missing Persons and Dan have nothing. Same with us. Simply nothing."

Cy shrugged. "Chief called to check in and told me even the asshole father seems almost contrite and distressed now."

"Did Chief happen to mention the gun he was getting for me?" Ginger asked.

"No. I guess my secretarial skills are slipping. Chief didn't mention it."

"Let's catch Jack up on our meeting this morning with Bailey Lee about Carter Ellis," she suggested.

Jack looked up quickly from his donut. "What happened to Carter?"

"You know her?" Ginger bristled.

"Around," he answered.

"Where were you last night after 10:30 p.m.?" she asked. And the two detectives dissolved into laughter, while Cy just looked at them, puzzled.

Jack listened intently as Cy quickly caught him up on that morning's meeting with Bailey Lee, occasionally tossing a glazed donut hole to Barnum.

Cy finished. "Anything to add, Ginger?"

"For Jack's illumination or for Barnum's stomach? No, that was fine."

She turned to Jack. "Jack, what do you know of Carter?"

"I see her around town several times a year at bars and restaurants and at some parties. But not last night, wise ass. Do I need to corroborate my alibi?"

"Oh, is it Betsy again?" Ginger asked, keeping up their agreed-upon pretense.

"Children," Cy said. "Let's stick to Carter."

"Since I don't know her and you two do, let me push this one," Ginger suggested. "Current boyfriend? Former boyfriends?"

Jack looked over at Cy. "She lived with that lawyer...with the firm on Broad Street off Church, for years. Right?"

"Yeah, something Carter... I think Desmond."

"That's right. That's right. We all used to tease her it was going to be Carter and Carter someday. They broke up after four or five years back in '98, right after she sold her hair salon I think."

"Almost," Cy said. "She graduated from high school in '85, spent a year in beauty school in North Charleston, was a hair dresser for about three years and then opened her shop which she sold to her partner around 1993. Then she spent two or three years as a carriage driver before deciding to go to college as a 30-year-old in '97. Shortly after that she and Desmond split up. And she's still not over that."

"What happened?" Ginger asked.

"She said Desmond was tired of her never being content," Cy said. "Always searching. He thought college was a waste of time."

"Any current boyfriends?" Ginger asked.

Jack shrugged. "She's usually alone. Sometimes I see her with a guy but nobody steady."

"Well," Cy added, "not really boyfriends. But, there are two guys she sees more than others. I don't know either one of them. Do you, Jack?"

"No," he shrugged.

"Does she know Clyde Culp?" Ginger tried.

Both Jack and Cy looked up sharply. "Don't know," they replied simultaneously.

"That's good, Ging," Jack added.

"Damn!" Cy said. "I've known this family since I first came to Charleston. She's like my little sister. Ginger, you want to check back with Clyde? See if he knows Carter and while you're at it, you may as well see if he's heard anything new on Cindy?"

"Sure," she said. "What about Carter's father?"

"There isn't one," Cy said.

"Dead?"

"I don't know," Cy replied. "He was there when I left for Charlottesville in '74 and he was gone when I got home in '78. He was a prick and mostly mean to Carter. Nobody ever talked about it much, but it seemed like he just left. Nobody wanted to talk about the circumstances. Even my mom dismissed it with a spiteful 'good riddance.'"

"Could Carter's disappearance be related in some way to her dad's?" Ginger asked.

"Hardly," Cy said. "We're talking about a guy who left his family almost thirty years ago. If he were back, Bailey Lee or Carter would have mentioned it to me."

Jack was suddenly interested. "But it *is*, at the very least, an odd coincidence that the father left and now the daughter is gone, too? Don't remember that ever happening before."

"Look," Cy said, "we don't know anything about the father's departure. But you're right, we should look into it. For all we know, he was murdered, or died here or in South

America years ago, or he just disappeared. And we know even less about Carter. But I'd bet they're totally unrelated."

"Are you too close to this? Is it personal?" Jack asked with concern.

Cy, clearly angry, flared up. "Look, let's move on. *You two* look into it. What else?"

"Which Ghost Tour was she running? Who's her boss?" Ginger asked.

"Wasn't she working for Spirits of Charleston?" Cy said. "The one that does ghost tours and tours of the bars. The one run by Henry?"

"Who were her closest girlfriends?" Jack asked.

"Well," Cy said, "there's her former partner and best friend, Julie Hodges, who still owns Shearly Chic. She'll know of any other close friends. She and I have known each other forever."

"We can ask Bailey Lee," Ginger offered.

Cy finally laughed. "I don't think Bailey Lee is going to be a good source of information on Carter's friends." Tossing a chocolate donut to the chocolate Lab, he continued. "Let's split up the work. And the remaining donuts."

# Chapter 9

## October 13, 2007

As Jack and Cy uncomfortably entered the foreign world of the hair salon and nail spa early the next morning, they were greeted by an effusive young man with "Shearly Chic Emile" embroidered in gold on his black shirt.

"Oh my, oh my. Did anyone see you come in here? What on earth happened to you? This must be an emergency. No one looking as scraggly and desperate as you two have come in here in, like...well, like in ages. I may have to call all hands on deck."

"While you're calling in the Cavalry," Jack said, "ask for a crowbar. You're not giving this guy a cut and a blow dry without getting that Braves cap off his head."

Emile waved both hands flightily in the air. "Well then, we'll start with the junior partner. Hi," holding out both hands, "I'm Emile! You look almost as bad, and Janice will do wonders with that beautiful, beautiful black hair."

"If you two are done," Cy interrupted, "we're here to see Julie."

"Oh, she's in the back with a client. Who should I tell her is here?"

"Tell her Cy Fapp and," gesturing to Jack, "Jack Crisp are here to see her."

"Does she know why you're here?"

"She knows me," Cy responded.

"OK, then. Make yourselves comfortable. Have as much candy as you want. I just filled the bowl. Do keep us in mind when you have a change of heart because you simply must do something about that hair." He glanced at Jack. "Both of you."

As Cy and Jack watched Emile bustle to the back of the salon, Jack looked pointedly at the top of Cy's cap. "He's right. You really do need to do *something*. You could always get a make-over while we're talking to Julie."

"Is everything all right?" Julie asked, a concerned look on her face as she hurried out. "Emile's in a dither. He always is so undone when men need help and don't know it."

Jack stood as Julie entered and smiled. "Well, that would make Cy a lifetime project for Emile."

"Cy, why are you here? Is everything all right?"

"Julie, this is my associate Jack Crisp," Cy offered as the two shook hands. "According to Bailey Lee, Carter is missing. She didn't come home night before last."

"Well, that's interesting."

"Interesting as in not unexpected?" Jack asked. "Or interesting as in news is slow at the salon today?"

"No. Just interesting, Jack." Julie looked amused, looking Jack up and down.

Her appraisal done, she continued, "So what's going on Cy? Do you really think Carter is missing? What did Bailey Lee say? Where does she think Carter is?"

Cy quickly related the basics of yesterday morning's meeting to Julie.

Julie paused before responding and looked thoughtful. "I'm working with a client now. Cy, can we meet for drinks tonight at the Blind Tiger? Carter swore me to secrecy but she's been talking about going to a better place. I can't talk here."

"But do you think she would really just go without leaving a note or calling to say goodbye?" Jack asked.

"I'll talk to you tonight, guys. I gotta go."

"Anyone else we should talk to between now and then?" Jack smiled down at her.

"Well, there's always Emile, but if we're going to be all business, try Desmond and Johnny."

"OK then. Tell Emile we'll take a rain check," Jack said.

"He'll be so excited!" Julie said over her shoulder as she walked back to her impatient client.

As Jack and Cy pulled themselves away from the salon, about a half mile away, Ginger spotted Henry, Carter's boss, alone, facing the door at a booth for four in Jake's Café. He had a cup of coffee and some paper work in front of him. Jake's looked like a breakfast diner straight out of the 50's, straight out of a faded print of a Hopper paining. "They said over at your office that you'd be here, Henry. You gotta minute?"

Henry looked up from his work, and the two other customers and the waitress looked over idly. As usual, not much was happening at Jake's after the early morning student rush. Henry motioned her to sit down across from him.

"Want anything, Ginger? I'm going to have Susie bring me more coffee."

"No, thanks. This won't take long," Ginger shrugged. "Carter disappeared after her Ghost tour night before last."

"How do you know she's missing, and not just out with somebody?" Henry asked, looking truly surprised.

"She didn't come home that night and she's never done that before. Nobody's heard from her since. When's the last time you talked to her?"

"That afternoon when I called her to give her the starting time and number of people on her tour."

"Did she call you after the tour was over?"

"No. Nobody ever calls afterward unless there's been a problem."

"OK then, tell me what happens at the end of a typical tour."

"The guide finishes with a favorite story and thanks the people. Some give tips, some don't. And people leave."

"Where do the tours end?"

"They end in different places. That night, Carter's was supposed to end in Philadelphia Alley between Queen and Cumberland. Are you sure about this? Who says she's missing?"

"Her mom called the police, and then came to see Cy. Did you hear about anything unusual on that tour?"

"No. Nothing. In a sense, you're right. I would have expected to hear from Carter today, telling me that all went well. They're supposed to, but sometimes the guides get lazy."

"How do we get in touch with the people who were on the tour?"

"We don't give out that information." Henry slowly sipped his coffee and looked over at the cook behind the counter, as though he expected Carter to be over there cooking his breakfast.

"Henry. Get real! If Cy and I can get this settled quickly, you won't have to deal with the police. Missing Persons is treating this like Bailey Lee's overreacting for now. Once they change their minds, it's only a matter of days until they come to you. And you know we can get the information without you with three days' leg work from the hotels."

"I'm assuming you want to help us find Carter as soon as possible. If anything should happen to her in the next couple of days, it won't be very good for your business. Or for you, for that matter."

"Actually Ging, if she disappeared in Philadelphia Alley, it will only *help* the Ghost Tour business!" Henry immediately regretted his comment. He leaned back when he saw Ginger's expression. "Hey, you know I like Carter and, of course, I want to help you. Give Jan a call. Tell her I said you could have the list. Jeez, cut me a break. I didn't know."

Jack stood up as Ginger, uncharacteristically late, entered the Blind Tiger. Jack pulled out a chair for her to join them. "I was getting worried about you, Ging. Julie, this is our partner, Ginger Grayson. She's working the case with us."

Julie looked at Cy, amused. "Isn't that cute? Your partners are Jack and Ginger! Is that the Agency drink or can I get whatever I want?"

Ginger gave her an icy glare. "You can have whatever you want."

"OK," Julie said, "I'll have what you're having." Ginger signaled to Sean at the bar, and held up two fingers, pointing at Julie and nodded back when he gave her the thumbs up.

"Julie was just telling us a little about Carter," Jack said, trying to get things back on a more amicable footing.

"Yes," Julie said. "Cy knew her as an unhappy little girl who has grown up to be an unhappy young woman. But as her closest friend, I see a totally different side to her. Everybody knows people who are dreadfully unhappy, and yet can put on a happy face. But Carter was almost the opposite. Her unhappy and gruff exterior masks a sensitive, caring, almost sweet friend you can always depend on."

"Wow!" Jack laughed. "You just described a female version of Cy." Julie laughed with him and Cy shook his head in mock exasperation, suppressing a smile. Ginger remained strangely silent.

"Oh, God. You guys need another round," Julie said, faking a drink signal over at Sean. "But seriously. Ask around---you probably already have---Carter is one of the most real people in town."

"But she is generally unhappy," Cy added.

Julie shrugged.

"What can you tell us about her father?" Ginger asked.

"Not much, but let me tell you something I wanted to say before Jack interrupted. When we were running our business together, David, one of our hairdressers, had a landlord who claimed to hate gays. And Carter went out of her way to work with the landlord to stop him from harassing David, who was the most wonderful guy you can imagine. In the end, the landlord came around---it was just a case of Julie taking a stand. Most people would have stayed out of it or just helped him find a new apartment. But Carter wouldn't back down."

"Yeah, she's unhappy in *her* life," Cy said. "But she's always there for others."

"Do you remember the landlord's name?" Ginger asked.

"No," Julie said. "That sure is a long shot. But I can get it for you." She paused, looking undecided, then went on. "OK, getting back to her father. I only know what she told me. She has no fond memories of the guy. He left them when she was about nine. As far as I know, she's never seen or heard from him since. There's no question that that's the way she wanted it."

"Was he abusive to her?" Jack asked.

"It's hard to know for sure. My sense was yes. But she never told me that he did anything. It was just a topic that you couldn't get close to. A few years ago, we went to a movie and she was shattered by it. It was about a girl being abused by her father. I'd never seen her react to anything that way."

"What do you mean the father left them?" Ginger asked. "Did he abandon them? Run away with the circus? Did he get a divorce? Did he disappear? What?"

"Disappeared."

The four of them sat and stared at their drinks in silence.

Finally, Cy turned to Julie. "I've known the family since she was four and I remember the father. I remember not liking him. I remember Carter was afraid of him. But it never occurred to me 'til now that he hadn't just divorced Bailey Lee and moved away. That's preposterous. Bailey Lee must know something. The police must have checked into it. He didn't just disappear."

Julie shrugged. "I can't help you there. Carter said one day he was there, and the next day he wasn't. They've never heard from him since. I don't know any more than what Carter told me."

Cy was thinking backward. Rapid fire. Thinking back through long-dormant memories. Back to when he was around ten or so and his own father had just disappeared. "One day he was there, and the next day he wasn't." Had Mom known about Carter's dad's sudden disappearance? Would she have never told me? How could she not?

Ginger noticed that Cy had gone a sickly grey. Alarmed, she reached out and took his arm. She was looking into his face. "Cy, are you OK?"

Cy continued to stare into his drink. Some color had come back to his face. "Yeah...I thought I knew Carter. I just.... I would have thought someone---Carter... Bailey Lee... my mom. I would have thought someone would have told me about this long before now."

"Is it important?" Ginger asked him.

"I don't know. I'm afraid it might be."

Jack finally broke the ensuing silence. "Julie, let's set aside the apparently twenty-five year-old missing persons mystery that we haven't been hired to solve. Can you help us any more with Carter's disappearance?"

"Twenty-nine," Cy corrected.

"Twenty-nine what?" Jack said.

"Twenty-nine years. It was 1978, while I was at school."

"Do you want us to get back together with Julie some other time?" Jack asked Cy, looking concerned into his boss' face.

"No, go ahead, Julie."

"Did you talk to Desmond and Johnny like I suggested?" Julie asked.

"Yes," Jack said. "They weren't much help. Desmond said he hadn't seen much of her lately and when he did, she was distracted. But he seemed very concerned and wants to help. And Johnny, who we all thought was her current boyfriend, turns out to have been seeing her less and less. By his body language, it seems clearly of her choosing. I would characterize him as alarmed at the news."

He looked over at Cy and paused. "Unlike Julie, neither one of them found the news *interesting*."

"Interesting?" Ginger asked, looking up from her drink first at Jack, then at Julie.

"Alright," Julie interrupted. "It's like Desmond says--- except that I've seen her almost every day---she has definitely seemed distracted lately, but somehow more hopeful. She hasn't been as focused as usual. She had started having conversations with me about leaving and going to a better place a few weeks ago, maybe a couple of months ago."

"What do you mean by a better place?" Jack asked. "Did she mean she was going to California? Hawaii? A vacation in the south of France? Some people come to *Charleston* to find a better place."

"It's hard to describe. It was like someone who'd just got religion or someone who just, quote, had seen a vision of a better place."

"Didn't that make you worry a little?" Ginger asked.

"Very much. In fact, it frightened me. I was worried for her. But when we talked about it, she was focused on how positive it might be and she would cut off the conversation the moment I showed any concern."

"Could she have been going off to join a cult or an Ashram or something like that?" Jack said.

"I don't think it was a religious thing or something to do with a group or cult. She said she might have an opportunity to go somewhere where she could be a happier person. But I don't think she meant geographically. I don't think it was about Charleston. It was like a happier place for her. Like a concept."

"It sounds to me more and more like a cult," Ginger said. "Was there a new group of people she was suddenly running around with?"

"No, not a group. But there was a guy."

"Go on," Jack said.

"I don't know how important this is---or if it's even important at all---but she met a guy a few times here."

"Here, as in here at the Blind Tiger?" Jack said.

"Yeah, the time I saw them together was at that table over there." She pointed to a small table by the wall just opposite the bar. "It was about the same time she started acting so distracted. She wouldn't tell me anything about him either. She was really secretive. She wouldn't even introduce me."

The three detectives suddenly became all business.

"Julie, what do you know about this guy?" Cy asked.

"Not much. She wouldn't tell me anything."

"What did he look like?" Cy asked.

Julie was clearly uneasy. "I only saw him that once, sitting at that table. But he was short, dark and looked like he was even older than he appeared. I know that sounds really weird, but I don't know how else to put it."

"Was he from here?" Ginger said. "Did he have an accent? Did you get his name?"

"Well, it was funny. Carter wouldn't introduce us, so I introduced myself and he sorta half stood and bowed, and said something I couldn't understand. It might have been his name. It wasn't English."

Ginger became more aggressive. "Dark as in black, South American, LA tan? Mediterranean?"

Julie paused for a second. "I'd guess Mediterranean, not an Arab, maybe Turkish, maybe Spanish or Italian."

Jack started to speak, but Ginger cut him off. Both Jack and Cy looked questioningly at her.

"When did you see them here?" Ginger asked.

"About two or three weeks ago."

"Do you mind if we call Sean over?"

"No."

Ginger signaled Sean to come over.

"Another round?" Sean asked.

"Do you know Carter Ellis?" Ginger said.

"Sure, I know Carter. Everybody does."

"Have you ever seen her here with an older, foreign looking man?"

Sean concentrated for a second. "Sure, I remember him. He's been in three, four times, always sat at the table over there, facing the door. Carter would join him. Sometimes they'd talk for hours. The guy really talked with his hands a lot."

"Did it always seem friendly? Did it seem romantic?"

"Not romantic, but friendly. More like a professor and a student. She seemed to ask him lots and lots of questions."

"Do you remember when these meetings started?"

"I'm sure I didn't see them all. But it seems to me late spring, early summer. About three, four or five months ago. Is Carter in trouble?"

Cy shrugged and looked around the table. "We don't think so. But we don't know."

"What was his name?" Ginger persisted.

"Who knows? I never got his name. He always paid in cash."

"They came in separately? Did they ever leave together?"

"No. Carter always left alone, or joined somebody else at the bar. He'd pay the bill and leave."

"When is the last time you saw them?"

"Ahhh, a week---maybe ten days ago."

"Can you describe him?"

"He's short, clearly foreign. Black hair, dark eyes, dark complexion. His English is odd. He has a very heavy accent. Always wore dark clothes. He looked European to me."

"If you had to guess, where would you say he was from?"

"Maybe Spain, Italy, Greece?"

"How about Brazil or Mexico?" Jack asked.

Sean looked thoughtful. "No, I think most likely European. He just had that manner."

Ginger, looking satisfied, grabbed some peanuts, leaned back, and sipped her whiskey sour.

"Sean, how did Carter appear after their meetings?" Cy asked.

He shrugged. "I didn't notice. Are you sure she's not in some kind of trouble?"

"No, Sean," Cy said. "You've been really helpful, thanks. Let us know if you remember anything else."

Cy turned to Julie. "Is there anything else that might help us?"

"In my opinion, you're on the wrong track. I doubt she ran off with this guy. From the little that Carter told me, I believe he was just helping her with the things in her life that she was unhappy about. It didn't feel like he was talking her into anything."

"At any time did you feel that this thing---this, better place---was a place she could go to without so much as a goodbye to you or to her mother?" Cy said.

"No. I don't think so. Now you see why it struck me as *interesting* when you showed up at my shop this afternoon, and told me she had disappeared. And besides, we don't know now for a fact that she is gone for good. She just might not want to deal with her mom or anyone else right now."

"Oh, trust me, she's gone," Ginger said flatly. The three turned to look at her. Ginger just looked back silently, and Jack and Cy knew immediately that their partner had been holding back something important during the discussion with Julie.

After Julie left and Dan joined them, the four walked over to Cypress for dinner.

"So, do you think the Braves will start winning again? Or is their streak over for good?" Dan said idly to Cy, as the two fell behind Jack and Ginger, walking up Broad Street.

"Not as long as they've got Bobby Cox . Every year was always going to be the year they were going to fall apart, and every year they figured out a way to win. The players change---just not the results. Cox is amazing---he'll get them back up there!"

"You think the Sox'll win the Series this year?"

"You mean win again!?! Hell, the playoffs are random. You can clearly be the best team going into the playoffs, but once in, it's clearly random. One in eight chance! Even Steinbrenner's money doesn't get the Yankees better than eight to one. You can spend a team like the Yankees, and now the Red Sox, into the playoffs, but you can't buy the Series."

Something in the byplay between the two friends brought Cy abruptly back to his days as a child, walking with his dad to the ballpark. He remembered the smells most of all. Old County Stadium.....the crowds....the men always in their suits.....the hot dog and roasted peanut vendors outside the park, always promising a preview of the wonders, the noise, the smells of the concession stands inside the old concrete underbelly of the park itself.

He remembered going inside, walking through crowds of people. Always different people, but always the same crowd. Bustling, jostling, standing in line, juggling all manner of food and drinks as they headed to their seats. Again, it was the smells that came back---fresh beer in cups, stale beer in corners, and the rich aromas of all different kinds of sausages and frankfurters and onions grilling. Everything all mixed together. All one memory, but each smell as distinct as if he were there now.

And then, there were the comfortable pre-game rituals.....his dad filling out the lineup cards with him.....watching the players. Giants, preparing to play a game, at a level that a kid could dream of, could hope for, could almost plan for. The visitors, to be secretly admired, but only in silent tribute. Clemente and Mays, McCovey and Allen, Koufax and Drysdale and Marichal, a young Rose, arrogant and hated, and yes, copied. And there were the Braves, always the Braves. Always just *this* close to being *the* Braves once again. '57 and '58 talked about as though it were just yesterday, and would be today, just around the corner, maybe tomorrow. Meeting his father's friends....everybody around always towering over him. The belts, the ties, the cups of beer, the half eaten sausages. Hearing the men talk: "The game was so much better back in the '40's....the '50's....the players really cared back then....played hard." "So this is your kid?" "Looks like a future ballplayer, right?" "Is it really true you named him after Cy Young?"

Odd, Cy thought to himself, he could never remember saying anything himself at a ball game. Not a word, not even that day he met Hank Aaron. It was all vivid images and smells.... Startled, he realized that he had always been like a voyeur at a series of defining moments in his own life. Just watching, listening, smelling. Never talking. Wanting so badly to be a ballplayer that he had never acknowledged a role as an active spectator. Just passive. Just watching and listening, and, above all, smelling the ballpark. And the game.

"We'll see," Dan chided his friend, unknowingly interrupting his secret return to his childhood. "I think it's finally the Rockies' year."

Once in and seated, they briefed Dan on where they were. Dan interrupted. "Do you all think Carter's been murdered?"

"If you take on faith what Julie told us, it doesn't seem likely," Jack said. "We don't even know if this foreign guy at the Blind Tiger is involved in her disappearance."

"Hell," Cy said. "We don't even know for sure that she's disappeared."

"Well," Dan said. "Bailey Lee sure thinks something's happened. She called Missing Persons again this afternoon. What have you got, PI?"

Jack looked up, annoyed, from his garlic soup, only to see Dan wink at him conspiratorially.

"I couldn't talk in front of Julie, but I found out something just before we met for drinks that changes everything. It's why I was late. And I've been mulling over exactly how to lay this out for you guys. I'm a little excited but I'm also a little scared."

All three men were completely focused on Ginger.

"Did someone threaten you?" Jack asked.

"No, let me just tell it to you my own way."

"Do we really need all this drama?" Cy said.

"Come on, Cy. Let Ginger tell us," Jack intervened.

"I can take care of myself, Jack," Ginger snapped. "I talked to Henry, her boss, this afternoon and he never heard from her after the Ghost Tour. But he cautioned me that it's not unusual for the guides to not touch base after a tour."

"Was it unusual for Carter not to call in?" Cy asked.

"He said 'no.' He was good enough to give me access to the tour list from last night. There were eighteen people on the tour---two families, a honeymoon couple, and a single guy."

Ginger smiled as both Jack and Cy looked at her sharply, but she cut off both of their questions."I was able to get in touch with the two families and the honeymoon couple through their hotels. The couple was at Charleston Place, one family was at the Holiday Inn downtown, and the others are at the Sheraton in North Charleston."

"They all told the same story," Ginger continued. "It was a ghost tour, scary for the kids, informative for the adults, and fun. Nothing unusual happened---they all said Carter was a great guide. The groom thought she seemed distracted and she made more eye contact with the lone guy toward the end of the tour. But, none of the other adults noticed anything unusual about Carter's behavior."

"OK," Dan said. "I'll bite. What about the lone guy?"

"I'm getting there. Everybody described him pretty much the same---a dark, European with odd English and a very heavy accent. A real gentleman---didn't talk much. In fact, he pointedly didn't give his name when they all introduced themselves, and ducked any questions about himself."

Ginger now had their full attention. Nobody touched their appetizers. "The tour ended in Philadelphia Alley just before 9:30. People headed back to their hotels and dinner on their own. But each of them clearly remembers that the foreigner stayed behind and didn't leave. In fact, the honeymoon couple had a few questions for Carter and were the last to leave. As they turned onto Cumberland Street looking back to wave, they saw Carter and the man engrossed in conversation."

"Come on, Ging. What else have you found out about this guy that you haven't told us?" Jack asked.

"I know he paid in cash. I know he didn't leave an address. I know he didn't leave a phone number. But they asked him for a name when he paid." Ginger paused and looked at each of the three men separately. Cy last.

She finally spoke. "He registered as 'Cy Fapp'."

Nobody said a word. And then they each started talking at her all at once.

She held up her hands as the waiter wandered over. "Is there something wrong with your appetizers?"

"Why don't you bring our main courses?" Cy said. With a wave of his hand, he turned to Ginger. "That's ridiculous. Is this a joke?"

"Look, I've been a little spooked about this for the last two hours. I'm the least likely practical joker in this group. I saw the name on the list, in his own handwriting, with my own eyes. I'm still shocked. I've been asking myself what it could possibly mean while I waited for the chance to tell you guys."

"Look, let's not get carried away," Dan said. "Let's look at this. What are the possible explanations that we've got here? Can we reject that Cy went disguised as a foreigner to scare Carter in the alley?"

Cy glanced at Dan. "This is starting to feel too serious to joke about."

"Ginger," Jack said, "you've had two hours to think about this. We've had only seconds. What is your gut saying here?"

"Something has definitely happened to Carter, but it isn't only about Carter. This is broader and somebody---presumably not Carter---is either after Cy or wants to bring Cy into this."

"Unhappy past clients?" Dan asked. "Past kidnapper just released? Anyone put away while you were a cop? Anybody out there, Cy, who has it in for you? Or who wants to hurt those around you?"

"Jay Sanderson from Summerville just got out on that grand theft charge, but I doubt he could spell my name let alone impersonate a foreigner."

"Were any of the people on tour from New Jersey who might mistake a South Carolina southern accent as a foreign accent?" Jack asked.

Dan and Ginger laughed.

"Any recent threats?" Dan asked, looking at Cy.

"No, not really. But Chief called and left me a message that I should get back to him. It sounded important, but I was late for the meeting with Julie so I haven't called him back yet."

"Does anybody think it could be Carter's father?" Jack said.

"Very unlikely, but not impossible," Dan said. "To be sure, in about seventy percent of missing persons cases, someone in the family has made off with the kid. Not that Carter's a kid, of course, but the father *could* have come back to strike up a relationship with her on the QT, win her confidence, and convince her she'd be happier going with him to where he's made a new life for himself."

Cy was incredulous. "After twenty-nine years?"

"I said it was very unlikely. And she certainly would have told Bailey Lee something. And then there's the problem with the disguise and the accent. What's the point? Even if he's recognized after twenty-nine years, unless there were pending charges, and I would remember hearing about that, he wouldn't need a disguise."

"What if he meant her harm?" Ginger asked.

"And spent three months meeting her in public and talking?" Dan said.

"OK," Jack said. "So the father's a long shot. But, Dan, as we agreed, you'll check through all the old files on his disappearance. And Cy, you're going to confront Bailey Lee. We've got the possibility that someone's really after you. Cy, why don't you think about it and we'll start looking into various leads in the morning. We're still left with the most likely case that the dark foreigner is someone totally unrelated to anybody we know or have thought about."

"Or he's not involved in Carter's disappearance," Dan pointed out.

"This guy has to be involved," Ginger said. "His use of Cy's name isn't just a coincidence. Tomorrow I'll start investigating where he's lived the last three to five months, what his real name is, what he's been doing here. Try to dig up any information I can."

"Have we ruled out Carter's ex-boyfriends?" Dan said.

Ginger looked at Cy, "I think so." Cy nodded back in agreement.

"This feels serious enough that I'll push the skeptics in Missing Persons to get back on this tonight," Dan said.

Jack leaned back in his chair. "The only possibility we've left out is that it could be the famous "whistling doctor" who supposedly dueled in Philadelphia Alley back in 1786. After haunting the alley for over two hundred years, he's finally come back and made off with one of our tour guides."

"Well," Dan laughed, "as usual, if it's one of Charleston's ghosts we can't prove anything. Can we rule out Bailey Lee, Cy?"

"Well...you can never rule out the person reporting the crime as having committed the crime. It's always possible that Bailey Lee knows more than she's willing to admit. But I know her almost as well as I knew my own mom, and my read is that under that polished veneer, she's terrified something really *has* happened to her daughter. And, frankly, I'm disturbed sitting here listening to the three of you. I'm worried now that something *has* happened to Carter. I'm worried some guy came into this town and promised to take a troubled person to 'a better place,' whatever that means. And she's run off without a word to anyone. There's nothing funny about this.

"And I'll be damned if I know why that man, whoever he is, used my name."

# Chapter 10

## October 15, 2007

Bailey Lee answered the knock at her door early Monday morning to discover a haggard looking Cy Fapp with Barnum at his side.

"Cy," Bailey Lee exclaimed, "I'm so glad you're finally here. Any news about Carter? What have you found out? Any idea of what happened? Oh, come in, darling. I don't mean to quiz you on the door step. Oh, my goodness, all I can think of is Carter and I'm being so thoughtless. Do come in. You look just terrible. Are you alright? Can I get you some coffee? Come on in. Barnum, I'll get you a treat, too."

Cy noticed that Bailey Lee didn't look so good herself--- her face was drawn, and dark shadows under her eyes showed through her heavily-applied makeup.

"Dan is pushing Missing Persons hard now."

"I should certainly hope so, given all I've done for that boy and his family."

Cy ignored this and pushed on. "Bailey Lee, tell me what happened to Richard in 1978."

Bailey Lee gasped. "Cy, what on Earth does that have to do with my daughter? What have you found out about Carter?

Has something terrible happened to her? Does Richard have something to do with this?"

"Nothing concrete. But in order to put what we have learned in perspective, I have to know what happened to Richard. And I need to know now."

"Cy, you are frightening me. There can't be a connection."

"Bailey Lee, up until yesterday I thought you and he split up while I was away at college. Yesterday, I found out that Carter believed he simply disappeared rather than left. This morning Dan showed me the police report. You're going to have to tell me what really happened."

"Your mother and I decided at the time that there was no point in telling you about it. I didn't even discuss it in detail with Carter until she was an adult. It has nothing to do with my daughter. Why won't you tell me what you've found out?"

"Setting aside the personal annoyance I have that you and Carter---not to mention my own mother---kept this all from me, you need to understand that the police don't like coincidences. Bailey Lee, look at me! *I* don't like coincidences."

Hearing the tone of Cy's voice, Barnum looked up, startled. Bailey Lee looked frightened.

Cy continued. "I've read the police report, and it states Richard and you fought a lot and you claimed he was extremely abusive to Carter. He disappeared on a Friday night and you didn't call the police to report it until the following Tuesday when he was missed at the office. His body was never found, and according to the police report, they found nobody with a potential motive to murder Richard except possibly you or Carter. When they officially closed the case, they noted that he had left no message to anyone personally or professionally, that nothing was missing from his home or office, and that he's never contacted anybody ever again.

"Bailey Lee, when he left that means he needed no clothes, no shaving kit, no passport, no money. No need to ever again contact anyone for anything. He didn't say good-bye to anybody. He left business deals hanging and loose ends everywhere.

"And now the exact same thing has happened to Carter. Within days---maybe even today---there are going to be police all over this house and in your gardens again. And this time they'll be much more thorough. In fact, in case I missed something the first time, I've asked Jack and Ginger to go through the Carriage House to look at Carter's things right now. They should be here any minute. Is that OK with you?"

"Of course. If you think it's necessary. I'll do anything to help find Carter. You know that. I didn't do anything to Richard. Or to Carter."

"In the experience of the police, and in *my* experience, these characteristics suggest murder, not abandonment. And the police saw you as the only possible suspect back then. But, there was no evidence of a murder and they eventually dropped the case."

"I had no idea the police ever suspected me. That's ridiculous. He walked out the door in anger and we never saw him again. I went through all this with the police twenty-nine years ago. Richard could have had a girlfriend; they could have been taking money a little at a time. I told them I thought he could have had a girlfriend and that they had run away together. Maybe she was wealthy, maybe he was quietly siphoning money out of our accounts, maybe he got a new identity or stayed in the United States and didn't need a passport."

"Yes, it's all in the police report and the police investigated all of those angles for months and came up with nothing. None of it made any sense. If he was planning to leave, he was too responsible an executive to have left so many things at the office totally up in the air."

"The police are coming here to go through everything, Cy? Again? They already went through everything."

"Yes. You were the prime suspect back then. And this looks just as bad. If you have anything to hide, you can be sure they are going to find it. *Do* you have anything to hide, Bailey Lee?"

"Of course not, Cy. I mean what...well, of course everyone has things they don't want others to know. I mean this is going to be damned inconvenient if this girl has just gone off for a few days and the police are going to be going through all my things."

"Bailey Lee, you are making me very uncomfortable here. Are you in over your head about something? Do you need some help?"

"I just don't want people---especially the police---going through my things. Can't they just confine themselves to things that will help them find my daughter?"

"Look! Both your husband and daughter have disappeared into thin air from under your roof. The police will leave no stone unturned to try to find out what's happened. Your feelings are of no consequence to them. Let me make this really clear---did you or Carter kill Richard? Or do you know where they are?"

"Cy, this is awful." Her eyes were tearing up. "You of all people should be sensitive to a disappearance like Richard's. He was a horrible man and I was frankly relieved he was gone. It was a blessing to both of us to have him out of our lives. He was terrible to Carter. He beat her. He beat me. You didn't talk about those kinds of things back then. You just lived with them. Teachers at school were starting to ask me about her bruises.

"I always hoped he wouldn't come back. And no, I haven't heard anything from him ever again. And no, I have no idea where Carter is. I'm hurt you would even suspect me."

She absent-mindedly had started to pet a suddenly attentive Barnum, who had stood up and was leaning into her. "Would you please tell me now what you've learned about Carter?"

Cy was struck at how much of her concern about Carter seemed an afterthought. "I wish I had some good news on that score." He walked Bailey Lee through everything they'd uncovered in the last twenty-four hours, leaving out the dark foreigner's use of his name.

"What are the chances that this stranger could be Richard with a foreign accent?" Cy asked.

"I have no idea. Why would he ever come back to town? What would he want with us? I'm sure Carter didn't see her father. If she had, she would have been frightened. She would have had nothing to do with him. And she would have told me."

"What about all this talk about going to a better place? Did she mention that to you?"

"Oh, that's just Julie being dramatic. You know how happy Carter was living here in Charleston. You know Carter. She won't even vacation outside the Lowcountry. She used to tease your mom that when the two of you came here to Charleston you'd died and gone to Heaven."

Cy frowned. "OK, now tell me about my mom's reaction to Richard's disappearance. I'm not a young college kid anymore."

Jack inserted the key Bailey Lee had given them and stood back so Ginger could enter Bailey Lee's carriage house first.

"What a change in Bailey Lee in three short days," Ginger said. "Cy really got to her. You didn't see Bailey Lee when she was the flighty Charleston matron. It's a complete turn-around. Today she's not just playing a part---she's a distraught and anxious mother."

"Did you see Cy?" Jack asked. "From the looks of him, this case is starting to get to him, too, just as you feared."

"My sense is that there's more to this than Carter's disappearance."

"Maybe. But you know Cy. He likes to puzzle things through himself before he lays it all out for us."

"No, this is really bothering him," Ginger paused to look around. "Hey, this is a pretty neat little place, even by Charleston carriage house standards."

They both looked around at the old Charleston brick walls and the French doors opening out to the garden beyond. Bookcases lined the main room where bright braided rugs gave the old heart pine floors a homey look. A delicate wrought iron spiral staircase in the corner led up to the second floor. The fireplace with its aged slate hearth sent up the rich smell of recent wood fires---a nice change from the lifeless gas logs now installed in almost every fireplace in town. The kitchen room beyond was sparse---a simple chestnut drop-leaf table, stove and fridge. It may have looked simple but, characteristically, Bailey Lee had gone top-of-the-line with appliances and kitchenware. There were no signs that things had been neatened up or that anything had been disturbed. It was as if the occupant would be back at any moment.

"Ging, why don't you take the downstairs and I'll spiral myself up to the second floor."

Ginger headed to the kitchen and began looking through drawers and cabinets to see if there was any indication that Carter had planned not to return, or if there was a clue to where she might have gone. She opened the pantry and took a very hard look---nothing alone was interesting or out of place, but taken altogether, it told a story.

"Ging, you really ought to come up and see this."

"Is it an emergency or can I finish up down here first?"

"Go ahead and finish up."

She continued looking, trying to get a sense of who Carter was. She made a mental note to ask Bailey Lee when the cleaning lady had last been in. She leafed through the phone note pad, studied the photos and scraps of paper attached by magnets to the refrigerator, and checked for notes and doodling on the Southern Bell phone book.

Everything was meticulous---even the counters looked scrupulously cleaned and waxed. Everything seemed to be in place. Even the newspaper from the day Carter disappeared was neatly stacked in the recycling bin.

The living room mirrored the kitchen in neatness. As Ginger looked at framed photos on the small writing desk by the window, she began to get a sense of the young woman they were seeking. Her books and magazines seemed the usual mix for a single woman her age: *Cosmo, Vogue, People;* Grisham, *Histories of Charleston*, poetry volumes and a whole section on horses. There was an entire shelf of Edgar Allen Poe. A small stereo system was wedged into a corner with CDs of 80's vintage rock bands and country collections.

There wasn't much more to see downstairs. Ginger headed up the spiral staircase to join Jack. As she emerged from below, the room took on shape bit by bit. "What a shock! It's a mystery how someone described as being as morose and sad as Carter could live in a room this bright and cheerful. This is wonderful; it's a haven."

The room extended into the high-pitched rafters above and the original terra cotta roof tiles were exposed. Oversized windows looked down on the garden below and into the trees above. It was like being in a magical treehouse. You could even hear the water splashing in the garden fountains.

Jack saw the look on Ginger's face. "Yeah, I thought you'd feel that way."

"It's so beautiful. If there were mountains....as a little girl, this is how I always imagined it was for Heidi visiting her grandfather."

"Well, am I old enough?"

"Oh, shut up!" Ginger laughed.

Jack smiled. "It's more like being at a resort than being on a case isn't it?"

"That reminds me," Ginger said, suddenly excited about something. "I heard about a romantic trip on the Edisto River that some company provides called 'Treehouse Trips' or something like that."

"And?"

"And they give you provisions, directions, a canoe and a paddle, and we paddle ourselves up the river to our private treehouse with a fireplace and everything."

Jack frowned.

"Oh, c'mon Jack. I promise we'll both paddle!"

"That's not it. Somethin' about being up the creek without a canoe comes to mind. How about if we deal with Cy first, *then* start planning our adventures in the wild, OK?"

"Oh, all right. But don't be such a stick in the mud," and she laughed at her own inadvertent joke.

"Precisely! Getting back to business then, did you find anything downstairs?"

"I left everything exactly like I found it. No evidence of a struggle or things packed up. Her suitcases are neatly stored in the closet, no good-bye notes or letters."

Ginger looked around, seeing pretty much the same story as downstairs.

"There are two things worth spending some time on," Jack said.

Ginger waited.

"First are the contents of the third drawer." Jack sat on the bed and gestured toward an armoire across the room.

Ginger walked over and opened the drawer and burst out laughing. "Any of these toys catch your fancy? Or are you more taken with the leopard things?" Ginger asked as she held them up in front of her.

Jack laughed and grabbed for the flimsy piece of lingerie. The two of them wrestled with the miniscule piece of silk. Ginger, off balance, fell on the bed next to Jack. "Stop that," she yelped. "Let me have them. How's it going to look if we shred the evidence?"

"There's not enough here to shred."

"Oh, come on now. Let me have them."

"No, I saw them first."

"Yeah, but they'll look better on me."

"We definitely can *not* go *there* right now."

"Oh. Damn! You're right. Looks like you lost your big chance at our first nooner. Besides, how would it look if Cy or the police walked in on us right now," she said as she expertly sling-shotted the offending garment into the open drawer across the room and winked at Jack.

"Nice shot. I'll definitely have to remember that."

"Now should I be afraid to ask? What was the second thing?"

"OK," Jack said, "Take a look at her bookshelf and see if you notice anything unusual."

Looking over at the bookcase, she saw more horse books and beach fiction, but a disheveled set of books on the work table by the window caught her eye as well.

She turned back to Jack. "Why on earth would Carter be reading theoretical physics? Nothing anyone's told us about her is consistent with that."

"My thoughts exactly. Do you remember any of her friends or acquaintances associated with the college? Is there a possible link between Tommy and Carter?"

"It's far-fetched---but worth checking out. It can't hurt to push on him a little more and see what happens. But just because someone has a surprising interest in physics doesn't mean they know every graduate student around."

"I agree it's unlikely but let's look at what we've got---two missing women, one of whom knew a physics grad student but nothing about physics, and the other of whom seems to have an interest in physics but, as far as we know, has no contacts with physicists."

"And add in one dead physics professor," she added.

"Where's Dan on that?"

"Last I heard they have no evidence of a homicide. But they've told Tommy to plan to hang around. But frankly, I don't see someone killing his thesis advisor."

"I think we're off track. Anything else you've noticed as you looked around?"

"The place has a feel of someone getting ready to leave. Her cupboards and refrigerator look like someone heading off on a trip – no leftovers, no containers just opened, nothing restocked."

"Yeah, but her closet has four suitcases and two dress bags in there. No room for any others---full dressers and cosmetic drawer. Doesn't look like she packed anything at all. Or even took a suitcase. Hopefully, Bailey Lee will be able to tell us if anything is missing."

"Certainly no evidence of an actual departure, but perhaps evidence of an intended departure. Wherever else she was going she didn't think she needed the contents of that third drawer."

Jack grinned. "Well, there's that."

# Chapter 11

### October 16, 2007

Ginger rushed around the corner into Bedon's Alley the next evening just in time to see Jack open the door to Cy's house to let in the Chinese food delivery man. She wasn't in such a hurry that she couldn't take a moment to look with her usual fondness on Cy's little sloped-roof cottage, peaking through its unruly front garden. Built just after the Revolution, possibly as an out-building for a larger house on the now prestigious Rainbow Row, it had passed down to Cy through his mother's cousin.

It fit Cy's quirkiness perfectly---the old window box hung at an angle, the door was painted, uncharacteristically for Charleston, a dark blue, and the Confederate jasmine grew in wild abandon over the entry arch. All in all, it looked quaint---not run down. Cy retreated to the local phrase that he was too poor to paint but too proud to whitewash---but the truth was he just liked it the way it was. His place was never a candidate for the house tour circuit, for which he was eternally grateful.

As she entered the door, her senses were happily assaulted by the smell of the food and Barnum's exuberant greeting.

"Barnum," Ginger said, "I know you'll forgive me for being late. Cy, can't you outfit Barnum with a drink keg like in the cartoons so I can have my whiskey already shaken when I arrive at the door after a day like this?"

"I did, but Jack drank it a half hour ago," Cy grumbled.

"I doubt it, unless it came in a beer bottle," Ginger laughed as she playfully poked Jack in the ribs.

Cy looked at the two of them and frowned. "Hey, let's get a move on---Jack, pay the man for the food. Ginger, get in here and give me a hand putting it all out. I'll make the second round of drinks," he added, looking pointedly at Ginger.

Ginger whispered conspiratorially to Jack. "Whoops, have I missed something?"

"No, this whole Carter thing has him grumpier than usual."

Ginger scooted into the kitchen, the only room in the house to suggest Cy knew he was living in the 21$^{st}$ century. The old brick fireplace provided an alcove for a small red-knobbed Wolf range, and a microwave and Cuisinart sat on the worn butcher block counter.

Ginger pulled plates out of the glass-front cabinets. "This search for a dark foreigner is going nowhere," she sighed. "There's not a single hotel or inn in the downtown area that has had a dark foreign male as a regular or repeat guest for the last three months. No bartender or maitre d' outside of the Blind Tiger has seen anyone of that description for the dates I'm checking. This doesn't, of course, rule out his staying in a different place each time he comes to town."

"And it doesn't rule out an obscure rooming house or apartment rental," Jack added.

"Right," she said.

The three of them sat down at the table and began doling out the food, Barnum faithfully settled himself down between Ginger and Cy.

"And," Cy pointed out, "it doesn't rule out that he's in disguise whenever he visits the Blind Tiger."

Ginger was clearly startled. "Right again. I hadn't thought of that."

"Speaking of dead ends, did anyone see them leave Philadelphia Alley together?" Cy asked.

"No," she said. "I rechecked and nobody in the area saw either one of them leave the alley that night."

Jack deftly held his eggplant and garlic with his chopsticks in mid-air. "I also checked with the Playhouse Theater and the homes around the Alley. All those doors are locked at night and no one knows of a break-in or anyone coming through their house or garden from the alley that night."

Cy swallowed his fork-full of General Tso's chicken. "Yeah, I had the police do a routine search of the alley, the gardens and the houses, and they came up empty as well."

"Of course," she pointed out, "they could have left the alley together or separately by either end or the East side onto State Street without anyone taking notice. But nobody saw them anywhere around there, or for that matter, anywhere since."

"So that leaves us with where did they go and how?" Jack said.

"Oh yeah," Ginger said, "I checked with the bartender at Norman's and our guy does not fit the description of the man Cindy was talking to at the bar the night she disappeared. Could you please pass the plum sauce and the mu-shu pork?"

Jack stabbed at a piece of chicken. "I checked with Julie and Clyde and Tommy and Bailey Lee, and it doesn't seem Carter knew Clyde or Tommy. Julie thinks the physics books must lead to the foreigner."

"Give us a little more flavor on Julie's take on the physics books, Jack," Cy said.

"She just felt it was consistent with how distracted Carter's been. As if she had a new interest she wasn't sharing with anyone. She, and Tommy for that matter, were both adamant that Carter didn't know any of the college physics community. Tommy---the arrogant little twit---thanked us for our ongoing interest in his graduate work."

"I thought about the physics books after you told me about them," Cy said. "I went in with the police and had a look at them myself. It doesn't fit the Carter I knew. I looked through the books. They're all used copies and either she or previous owners were marking passages on quantum mechanics. The cops said it would be OK, Ginger, if you also took a closer look at them. Maybe you can figure out what she was after."

"Are we reading too much into this?" Jack asked. "She just had some physics books around."

"Well," Ginger answered, "at the very least, if she was infatuated with the foreigner and physics was an interest of his, she may have been reading up on his field just to impress him."

"Granted," Jack said, "but where does it lead? We already know we have a missing foreigner. There may have been someone else in her life interested in physics. Reading the books takes us nowhere."

Cy downed a mouthful of fried rice. "Most facts take us nowhere, but we push everything as far as we can and in the end see what fits. Do I need to remind you that that's what we do for a living, Jack." He winked at Ginger.

Ginger smiled despite herself. "My sense is that this is related to Carter's disappearance, but it's no help in finding her." She speared a piece of the General Tso's Chicken with her chopstick.

"No, but it may help us figure out what happened," Cy said thoughtfully.

Jack broke through the short silence. "Cy, did you learn anything from Bailey Lee that we need to know?"

"Yeah. Mostly we talked about her husband's disappearance. It turns out he really did just disappear one night. Neither Bailey Lee nor Carter was sorry to see him go. She confirmed he was extremely abusive to Carter. It seems there's a whole lot people weren't telling me about this family."

"Abusive? Sexually?" Ginger asked.

"No. Physical abuse. He beat her a lot, enough for the authorities to notice. I put the fear of God into Bailey Lee by pointing out that she is now a double suspect."

Jack looked up. "Given what you know now, do you think Bailey Lee's involved in either disappearance?"

"Well, that's the funny thing. I'm convinced she isn't. But, I'm equally convinced she's hiding something."

Ginger reached for more plum sauce and some hot chili oil. "Where are we on whether or not there's any connection between this guy who used your name and a past case?"

"Damn!" Cy said. "I asked Dan and Chief to check into that for me. I forgot to listen to my messages." He punched the numbers in on his cell phone, listened, then looked up. "Dan says there are no recent prison releases related to my past cases and Chief was calling to confirm what you found out about Cindy's father's alibi. And, hang on, I've got a message from Bailey Lee."

Cy frowned into the phone and his face darkened as he listened. He slammed the phone shut. "How stupid of me not to listen to my messages. Something's happened and Bailey Lee seems terrified."

"Something the police did?"

"No, I don't think so. She wouldn't talk about it on the machine. She thinks she caused something, but it's not likely the police put her into this kind of panic. She left several messages pleading for our help over the last couple of hours. Why don't you two clean up and amuse Barnum? I'll call if you need to come over."

Cy headed to the door with Barnum at his heels.

Jack called out. "Don't forget this!" He tossed him a fortune cookie.

Cy started to put the cookie in his pocket, but thought better of it. He broke the cookie open, gave all but the paper fortune to an effusively thankful Barnum, and read the message. He scowled at Jack and Ginger as he dropped it on the table and walked out the door.

They both leaned over and read: "Things are often as they appear."


The two started cleaning up. "Hey, Ging," Jack mused out loud. "Have you ever been in a town in this country that didn't have a Chinese restaurant?"

Ginger paused. "No. In fact, everywhere in the world, no matter how small the town, there always seems to be a Chinese restaurant."

"Did you ever wonder how.....where they all come from??"

"Like, maybe China?"

"Come on, I'm being serious. There's always at least one in every town. How did they get there? How did they choose that particular town? Is there, like some central commissar that tells them which town they have to go to? Think about their kids, their cooks. They live in this town or that, totally isolated, no other Chinese. Do they network with each other? Do their kids assimilate? Home school?"

Ginger laughed. "Are you suggesting this is a vast international conspiracy? Why can't they just come? Why can't it just be random?"

"The menus always seem the same---the same dishes. People who've been to China say it's different from food in China."

"Well, how do we know the families don't rotate from restaurant to restaurant around the country, like a Foreign Service or Army Posting?"

"That's interesting." He looked thoughtful. "Maybe it *is* a conspiracy. So what are all these Chinese going to do? Deprive us of Chinese food? Once we're dependent on it, they're going to rise up and what?"

Ginger got into the spirit of it. "Maybe it's in the fortune cookies. Maybe they are brainwashing us with the fortunes. Which one of these do you want?" She held up the two cookies.

Jack lunged for her right hand as she pulled the cookie out of his reach. He grabbed her from behind and they wrestled to the floor, laughing. Ultimately, Jack succeeded in prying the now-broken cookie out of Ginger's clutches. They sat side by side on the floor, laughing and catching their breath.

"What does it say? I'll show you mine if you'll show me yours," she said.

"No, you first."

"OK," she groaned and reached up to the counter above her head, opened the cookie and read out loud: "Beware of risky romantic entanglements."

Jack laughed. "No way. It doesn't say that."

He reached for it, but she pulled it away.

"Alrighty then. With a dramatic flourish, he said, *Mine* says....'Follow your heart.'"

Bailey Lee and Cy sat across each other at her kitchen table, a half full, steaming pot of coffee between them. Cy, exasperated, slammed down his cup.

"Bailey Lee! Dammit, you've hired us to find Carter. Unless you level with us and tell me what's going on, we're not going to be able to find her. Time may be critical. We need to know everything you know."

"I *have* told you everything."

"All you've told me is that the phone rang and a man threatened to hurt Carter unless you stop talking to the police. It doesn't make sense. Did you recognize the voice?"

"I couldn't be sure. It was muffled."

"Did he say how he knew you'd gone to the police?"

"He said they'd driven by and seen all the police cars here."

"They?"

Bailey Lee was clearly flustered and shaken. "Well, I think he said 'we' but he might have said 'I.' What difference does it make?"

"I don't know what matters and what doesn't. I need to know everything. Even things that you feel are insignificant might be important. Did they say where they have her?"

"No."

"Was there any background noise that would give us an idea where he was?"

"Sounded like he was calling from a truck."

"Did it sound like there were other people in the truck?"

"No, he wasn't talking to anybody but me."

"Did he have a foreign accent?"

"No."

"Wait a minute. Did you say he called from his truck? How do you know it was a truck?"

"I just...I just don't know. I just....well it sounded noisier than a car...I don't know. Maybe it wasn't a truck."

"Had you heard from them before this?"

Bailey Lee was now clearly flustered. "No."

Cy was visibly controlling his temper. "Bailey Lee, this doesn't make any sense. A kidnapper would call you making demands and then get upset if the police were involved. They wouldn't call you after the police were involved."

Bailey Lee started crying softly.

Ginger finished wiping the rice and goo off the counter and sat down on the couch just as Jack reemerged from his walk with Barnum.

"Jack, while we wait for Cy, I suppose this is as good a time as any to talk about us and Cy."

"In front of Barnum?" Jack teased.

Getting only a blank stare in response, he plunged on. "OK. But what if your interest in me is purely physical?"

"Jack, I'm serious here."

"OK. What if it turns out to be a short-term fling or a passing fancy?" He held up a hand when she tried to interrupt. "You asked. Let me answer, Miss Detective."

She stuck out her tongue but didn't say anything.

"What if we tell Cy, he fires one of us, which he almost certainly will, and then, later, we break up? Maybe he'd take back the former partner, maybe he wouldn't. Somebody's career would be toast. Who are you nominating for the martyr role? You or me?"

Silence.

"Under normal circumstances, I'd tell him now. But I don't see how we do that given our professional responsibilities and given his expectations."

"One thing that's really annoying is that everyone in town already assumes we're lovers. Dan's starting to really piss me off. Pretending it's not there in a way that clearly suggests he 'knows.' Hiding it from everybody just gives us downside."

"You're right, but *we* can act like we aren't. I don't want this to get in the way of our working relationship. I really enjoy working together." He winked. "I don't want it to get *too* tortured."

"Oh," she said. "So a *little* tortured is OK?"

Jack reached out to take her hand. "Look, I agree it'll be hard, but I think we can be mature enough to have both. For a little while. Until we agree it's time to tell Cy."

Ginger brushed the back of his hand with her cheek. "I just don't know. It feels so right. I don't want it to be wrong. And I certainly don't want it to *become* wrong."

Jack leaned down to kiss the top of her head. "I know we can make this work."

Ginger sat up and pulled away. "We know that Cy can't deal with this. I've gotten *the lecture* at least five times. Like everybody else, he already suspects we've gone too far."

"Well, we can still get away with pretending that we haven't. If we get to the point where we can't any more, Cy's just gonna have to grow up and deal with it like everybody else."

"If??"

"OK then," Jack smiled. "When."

She giggled and swatted his hand away. "You'll have to be the one to tell him."

Jack leaned in to kiss her.

She pushed him away teasingly. "God, no!!" she said. "Not here. Not at Cy's. Not in front of Barnum!"

At that, Barnum, hearing his name, leapt to his feet and trotted back to the door, looking expectantly over his shoulder.

It was getting late and Cy felt he was getting nowhere with Bailey Lee. She was clearly holding back. But what? "Have you had calls from anybody else since the call from the truck?" Cy asked Bailey Lee.

"No, I don't think so."

Cy walked to the phone and punched in *69. He wrote down the number. "Does this number look familiar?"

"No. It might have been the number I saw on caller ID when the call came, but I didn't think to write it down."

Cy picked up her phone. "We need to go to the police with this. The behavior doesn't make sense. Carter may be too much at risk."

Bailey Lee gave Cy a beseeching look. "Cy, you can't do that."

He put the phone down and glared at her. "Until you start telling me what's going on, I can't help you."

Bailey Lee backpedaled under Cy's unrelenting stare. "I don't know if this is important, but I *did* notice a white panel truck going by several times when the police were here. Then after that call came, I got suspicious. And then it went by again. I got part of the license number." She gave him a torn scrap of paper. "And oh yeah, I don't know if this will help or not, but it had a very strange bumper sticker."

"Yeah?"

"It said: 'I know Jack Shit.'"

Cy, smiled despite himself. "Well, I knew that somebody involved with this case eventually had to."

# Chapter 12

## *October 17, 2007*

**Charleston**

Cy reached out to the dash for his cup, took a sip of now cold coffee, and grimaced. Experience told him that after two hours on any surveillance gig, the refreshments started to go bad, and you needed another diversion to stay sharp.

"Cy," Ginger said, "I don't know how you can drink that sludge you brew."

"At least it's the real stuff---not some frou frou brew from a list of thousands at one of those stupid coffee boutiques. Here, try a sip. It'll cure whatever ails you."

"Ugh! Cy! No, thanks! I'll stick to herbal tea. But thanks."

"You know, Ging, after two hours of following furniture pickups and deliveries, and now two hours of nothing, my professional opinion is that these two dopes don't seem to be hiding out from anybody."

"And with that bumper sticker they'd sure have trouble not standing out."

"Anything new from Jack?"

"He's still doing surveillance---and 'seein' nothin'---at 'Antique Jack's' home. He's the registered owner of both the van and the shop. Jack's been there since you and I checked out the vacant antique shop and spotted the van. You know, Cy, I just don't get this. We checked these guys out and they've been in business with Bailey Lee for seven years. There's no way she just happened to spot this van hanging around her house. She knows these guys."

"Yup! I'm not happy with Bailey Lee. She's not telling us what's going on. There's no question she's hiding something from me and the police. I'll be damned if I know what it is, *or* what it has to do with Carter's disappearance."

"Do you think they're muscling her over some failed business arrangement?"

"She'd turn 'em in in a heart beat. It doesn't make sense. Unless she's involved in something worse and is already in too deep."

"I can't believe she'd let her daughter go just to save her own skin."

"Maybe she thought it would never go this far. In her defense---even though reluctantly---she put us on to these guys. Everything else has turned up a dead end. This is all we've got."

"OK. They're off again." Ginger grabbed their two cups off the dash just as Cy slipped back into traffic, well behind the van.

Heading north onto Remount, they followed them up onto I-26 heading west. The van picked up speed and Cy shifted lanes, easily keeping them in view.

"Do you think they've spotted us?" Ginger said.

"These guys are clueless. They aren't acting like they have a thing to hide."

At that point, the van exited onto Ashley Phosphate Road and swerved through the light and across the road, into the McDonald's.

Cy pulled into a distant space. After the two men entered the restaurant, Cy decided to try something. "Can you tell if they have a sight line on their van from within the restaurant?"

"No, they don't. From where they are sitting, neither one of them can see it."

"I'm gonna take a look at the van, then. Honk twice if they head back out."

Ginger watched as Cy approached the vehicle from the blind side. He disappeared. All she could see was his shadow underneath the van. In the restaurant, the lanky one got up and headed to the door. She started for the horn, but stopped herself quickly when she saw he was just getting a drink refill. She jumped as her cell phone rang.

"Hey, Jack," she answered. "Anything there?"

"Yeah, if nothing is something! The back door was actually unlocked. I hadn't seen any movement inside or outside for three hours. So, I just went in."

"Hang on, Jack." The short one got up with his tray. Ginger's hand edged to the horn. "Damn, where's Cy?" She couldn't see him anywhere. She eased her hand off once again when she saw the guy go back to the table.

"You sure the door was unlocked, Jack? You didn't pull a B&E? You know how Cy worries about us getting in over our heads!"

"It doesn't matter---no evidence I was ever in. There's nothing in the house that would bring suspicion to anyone. It's just a house. Nothing there about Carter or Bailey Lee. And besides, I'm out now."

"Well, Jesus! You're not going to believe this. Our big-talking, law-abiding boss just broke into the white van in broad daylight in a public parking lot. And oh shit, here come the two guys out of the restaurant. Gotta go, honey." Ginger flipped the phone off and hit the horn at the same time! Once. Twice.

The two guys, oblivious to her horn, got in the van, backed up and started to pull away. She looked wildly around. Cy was gone.

She circled the McDonald's once. No Cy. She saw the van just make the light and head left back out on to Ashley Phosphate.

"Shit shit shit!" Ginger yelled out to nobody, hitting the steering wheel repeatedly with her palms, as she sat fuming at the light, waiting to make a left turn---one eye on the light, one eye on the van now disappearing into traffic up ahead. She reached over to the glove compartment and pulled out her gun and reached back to slip it into the waistband of her jeans at the small of her back. She grabbed her jacket out of the back seat and, with a squeal of tires, careened into the intersection just ahead of the light change.

Weaving madly, she threaded her way through the double lanes of traffic. Straining to pick up the van ahead, she glanced quickly in the rear view mirror to make sure no cop had caught her act at the light. Just as she caught a glimpse of the van making a right onto Rivers Avenue, her phone rang. She fumbled it open as she hit the turn onto River, tires screeching.

"What?!?"

"Are you OK?" Jack asked.

"Hell if I know! I'm doing my best Jeff Gordon imitation. The guys took off. I'm following and I don't know if Cy's in the van or back at the McDonald's."

"What about his phone?"

"It's here in the back seat with his jacket and his gun."

"Shit, Ging, are these guys dangerous?"

"I certainly hope not."

Ginger followed as closely as she could until they turned left off Rivers Avenue into a deserted warehouse area. She had to fall farther back, creeping along the narrow two-lane road, going as slow as she had to and as fast as she dared. When she spotted the van backing into a delivery bay of what looked like a long-abandoned warehouse, she pulled the car over, out of sight and walked back to check out the area through a copse of trees.

If Cy was still back at the McDonald's he would have called by now. Think, she thought to herself. He had to be in the van or, by now, somewhere in the warehouse. So, what was her move---sit and wait these bozos out, or go in guns blazing to the rescue? That would be worth it, just to see the look on Cy's face. Or should she wait for them to leave and go in then? Of course that could be way too late. Or worse, she'd have to follow the van without knowing about Cy. She had no choice. She had to go in.

She took another long look at the building. No windows pierced its long rusted corrugated exterior. The only sign it was still in use were large compressors on the roof and the hum of an air filtration system. She checked both guns and started walking to the warehouse. As she approached from an angle, she saw for the first time a late-model green Dodge parked on the other side of the building. From the looks of it, she wasn't going to be dealing with anyone Bailey Lee socialized with. But she'd already guessed that.

She took a deep breath, and pounded on the sun-tinted glass of the door in what she hoped was a strong, authoritative knock. After what seemed like minutes, the door opened, and the tall guy looked out startled.

"Yeah?"

Ginger now noticed, close up, that he was black and probably in his forties. Skin too light to have picked that up from a distance.

Ginger decided to try charming him. "Hi. My car suddenly stopped, and I couldn't get it started again." She gestured toward the road with her left hand. "I was hoping there was someone here with a phone so I could call for help. Do you have a phone?"

"Ummm, yes ma'am," he said. "We do. But give me a second to talk to my partner."

He looked back into the depths of the building and called out. "Joe, there's a lady here wants to use the phone."

Taking the opportunity while his back was turned, Ginger stepped past him into the warehouse.

"Wait a minute, Lady. You can't come in here. Give me a sec."

Ginger quickly walked around. She saw the van and a lot of furniture in various states of repair and restoration. Tools, sawdust, littered work benches, and pieces of wood were everywhere. A pervasive, overpowering smell of amber wax filled the air. But there was no sign of either Cy or Carter. At least not at first glance.

The one called Joe hustled over.

"Hey lady," he yelled. "Who the hell do you think you are? What are you doing here?"

Unlike his tall, thin partner, Joe was only about 5'4", but stocky. He may have been in good shape at one time, but his beer belly and thick neck hinted at a weightlifter well past his prime. Ginger sensed his lifting was now confined to beer cans.

"Gosh." Ginger said. "I'm really sorry, guys. My car broke down and I was looking for a phone...Joe? I'm Amy Weeks and I live in Mount Pleasant, and...." She pointed questioningly at the other man....

"Sorry, my name is Andy," he said.

Joe looked at him quickly, annoyed.

"Sorry I didn't introduce myself earlier," Ginger said, "but Andy was kind enough to say you might be able to help me."

"Look lady." Joe said. "This is private property and frankly nobody's ever just out for a drive around here. What are you up to?"

"Sorry to trouble you. I was picking something up for a friend on Rivers Avenue, and my car started giving me trouble. I finally pulled over and it just stopped." She looked around. "What is this place? What do you guys do here?"

"Hey." Joe said. "I'm not buying some bullshit story about you just ending up on our doorstep. You're trespassing. Either leave or I'll call the cops."

"All I want to do is use your phone to call for help. I'll wait outside for someone to come pick me up."

"Aww, come on Joe. Let the lady make the call. We need to get back to work."

Instead, Joe grabbed Ginger roughly and pushed her toward the door. "Just get the hell out of here, OK." Then he stopped, a sly smile played over his pock-marked face. "On the other hand, maybe you wanna stay around for a little fun. Waddya think, Andy? She's good lookin'. Think she could handle both of us?"

Andy looked confused as Joe tried to grab Ginger's arm.

Ginger blocked Joe's clumsy grab, looked at Andy and squared her feet as she turned to face Joe. Time to go on the offensive. "What are you guys hiding in here?" Joe circled to her left as Ginger shifted into a defensive position and moved her keys into her right fist.

Andy, now sensing a situation out of hand, circled to Ginger's other side. "I think it would be best you just left now."

"You didn't just drop in here." Joe added."Who the hell *are* you?"

Cy stepped from behind the van. "Maybe you should ask me first."

Andy whirled toward Cy. Joe, sensing his opportunity, jumped for Ginger. But she leveled him with a right to his solar plexus and then, shifting, put her whole weight into a left chop to his kidney. Joe collapsed to one knee and looked up into the muzzle of Ginger's .45.

Andy jumped back, alarmed."Who are you guys? What do you want?"

Cy stepped toward them. "Help your midget friend over to the wall. Amy, are you okay?"

"Yeah, Ray." She said. "I'm fine."

"Are you guys cops," Andy asked uncertainly.

"Why?" Ginger asked. "Are you expecting cops?"

"We're private investigators," Cy answered. "Our client hired us to find out what you guys are up to here. You two stay nice and quiet for the lady and I'm going to take a look around."

"She's no lady," Joe sputtered, still on one knee.

"Good point," Ginger said. "Sit still anyway!"

Cy called over his shoulder as he threaded his way around the warehouse. "Hey guys, I thought Fast Jack was into antiques." Andy and Joe looked uneasily at each other as Cy walked back toward them. "What do you guys do for Jack?"

"You two are trespassing." Joe said. "And you, asshole," he gestured toward Cy. "You're going to go down on a B&E charge."

"You can call me Ray." Cy said. "But you've made another good point, shorty. Let's the four of us just march into the office over there, call 911 and turn us in for breaking and entering. The police already know we're here. They'll be glad to hear it's time to come join the party."

Ginger reached behind her, produced Cy's gun and tossed it to him.

Cy grinned. "Thanks. What took you so long?"

Ginger sat in the office, her gun on Andy and Joe, waiting for Cy to finish looking around. No sooner did Cy finish his circuit of the warehouse than the shrill ring of the phone broke the uneasy silence. Ginger pointed her gun at the two startled guys seated in the office.

Cy entered the office and stared at the phone. "Joe, answer it on speaker. Play it straight. Remember, you two are alone." Cy pushed the speakerphone button.

Joe and Andy nervously squeaked "Hi" simultaneously. A loud voice erupted from the phone. "Did I catch you two guys napping again?"

Joe looked nervously at Cy. Cy pointed the gun at the phone and shrugged.

"Hey, Ron." Joe said. "We were checking the address for the five o'clock delivery."

"Are you guys going to need me this afternoon?" Ron asked. "Or can I wait to come in 'till tomorrow?" Joe looked over at Cy. He shook his head.

"Yes." Andy blurted out. "In fact, we were just about to call you. We need you and Mickey here in about 20 minutes."

"What the fuck for?" Ron asked. "What's the hurry?"

Cy hit the mute button angrily and Ginger pushed the gun into Andy's ribs as Cy warned them loudly. "Don't push us."

Joe finally caught on to Andy's lead and released the button. "Fast Jack had us bring some new stuff over, and Miss Bailey Lee needs it done by morning."

Cy stood up menacingly, his gun pointed at Joe.

"Shit." Ron whined. "OK. This sucks! But I'll call Mickey and we'll be there in about an hour."

Ginger motioned to the phone, gesturing for them to hang up.

Andy smiled. "See you in an hour."

Joe hung up and looked back and forth between Cy and Ginger. "What now, pal?"

"Maybe you *are* as dumb as you look." Ginger said. "All you had to do was tell those guys not to come."

"Or else what?" Joe said. "You two are the ones on thin ice. You're risking your PI licenses on a trespassing and B&E, and you haven't even told us what you're doing here. And now, in an hour you'll be in over your heads."

"If you're not already," Andy added.

Ginger looked at Cy. "We're investigating the disappearance and possible kidnapping of Carter Ellis."

Andy looked completely confused. "That's ridiculous. Carter's a friend. She's a client. We didn't even know she was missing."

Cy and Ginger just looked at Andy.

Joe looked strained, as if thinking required his total concentration. And then he said, too late, "Andy's right. You guys are crazy. We refinish antiques. We're not thugs or criminals."

"You've already seen us in action!" Andy added, scowling at Joe.

"She sucker punched me," Joe said, glaring at Ginger.

Ginger decided to play a hunch. "OK, Joe. Then why does Bailey Lee think you called and threatened to hurt Carter?"

"I don't know what you're talking about. Maybe it was someone who sounded like me."

"Andy, what do you think?" Cy said. "Bailey Lee thinks Joe called her threatening Carter."

Andy looked genuinely shocked. "I don't know nothing 'bout any of this."

"Do either of you recognize this number?" Cy asked as he showed each of them the result of his *69 inquiry.

Andy visibly winced. "Isn't that your cell phone Joe? Maybe we should call Jack and clear this all up."

Ginger reached over to hit the phone speaker button--- noise of the dial tone filled the office. "Yeah, Joe, why not call Fast Jack and have him explain why one of his clients thinks one of his workers called up and threatened her daughter."

Joe angrily pushed the speaker phone off. "You two are full of shit. You need to get out of here."

Cy silently motioned with his gun for Joe and Andy to get up and move over to the wall behind the desk.

Andy took two steps back, but Joe sat defiantly in his chair.

Cy hooked his foot under the front rung of Joe's chair and pulled him over, backwards into the corner. With his gun pointed at both of them, Cy picked up the phone and dialed.

"Hello Sally. This is Cy. Is Dan in?"

They used their next hour as productively as possible. It was clear to both of them that this was not just a warehouse for future antique sales. Cy was pretty sure he could see what was going on, but he would have to talk to somebody much more knowledgeable about the business to be sure. No sign of Carter, but they needed to follow up to see how much each of these four guys were willing to talk, before heading back out.

Ginger, stationed at the door, suddenly called out to Cy. "Here they come!"

Cy came trotting over from the other side of the warehouse, and the two of them flattened themselves against the wall to the left of the door. Two huge guys in their 30's pushed through the door.

"Thanks for being so prompt," Cy said as Ginger secured the door behind them.

The men whirled around and stared down the barrels of the two pistols confronting them. The heavier of the two, clearly the leader, spoke first. "Who the hell are you?"

"Funny, that's precisely what Joe asked," Ginger said.

"I make you to be Mickey," Cy added, pointing his gun at the silent one.

Ginger pointed at the blond. "That'd make you Ron."

"What's going on?" Ron said. "Who are you guys? Where are Joe and Andy?"

"We're private detectives," Cy said, "looking for information about a kidnapping, and Joe and Andy were kind enough to spend an hour with us after they invited you here."

"Where are they?" Ron said.

Ginger gestured toward the office. "They're tied up for the moment. We have a few questions for you. It'll just take a minute"

Ron looked over at Mickey. "We don't know nothing about no kidnapping. We haven't done nothing. Why the guns?"

"Joe jumped us," Cy said. "It's been a little dodgy since then."

"How do we know you're really private dicks?" Ron asked, looking pointedly at Ginger.

Cy pulled out his wallet and showed his license, too quickly for either of them to catch the name. "Why don't you two take a seat over there so we can see if your stories are the same as your buddies?"

"We don't have to talk to these guys do we, Ron?"

Ron clearly ignored him. "Look, we don't know nothing, girl. If Joe's in trouble again it ain't got nothin' to do with us. We do part time work for Jack when there's too much for Joe and Andy to handle alone."

"Tell us what you know about the disappearance of Carter Ellis and the threats by your friend in there," Cy said.

A flicker of recognition crossed Mickey's face. "You mean Bailey Lee's daughter? I haven't seen her in years. Last time was at a bar downtown." He looked at Ron, puzzled.

Ron shrugged. "I have no idea who she even is."

"How about Cindy Boisseau?" Ginger asked.

The two looked at each other blankly. "Never heard of her," they both agreed.

"Look, there's no point in trying to scare us." Mickey said. "We don't know nothing."

"Hey," Ron asked. "Do the cops just let you two go around pointin' guns at innocent people?"

Cy saw that this was fruitless. These guys were clueless. "OK. You've made your point," Cy said."Just one more question. Do you know of any short, dark foreigner with a heavy accent who works with Jack?'

"No," Mickey answered without too much thought. "Not that we've ever seen. Unless you mean his secretary. I think she's Mexican or something."

"Amy, go ahead and tie them up in the van."

"Are you out of your fucking mind?" Mickey yelled. "Tying us up when we haven't done anything?"

"By the way," Ginger asked as she pushed them toward the van. "Both you and Andy have mentioned that Joe's been in trouble before. What for?"

"He's always getting into fights," Mickey offered. "He's in and out of jail. I don't know why Jack keeps him around. Jack spends more money on bail for Joe than he saves by antiquing the furniture."

Cy looked over. "You mean these things aren't original?"

"No," Mickey said. "I mean, I don't know nothin' about this. I just carry stuff for Jack."

Cy motioned with his gun toward the van. "Get in the van. Call me sometime when you know somethin'about somethin'.'"

Ron tried to look tough. "The next call we make is to the police, Jack."

"I seriously doubt that." He pushed them into the back of the van. "And you can call me Ray."

Only five minutes after closing up the warehouse on their way out, Cy pulled over to the first pay phone he saw on Rivers Avenue before they got back to Ashley Phosphate. "Surprised there are any of these things left," he said to Ginger as he dialed 911.

It was answered immediately. "911 emergency. Can I help you?"

"There's been a break-in at a warehouse just off Rivers Avenue, east of Ashley Phosphate." He gave the specific directions.

"Is anybody injured?"

"There're people tied up and panicky."

"I see you're at a pay phone. What is your name?" Cy hung up.

Meanwhile, Ginger was punching in Dan's number on her cell. "Hey, Dan. It's Ging. This is the call Cy told you would be coming. Cy and I just left a warehouse in North Charleston with four employees of Jack's Antiques tied up. Two on the floor and two in a van."

"What happened and where are you now?"

"We were following a lead on Carter's disappearance and these guys were gracious enough to invite us into their warehouse. Then the four of them jumped us and I single-handedly overwhelmed them and hog tied them while Cy looked on approvingly."

"And lemme guess, these guys' versions of this story are not going to be identical to yours?"

"Well, let's just say they aren't going to be comfortable saying anything at all. In fact, we're so concerned about their unwillingness to share what they know that we've called 911 just to save them a dime."

"Geeze, Ging. What's really going on?"

"Just alert North Charleston police that this may be linked to Carter's disappearance. I'd be surprised if the four guys ID us."

"Did you find Carter?"

"No, but we're headed to see Bailey Lee and we want you to join us there."

"Fine. I'll be there in twenty-five minutes. This better be good. What about Jack?"

"Jack the partner or Fast Jack the antique dealer?"

"I meant Jack the antique dealer."

"Jack has him under surveillance. I think it's premature for you to send someone over to Jack's Antiques."

"I'm afraid to ask which Jack is watching which."

It took them several hours to catch Bailey Lee and Dan up on what they had and hadn't discovered. And it took another hour to get a disconsolate Bailey Lee to admit what had actually been going on. When all was said and done, they were no further along on finding Carter than they had been before the day had started. They had a can of worms involving Fast Jack and Bailey Lee, and had started the process of turning it over to the fraud division of the Charleston Police Department.

But they were nowhere on Carter.

Cy reached for his cell phone as it went off, glanced at the caller ID and winced as he looked at Ginger.

"Uh oh," he said to Ginger. Then spoke meekly into the phone. "What you got, Jack?"

"All hell is breaking loose over here. Nothing happened all day and suddenly four police cars just descended on Jack's Antique Shop. What's going on?"

"Well, actually, Jack, in all the excitement we forgot to call you. A very unprofessional mistake. Sorry."

Cy then filled him in on what had happened at the warehouse. "Then Dan and Ginger and I met with Bailey Lee. Turns out that Jack fakes antiques and uses interior decorators like Bailey Lee to pass them off to unwitting clients in the Charleston area. When Jack saw the police yesterday at Bailey Lee's he had one of his goons call her to threaten Carter as a way of reminding Bailey Lee to never reveal what they were up to."

"So do they have Carter?"

"No. The call came in after she disappeared. They didn't even know she was already gone. Talk about the gang that couldn't shoot straight. They have nothing to do with her disappearance. I wish they did. This'd be the easiest case we ever had"

"How long were you going to keep me hanging out here? I had already finished *The Baseball Encyclopedia* and I was just getting started on Volume I of Gibbons' *Decline and Fall of the Roman Empire* when Charleston's finest arrived!"

"Gimme a break. We've had our hands full all day, and this just broke. Tell you what. If it makes you feel better, you can go out to the warehouse and help the cops untie Ginger's four newest friends if you want."

# Chapter 13

## *October 18, 2007*

Cy sat in his office the next morning thinking through what he knew about Carter's disappearance, which wasn't much. This whole mess with Bailey Lee only added to his frustration. Another dead end. Carter's gone, and now he and Dan were stuck with how to manage Bailey Lee's future on top of it all. Could they keep her out of jail? *Should* they keep her out of jail? Nothing they'd unearthed about Carter's last few days had led anywhere. Nobody in town seemed to have a clue, and Jack and Ginger hadn't come up with anything else on the dark stranger. Except for being seen at the Blind Tiger by the staff there, and always in the company of Carter, it was if he'd never existed.

Cy started at the shrill ring of his phone. He swiveled his chair and reached for it. "Hey."

"Cy, it's George Foster. Out in L.A."

"George! How the hell are you? What's it been...two, three years since we've talked? At least three years since we got together in Santa Monica that time, and over four since the FBI 'I-SPY' session at Quantico. How've you been?"

"Good. Great, actually! We'll never be at a loss for missing persons out here in L.A. And you?"

"The usual frustrations. I had to take on two new hands to help out. Between training them and a backlog of cases, my hands are always full."

"Cy, cheerful as always."

"Yeah. I think the last time I laughed, really laughed, was the caper you pulled in Quantico."

"Oh, yeah. I forgot about that," George chuckled.

"Are you finally coming to Charleston?"

"No, actually I'm trying to avoid coming to Charleston. That's the reason for this call. I've got a puzzling case. A guy named Tim Johnson. Divorced. No current relationships. Free-lance waterfall architect. Disappeared without a trace a month or so ago. I pretty much followed all the leads out here. They're all dead ends. But, it turns out that last August he attended an architects' conference in Charleston."

"And, you want me to do what? See if he met someone here or came back here later?"

"I don't really know. A couple of his buddies say that when he's alone, he likes to hang around bars until the wee hours and it occurred to me you might be able to turn something up."

"What else can you tell me?"

"I've got a file I'll fax to you if you're willing to help and then we can talk about it."

"I'll take a look at it. See if I can come up with a reason why I'd rather have you come here than run errands for you in my own backyard."

Striding easily up East Bay that afternoon, Ginger turned onto Queen where old brick buildings with enormous arched windows and doorways told of the neighborhood's past. This was the old warehouse district where canals and piers preceded today's streets. She much preferred walking along this quieter cross street, with its narrow sidewalks and old lamps, to fighting the denser tourist traffic along the more boisterous, crowded Market Street just up the block. Even at a quick pace, she could enjoy the wrought iron balconies of the old French Quarter and the galleries and restaurants that dotted the way.

This was one of the carriage routes, and from time to time she could catch wisps of stories along with wisps of acrid horse fragrances as the drivers gave their tours. She'd once dated one of the Olde Towne drivers and she had been surprised at the rigorous training and studying he'd had to do to get his tour license. She still loved seeing those huge horses---the Belgian Drafts and the French Percherons---clopping through Charleston.

She reviewed in her mind how they'd agreed to approach Tommy on this. It was a long shot, but she knew that the physics connection was nagging at Cy as much as it was at her. Carter's interest in physics made no sense, and any link to Tommy and Cindy seemed really, really tenuous to her. But every time she pulled at this loose end it begged to be pulled further. She remembered enough college physics to be dangerous, but Cy said he was checking with an old school friend who was now a professor...where? Oh yeah, Berkeley. If she remembered right, he had said "she," causing her to immediately wonder if there was a romantic link there. Then she laughed at the thought. Of course, for all she knew, long distance romances might be the only ones that worked for Cy.

Smiling at the suddenly random thought, she turned right onto King and passed the Charleston Library Society, slowing as she always did to look at the two ancient Ginkgos dripping with Spanish moss. As always, she was intrigued by the sign on the library lawn, "Research and Annual Memberships Available." This was not the main Charleston library, and she was always promising herself that she would call and see what this membership implied. But now, as usual, she was in a hurry, late for the meeting with Cy and Tommy.

From this vantage point, King Street always looked to her like a movie set, with its Victorian and turn-of-the last century store fronts. Shops with apartments above were interspersed with courtyards and alleys. She spotted the Hat Cottage down the narrow passage and knew she was right next to the building housing Tommy's apartment.

Then she saw Cy pacing impatiently just ahead.

"About time," he growled. "What took you so long?"

"You shouldn't complain. You got an extra long smoke break. And I'll toss in a sweetener...I promise no 'Dangers of Smoking' lectures from me today."

Cy just grunted as they passed under the arched entrance and headed up the stairs to Tommy's. Tommy answered his door, saw them standing there and said nothing.

"Can we come in?" Cy asked. "We just have a couple of questions."

Getting no response, he continued, "Not about Cindy or Easler."

Tommy gestured them in without a word, obviously less than happy to see them.

The three stood facing each other awkwardly in the immaculate room. Finally giving up on being offered a seat, Ginger started in as they'd agreed, "Tommy, what's your dissertation on?" Trying to throw him off balance.

"What's that got to do with any of this? I don't see that it's any of your business."

"It probably isn't of any importance, but we're working on another case here in town where somebody had an interest in quantum mechanics that doesn't make any sense to us. We were hoping you'd be helpful to us on some background.

"Someone we're looking for, who had no previous knowledge or training, was reading and studying some physics material. She had underlined pages and pages of material in several books that we're trying to fit into a pattern. Humor me. Just give me the Cliff Notes version of your thesis."

"You guys are a bloody waste of time! I don't know what happens to my graduate work from here on, but I *was* working on extending some recent work on the extension of quantum mechanics to cosmology."

"Is that *still* a hot topic? My boyfriend at Boulder was working on something similar more than a decade ago."

"Well, sorry my work doesn't impress you," he answered sarcastically. "Can you just go now? Why don't you pick up a copy of 'Physics for Dummies' and leave me in peace."

Ginger ignored his dismissal. "I see you have Zukav's 'The Dancing Wu Li Masters' on your desk. Anybody make any progress on a less mystical explanation for particle disappearance and reappearance?"

Tommy looked over his shoulder at the book. "I never found it all that mysterious. I think Zukav is a drama queen."

"C'mon Tommy. Of course it's mysterious. Unless there's been a major breakthrough since I last looked in, physicists have been puzzling over this for nearly a century."

"OK, I'll concede that in their interaction with each other, quantum particles can behave, well, a bit strangely."

"Just as a pretense," Cy interrupted, "just to keep me in the conversation, somebody please refresh my ancient undergraduate memory on quantum mechanics."

"The study of the behavior of subatomic particles," Ginger said. "They have some quirky behavioral characteristics, like suddenly appearing and disappearing, that don't occur in larger objects. The kind of objects we can observe."

"Right," Tommy went on, clearly a little impressed with Ginger and warming to his subject. "These particles can literally appear and disappear and reappear out of nowhere and into nowhere. There are often sudden changes... quantum jumps...rather than continuous changes in their characteristics. Critically, particles and anti-particles can apparently be created out of energy, and then actually have the ability to annihilate themselves upon intersecting."

"And," Ginger urged, pretending to suddenly remember something, "Doesn't the mere act of observing these particles actually affect their behavior *and* their location?"

"Yes. And the behavior of one particle can be affected by the actions on, and actions of, another particle at long distances. Even, in layman's terms, at the other end of the universe. Essentially, it's meaningless to ask where something is until it's actually measured."

He looked at the two detectives. "But why is any of this of interest to *you*? Unless you believe somebody was plagiarizing somebody's work. And this stuff is Physics 101 kind of stuff, anyway. Who is it you're looking for?"

Cy interrupted again. "Tommy, you know we don't know what is and isn't important. You're essentially telling us that physicists believe………"

"Know," Tommy interrupted.

"………OK, *know*," Cy replied. "*Know* that subatomic particles come and go and interact randomly, some affecting each other, simultaneously, at great distances. And that until particles are observed, there's no way to know where they are?"

Tommy just nodded.

"So," Cy persisted, "Where do they go? Where do they come from? How can we affect the behavior of something millions of miles away? Instantly?"

"Those of us who are physicists spend our bloody lives looking for the answers to those questions. Nobel prizes go to those who…"

Cy interrupted Tommy's coming lecture in mid-thought. "And how big does something have to be to no longer be a 'quantum particle'? When does something start being too 'big' and start acting like what we see in the real world?"

"Same answer. Wait for my Nobel speech! Now, if you're finished questioning me, can you two please leave? Go back to something you're supposed to be good at. Finding my former girlfriend and discovering what happened to my thesis advisor. I didn't do anything to either of them, and I'm sorry I can't make it any easier on you by providing alibis."

Ginger suddenly cut in, trying once again to get him off balance. "Do you know Carter Ellis?"

Tommy frowned, looked thoughtful. "No." He looked back and forth between Cy and Ginger, and shrugged. "Never heard of her. Should I?"

"She's disappeared," Ginger replied. "And her interest in physics makes no sense. We were hoping you could be helpful. We now have three people linked to physics in Charleston who have suddenly come to some sort of mischief . Are you sure you've never heard of Carter?"

"Absolutely never heard of her. Now, would you two please go! Gimme a break? I have to figure out where my graduate education goes from here."

"And mourn." Ginger added.

Tommy looked up. "Oh. Of course...and mourn."

Later that afternoon, Cy cradled the phone between his neck and right shoulder as he doodled on a pad on his desk. "George, I thought you were kidding about this guy being a waterfall architect. Do you mean to tell me there really are guys who make a living designing waterfalls?"

George laughed. "You really ought to get out and see that there's a whole world outside Charleston. All the new hotels have 'em. Anybody who's anybody in Hollywood has waterfalls and fountains built into their gardens and houses. In fact, the talk that Tim Johnson gave in Charleston at the architecture convention was on waterfalls in the traditional home."

"Sounds like an oxymoron to me. So, you've been working the case. What do *you* think happened?"

"I'm at a loss on this one. He left without a trace. Poof. No evidence. No witnesses. Nada. No hint he was leaving. All the relatives and the 'ex' say that he's not the kind of guy who would just take off, though they admit he was usually unhappy. And, his drinking buddies find it hard to believe he wouldn't have said something to somebody if it was planned."

"So, you're hoping he met someone here in Charleston who...what? Who he stayed in touch with? Who he's run off with? Or, he's come back here to live with?"

"Hell, I don't know, Cy. You know how this goes. If it goes nowhere, it's a dead end. If it goes somewhere, it's a lead."

"And, this guy has no record at all?"

"None. Clean as a whistle. He was a nerd in high school, college and graduate school. And, whereas he's a regular in bars, he never connects with people, never gets into trouble."

"Well, we can certainly check hotels and bars and show his picture around. It's a pretty good picture and I have to concede that we could get this done faster than you. We can play the local angle. It should be relatively easy given that he has such a memorable face.

# Chapter 14

## *October 19, 2007*

### Berkeley, California

Mary Beth Bracken stood by her window, hand on the wall, looking out over the Berkeley campus, just thinking. She smiled at herself as she remembered the poster her office mate at Cal Tech had over his desk when they were in graduate school. It showed a student sitting at a desk in the left panel with the caption 'Sometimes I sits and thinks.' And, in the right panel, it had the same student in the same pose at the same desk but this caption read: 'And sometimes I just sits.' That poster had got Sid and her through a lot of rough spots for four years with their senses of humor in tact. She made a mental note to call Sid and see how he was doing in London, when her phone rang.

"Hello?"

"Hey! It's Cy."

"Cy! So good to hear your voice. How have you been?"

"Hi. Fine, fine, MB. The missing persons business in Charleston is booming. Things couldn't be better---I've had to bring on two young associates to help me out. And you?"

"I'm great, Cy. Mostly work stuff. Not much happening on the social front since you dumped me!"

"Hell, that was over twenty-five years ago, Mary Beth Bracken! Don't you think a twenty year, long distance relationship between Berkeley and Charleston would have been a bit hard to hold together?"

She laughed good-naturedly. "I bet it would've been easier for us than being together!"

"There's that!"

"What's up?"

"I'm going to be in San Francisco next week for a surveillance conference with an L.A. private eye I know, and I was hoping we could get together. How long's it been?"

"Six years, I think. Is there something specific, besides just catching up?"

"Yeah. Sorry. There are two cases we're working on that've bumped into theoretical physics in a way that makes no sense. Three, actually, but one's irrelevant."

"How so?"

"The relevant or irrelevant ones?"

"If you want me to help, stop playing games, Cy. Both."

"The two irrelevant ones involves a dead Professor.... Easler at College of Charleston....did you know him?"

"No, I don't think so."

"One of his graduate students is the former boyfriend and likeliest suspect in the disappearance of a coed, and possibly also in the death of Easler. The relevant one involves the disappearance a young woman, a college dropout, who had an odd collection of physics books on her desk before she vanished."

"Odd? Odd how?"

"Odd, as in she had no interest in physics and no training, and odd in that there was a suddenly mysterious, older man in her life just before she disappeared. We're trying to see if there's any link between her sudden interest in physics and her disappearance."

"What are the books?"

"Just a sec..........here they are. Zukav, *The Dancing Wu Li Masters*. Bell, *Speakable and Unspeakable in Quantum Mechanics*. Penrose, *Shadows of the Mind*. And Hawking, *The Universe in a Nutshell*."

"She should have had trouble with Penrose and Bell, unless her training is more than you say. The general public can get through Hawking and Zukav. Anything else? Notes? Dog-earing?"

"Yup, I was getting to that. The last twenty pages of the Hawking book...the stuff on a "Brane New World" if I got that right. All the stuff on spin and particle appearance and disappearance on pages 207 through 240 of the Zukav book. But mostly, she seemed focused on taking notes all through pages 237 through 278 of the Penrose book. Even the technical stuff on quantum mechanics and spin."

"I teased you a long time ago that we were in the same business. You look for missing people, and I look for missing particles. It was only a matter of time until we intersected. How do you think I can help?"

"Well, no surprise to you, this stuff has given me a headache thinking back to the days when you got me through Physics 100 in Charlottesville. But I think this is somehow related to the young woman's disappearance and maybe even her whereabouts. So I was hoping I could buy you a couple of lunches, maybe even a dinner, and you could give me a primer of sorts next week."

"Do you have any questions now?"

"A million, but I want to try my hand at plowing through this stuff on my own on the plane, and then organizing it in some way so it isn't too big a nuisance for you. Are you willing to help?"

"Cy, of course. Let me know times and dates. I'll pick the restaurants, and we'll talk and walk. Just like the old days........sort of!"

"Sort of."

# Chapter 15

## October 20, 2007

**Charleston**

"Tell me again," Cy whined," why we're sitting here in front of the Cooper River like a bunch of tourists eating our lunch out on a park bench."

Ginger replied sweetly. "You mean besides getting you out of the smoke-filled den you call your office into the fresh air? Well, because I really like it here! This is where I run every morning to begin my day. Each time, it looks a little different. This morning the fog drifted over everything, and the Pilot Boat going out on patrol looked like a ghost launch as it disappeared into the banks of clouds. All I could hear was the warning drone of the fog horns.

"And, now Cy, it's warm and sunny and I just like to sit and have a sandwich on these wooden benches and watch the children playing in the fountains. We'll work, but just for a minute, look at the sweep of the palms to the Pineapple Fountain. Come on, Cy. Admit that it's nice to get out. We all need it."

Cy pointedly didn't respond.

"It's a gorgeous day," Ginger tried again. "And the fresh air, when you're not smoking, will do you good."

Jack pushed on."It's more fun for Barnum chasing the seagulls and the tennis balls here than sitting in your office waiting for you to share your corned beef."

"Humph."

Ginger remained undeterred. "And the view. Look at the sail boats across the way. I love to see the pelicans skimming the water just beyond the marsh grass. I guess it inspires---or at least fills me up in some way."

"I'm not opposed to inspiration," Cy lied. "But speaking of which, did we ever get paid by the Abbots for finding their daughter out at Wadmalaw Island?"

Jack answered. "Yep. I told you a week ago we got the check."

"OK. *Moving on* ...we have a new case, but there's a problem."

Jack looked at him questioningly as Cy continued.

"Got a call from Miami from a..." he looked at his notes. "Lillian Sandler. She heard I'd found a brother of a friend of hers five years ago. She was hoping we could help her find---bear with me on this---her missing shoe salesman."

Jack rolled his eyes. "You've got to be kidding."

"I'd be really upset if I lost Catherine at Bob Ellis," Ginger jumped in.

"But, would you be willing to pay someone to find her," Jack asked.

"Damn right---especially if I had some big events coming up!"

Jack laughed. "Give me a break. You couldn't afford us."

"Come on, children," Cy continued. "Lillian and a couple of her friends apparently put a lot of stock in their favorite Miami shoe salesman. Name of Robert Flynn. According to her, he's more a friend than a shoe clerk. In any case, they are extremely worried and more than ready to pay us. The real problem is that I'm off to San Francisco tomorrow for the surveillance conference that I'm attending with George. And I've also been counting on spending some time with Mary Beth Bracken at Berkeley for the first time in years."

Ginger looked perplexed. "So, what's the problem?"

"I can't be in two places at once."

"Well, Jack and I'll go to Miami, Cy." She ignored Jack's not so accidental bump of her leg. "Neither Carter nor Cindy's cases have anything open or urgent right now. And we should be able to finish up the footwork on Tim Johnson by tomorrow night at the latest. Maybe even tonight."

Cy sighed. "OK, I guess we're just dead in the water on both at the moment. Hopefully temporarily. What I wanted to talk to Mary Beth about are the underlined passages in the physics books Carter had out on her desk. See if it goes anywhere. See if there's a link we don't see between Cindy's physics connections and Carter."

Ginger looked up, suddenly realizing what she'd heard. "You don't mean *the* Mary Beth Bracken at Berkeley, the professor of physics, do you, Cy?"

"Yeah. She and I went to Virginia together as undergraduates. I haven't needed it until now, but she's the one got me through undergraduate physics. It's time for her to pay the price!"

Later that evening, a lone man in a corner of the restaurant watched Ginger as she left the bar. His lips moved as he angrily thought to himself that he was getting really, really tired of that snoopy bitch. Maybe he'd get around to putting her down just like the rest. She may not have been like the others, but she sure was getting on his nerves. Not that he thought there was any chance she'd ever be on to him. But it would be nice to be able to relax, not to have to be on his guard around her. Women seem to be always getting in the way. She deserved it as much as the rest of them. That was for sure.

He waited until enough time had gone by, and then walked out. Just to see where she was going. He followed her back down to Broad, staying in the shadows, far enough back not to draw any attention. She hadn't seen him in the restaurant and now she didn't notice he was behind her. And she called herself a private eye!

He trailed her along Broad. Saw her turn into The Blind Tiger. Looked down at his watch. Damn! He was late. Just her luck. Well, time is running short for her as well, he laughed to himself. In a more final way of course. If she didn't start leaving him alone soon!

Ginger walked into the Blind Tiger, and took a stool in front of Sean. It was her sixth bar in an hour.

Sean looked surprised. "Where are the rest of the sleuths tonight?"

"I'm actually working solo tonight. No drinking. I drew the short straw checking out bartenders' long-term memories."

"Sounds like we may both need a drink before this is over."

"Not me---maybe you." She handed him the photo of Tim Johnson. "Have you ever seen this guy?"

Sean stared briefly at the photo. "No, I'm sure I've never seen him before. I know I'd remember that Fu Man Chu and those out-dated sideburns. When was he supposed to be here and from where? Was he visiting from the 70's or just from L.A.?"

"Well, L.A.'s a good guess. It was August."

"Mostly Bobby and I split the bartending duties in August. You might want to check with her."

"I already did and she came up a blank. This is going to be a long night. I may come back for that drink after all. But thanks for your help."

Sean shrugged as Ginger headed toward the door and stepped out onto Broad Street. A wall of heat and humidity lingering on from the summer hit her as soon as she left the air conditioned bar. Across the street, she could see the white and black shingles of "Lawyer's Row" reflected in the street lamps. Broad Street was still home to the legal profession and real estate agents, but the stately old columned bank buildings now housed galleries, condominiums, and restaurants.

Preservation was the watchword here. Charleston hadn't changed much since the "War of Northern Aggression," a mere hundred and forty-five years ago. But occasionally a project got approved by the Board of Architectural Review that infuriated the locals. Aunt Val was still fuming about her next door neighbor's successful third floor addition that blocked her view of the river. The approval was based on a set of documents purporting to show the original 18<sup>th</sup> Century third floor. Too late, it turned out the document was false. Ginger certainly understood the frustration of the preservationists in such cases.

But whereas many old Charlestonians railed against the surge of tourists and occasional inappropriate renovations, Ginger appreciated the influx of good restaurants and shops that came as a result. Property values certainly kept rising and she knew that a number of visitors returned to buy property and live in town. There were people who would argue the point with her, but she felt even in the few years she'd been here, the town had become more cosmopolitan.

After a short walk up State Street, she was slammed by an avalanche of sound as she entered Norman's. She snaked her way through the usual mix of the twenty-something crowd and businessmen to get to the dark bar with the famous painting of pre-Revolutionary Charleston, now partially hidden by the mountain of mini-bottles so quaintly still retained by some of the bars. It was only this past year that the South Carolina legislature had finally allowed restaurants and bars to move into the 20th century, and move away from mandatory mini-bottles. The 21st would come much, much later. She was sure of that.

"Well, well, well! Looks like you've traded in horse shit for bull shit," she yelled to Clyde who looked up from behind the bar.

"Well, if it isn't Dr. Watson."

"So you presume," Ginger laughed. "When did you start bartending?"

"Just the other day, actually. Things have been so slow in the winter carriage trade the past few years, that I knew it was either get a second job or move on after next month."

"Why didn't you decide to move on?" Ginger asked sweetly.

Clyde looked away. "It just didn't seem like a good idea......."

"......until they find Cindy," she finished for him.

"Yeah. Or whatever happened to her." Clyde fiddled with the top on a bottle of wine as the silence between them grew awkward. "What can I get you to drink?" He finally asked Ginger.

"Nothing. I'm working. I'm looking for whoever bartended here last August."

"Hey Tony," he yelled to the other end of that bar.

Tony lumbered toward them. "What's up? How ya doin', Ginger?"

"Trying to get some info on a guy who was in town last August." She handed Tony the photo. "Ever seen this guy in here?"

"We see a lotta guys in here. He looks a little familiar, but I don't think I've seen him before. You don't see a lot of guys looking like that these days."

"Wait a minute. Can I see that?" Clyde asked. Tony pushed the photo to Clyde, who stared at it as he idly dried his hands on a towel. "Yeah. I know this guy. Tony, you remember this guy. How could you forget him? He was here a couple of nights recently. Isn't he the guy Cindy spent all the time with the night she disappeared?" He looked expectantly at Tony.

Tony looked skeptically at the photo once again. "Well, he *does* look a little familiar, but I'm not sure. I guess you'd know more than I would, Clyde."

Ginger looked curiously at Clyde. "Are you sure?"

"He looks like the guy I remember. You can never be sure, but I'm pretty sure it's him."

Ginger looked down at her notes and was startled to discover that the dates matched.

"I thought you weren't working Cindy's case tonight," Clyde said.

"I didn't think I was."

# Chapter 16

## October 21, 2007

The three detectives sat in Cy's office, drinking their coffee. They were arranged so as to be able to see each other without squinting through the glare of the morning sun blazing through the windows, and Jack and Ginger, as usual, were trying unsuccessfully to stay upwind of Cy's smoke.

"So, Jack, where are we with Tim Johnson?"

Jack looked up at Cy. "I've got nothing. The people at the Mills House remembered him. Their records confirm he left the day after the conference and neither their records nor their employees remember seeing him since. I checked the major hotels and B & B's downtown. There are several Tim Johnsons who've been there, but none from L.A. No one else remembers him from the photo.

"One of the bellmen at Charleston Place thinks he may have seen him one night late at their bar. And, this is probably pretty inane, but the concierge at the Mills House said she helped him find local fountains and gardens with water features. Seems he spent his days wandering around the historic area, especially South of Broad."

"Well, at least we know he's our guy. Anything else?"

Jack gazed distractedly out at Fort Sumter out in the harbor, noting the blinding glare off to the right of the island."No, I think that's it."

Cy turned to Ginger. "What about you, Ging?"

"Yeah, as a matter of fact, I think I stumbled onto something...."

Jack interrupted. "Sorry, Ging, there is one other thing. I felt like an idiot at the Mills House when I suddenly noticed that he was here the night Cindy Boisseau disappeared. Had either of you noticed that?"

Cy nodded. "Yeah, I noticed. It's the reason I agreed to do this for George."

"Yeah, join the club," Ginger said. "I felt like such an idiot not putting it together until that moment." Ginger briefed the two on her bar hopping, ending with Clyde's ID'ing of Johnson.

Cy was brusque. "Where did you leave it with Clyde?"

"Frankly, I was so stunned by his revelation that I didn't make a whole lot more progress. If you're asking my gut feel, I don't know if he's telling the truth or not. It's in his interest---in the famous words of OJ---to 'leave no stone unturned until the real killer is found'. Tony seemed skeptical. The one thing I can say for sure is that every time I meet Clyde Culp he gives me the creeps."

"Did you check at Big John's?"

"Nobody there ever saw the guy."

"Tommy?"

"Nope. Says he never saw the guy."

Jack broke in. "I don't like coincidences."

"Yeah. Me neither. But there are always a lot of businessmen in town, even when Cindy disappeared," Cy noted.

"But," said Ginger, "how many of *them* disappeared, Cy?"

"Good point. So where does it go if your boy Clyde is telling the truth and it was Tim Johnson with Cindy at the bar that night?"

Jack tried it out first. "He follows her to Big John's, waits until she leaves and abducts her. When it doesn't go well, he kills her and dumps her body."

Ginger interrupted. "Who's he in this version?"

"Johnson."

Cy joined the fray. "How on earth would he know where to hide a body so that it's never found here in Charleston. In a strange town? And you really believe he then goes about his regular business in Charleston, goes back to L.A. as if nothing has happened and then he, himself, disappears a few weeks later?"

Ginger turned to Jack. "Do we know that he did go on with his regular business the rest of the visit?"

"Nothing in his behavior was noteworthy to the people at the Mills House or at the conference. But I'll check again."

Cy reached for a cigarette. Ginger held up her hand and gestured for him to stop. He just shrugged and ignored her. He lit up, drew deeply, and then looked at his partners. "My memory is that, according to George's report, none of his friends reported any unusual behavior preceding his disappearance. But, let's get George on the phone and make sure." Cy slammed his finger on the speaker phone button.

George answered brusquely. "Hello?"

"It's me. Cy. And Jack and Ginger. I'm looking forward to tomorrow! But first, we may actually have something on Johnson."

"Oh? You have any idea what time it is out here? I know you guys are used to snapping your fingers in South Carolina and getting the help to hop to. But us descendants out west are used to at least a 'Good Morning' before we're asked to start working!"

"That's gratitude for you. You've got three honkies busting their butts for you out here, and you expect manners, too! Good morning, George. Am I still invited tomorrow?"

"Sure. Go ahead. What ya' got?"

"Did any of his family or associates notice any change in his behavior after his trip to Charleston?"

"No. I can check again. But nobody ever *mentioned* a change in Tim's behavior. What sort of thing are you after? What are you thinking?"

"It may be nothing," Cy explained. "But I know how you love coincidences. He's been tentatively ID'd as spending an evening in a bar with a promiscuous coed who disappeared that night and who is one of our unsolved cases."

"Nobody, but nobody, makes Tim out to be a murderer. No violent behavior has ever been indicated. Is there another possible explanation? Did he leave the bar with her?"

"No." Ginger frowned as she looked at the phone. "But of course, they could have spent time together. She leaves to go to another bar. He does whatever he does and somebody else makes off with her."

George continued the scenario. "What if they liaise back at his hotel. Hit it off. She stays with him during the conference. Comes back to L.A. with him. And the two of them go off together later? Does that work? What's her name?"

Jack summarized. "Cindy Boisseau, age 19, Caucasian, flirtatious, promiscuous, loves the bar scene. Did any such person pop up in his life after Charleston?"

"Hardly," George laughed. "But I'll check the planes to see if she flew back with him. I think it's a long shot that they were an item for weeks and none of his family or friends knew about it."

Cy stamped out a cigarette angrily. "I'll bring her photo out to you tomorrow and we'll see where it leads. Frankly, I think it's a dead end."

"OK. Do you all think it's possible she stayed in Charleston pining away for Tim and they joined up later?"

"That's an easy one," Cy responded. "Not unless she spent those months hiding in one of the rumored Pirate tunnels on upper Church Street. She was never seen again after that night."

# Chapter 17

*October 22, 2007*

**South Beach, Miami**

Jack and Ginger, having checked into the Tides, were now sitting outside on the front deck, looking out over Ocean Avenue. Ginger glanced at Jack. "Wow, this is spectacular! How are we ever going to get any work done here?"

"I had the same thought. But Cy isn't going to be happy having us take a four-day South Beach vacation. Not to mention that it'll feed on his growing suspicions that your intentions toward me may not be so honorable any more!"

He ignored Ginger's kick under the table. "And," he went on, "Lillian was nice enough to put us up here at the Tides. I'll bet she expects us to have something to show for it."

"Did you see that?"

"The one with the cleavage or the guy?"

"Well. I don't know where to start. That was a guy with the cleavage and the slinky dress! But, did you see the two girls in spandex roller blading right through all the pedestrians? Look at the guy and the poodle in the old Cadillac convertible."

"OK, Ging, you win. Let's look at the beach and the people before we have to work."

A waiter glided up to them. "Are you Jack and Ginger? Bobby sent these two Mojitos out from the bar. Welcome to The Tides." He hesitated. "Unless you prefer Jack Daniels and Ginger Ale." He smirked as he set the tall frosted glasses on the table.

Ginger smiled sweetly. "No, we're fine with these. We'll switch later, thank you."

"Just one request," Jack added. "Can you ask Bobby to come out for a minute?"

After the waiter headed back, Ginger poked Jack. "Come on. How do you keep from staring?"

"You don't. People here are expecting to be looked at. And everybody's looking out over the beach in that general direction. You can't *not* look!"

"Is Bobby anything near what you expected?"

"Pretty much. A little older than I thought for a South Beach concierge, but we know so little about Robert Flynn that it's presumptuous of us to assume we can know anything about his former partner."

Bobby appeared silently behind them and startled them. "Is there a problem?"

"No. No. No problem," Jack stammered, clearly startled at the thought that Bobby might have overheard their conversation. "Thanks for the Mojitos. Lillian and her friends are going to show up any minute. If we end up having dinner on our own, where would you recommend?"

"Elegant? Gay Scene? Casual? Typical South Beach?"

"Well," Ginger cut in. "If it's just going to be the two of us, let's go with elegant and memorable."

"That would be the Blue Door at the Delano. I'll go ahead and get you seven-thirty reservations and we'll switch them to tomorrow night if Lillian's already made plans for you. And, *right on cue*, here's Lillian now. I'll scoot and let you detect without me. I'll see you at ten tomorrow on the beach right in front of the hotel where we arranged."

Lillian, dressed in stylish beach linen chic, approached with two grey-haired ladies following in her wake. "You must be Jack and Ginger. This is my sister, Dorothy Addamson, and our friend Ruth Geld who I told you about. Wasn't that Bobby you were just talking to?"

Ginger held out her hand to Lillian. "Nice to meet you. Yes, we're meeting with him in the morning."

"Have you had a chance to settle in?"

"Yes," Ginger assured her. "We're very comfortable. The hotel is perfect and beautifully understated….not what we're used to in Charleston. It's so nice. Are you sure you want us staying here during the investigation?"

"You need to spend time with Robert's ex-partner, and, since he's the concierge here, it seemed to make sense," Lillian explained. "Don't worry about the money. We just want you and Cy to find Robert."

Jack cut in impatiently. "Can we get you all some drinks before we get started?"

Ginger shifted her chair across the table. "Do you mind if I sit with my back to the beach so I don't get distracted?"

Ruth laughed. "It takes us all about five years after we move down here to stop staring at this scene."

Jack raised his glass toward the three women. "Bobby sent us over these Mojitos. What would you ladies like before we get down to business?"

"Three white wines," Lillian answered without a pause.

Ruth immediately jumped in. "I haven't had a Mojito in ages. Make it a Mojito and two white wines," as she gestured to the waiter.

"OK." Jack began. "Tell us everything you know about Robert that might help us."

## U.C. Berkeley

Mary Beth's door was open when Cy arrived at her office in the Physics Department. A couple of young men were asking her questions and she was at the chalkboard, so he walked right by and idly started reading the announcements on the bulletin board.

Time goes by, he observed to himself. But the college students stay the same age and the messy bulletin boards with all their scattered attachments somehow never change. Movies, lectures, tutoring.....

"Looking for a tutor, big fella?" A familiar voice behind him inquired.

"You bet," he replied, turning around and grinning as he hugged Mary Beth. "And I'm desperate.....as desperate as I was thirty years ago. *Professor* Bracken." He couldn't help but notice the amused looks the two students gave them as they walked by, hiking their backpacks up on to their shoulders.

"Thank you, *Professor* Bracken." They mimicked in unison as they grinned and walked by.

"You're welcome......you two'll be fine if you can keep your mind on your work." She laughed as they waved without looking back.

"How about a walk and a snack in Sproul Plaza," she asked Cy.

"Sure, MB. Just like old times. It'll make me feel a lot younger."

She locked up her office. The two walked down the stairs together and out into the beautiful Berkeley late afternoon. They started their walk across campus.

"How's the surveillance conference going?"

"Oh, fine. Really it was just an excuse to spend some time with George on a couple of his cases, and catch up with you. Did you have a chance to look through the specific pages Carter was working on?"

"I did."

"And?"

"And nothing. It's all pretty elementary stuff. I think I need some context and some questions before I can be helpful."

"Fair enough." Cy spent the next twenty minutes telling her about Carter's disappearance and the lack of any leads as they strolled along the stream and through the redwoods of the Berkeley campus. From time to time, she had to stop to talk to students and other professors along the way.

"So how and why has theoretical physics come up?" MB asked.

"It's mostly the books. Pure logic says they're irrelevant, but our intuition is that they aren't. What keeps coming up both in her notes and in the graduate student's work I told you about is the disappearance, sudden appearances, and re-appearances of particles. Or is it waves? How do you know where a particle actually is, if observing it actually affects its precise location or characteristics?"

"Well, actually, it's both particles *and* waves. Most simply put, they're both particles and waves at the same time, until observed. And it then becomes the observed particle only."

"MB, you're losing me. When it *is* observed, what happens to the other.....er, is it states? Give me an example."

"The same thing that happens to the 2 on a dice when you roll a 6, or the same thing that happens to all the remaining diamonds in a deck of cards when you get a spade that busts your diamond flush."

"You mean they're still there, just not visible.....er, observable?"

"No. They just don't exist in *that* hand or on that roll. All the other, unobserved, potential possibilities have essentially become the one, certain, observed outcome. Look, the analogy's not perfect, but think of it like being dealt 1,000 hands from the same deck, or rolling the same die 1,000 times. You'll get a spectrum---or a distribution---of results.

The same thing happens if you observe a large number of wave/particles. You'll get a spectrum, or distribution, of observations at each point. Each particle had some probability of being at the point you observed, and one of them actually was.

"But the busted flush happened, and no matter how much you'd wish for a different outcome, you got the busted flush *that* time. Next time, you'll observe a different outcome, probably! Although," she laughed, "maybe not in *your* case, Cy!"

"I thought Einstein said 'God doesn't throw dice'."

"Well, it wasn't his only mistake. Look, there's a famous historical paradox that we use in laying this out. It's called the paradox of Schroedinger's cat. Quantum mechanics seems to show it's as if you have a cat in, say, a box and you don't know if it's alive or dead. But you can't prove that it's not both."

"Both? As in at the same time?"

"Precisely. You and I, in fact nobody, can prove which it is until you lift the lid and observe it. Theoretically, it's simultaneously both alive and dead until it's observed."

"OK then, since we also know that observing particles affects them, how do you guys test the theories if the observations aren't independent of your meddling around?"

"How do you in *your* detecting? How do you tell if the behavior of a suspect is independent of your meddling? How many innocent citizens are convicted because their behavior, and the behavior---not to mention---the *memories* of their fellow citizens, are affected by your accusations, by the ongoing actions and observations of the police and the lawyers?"

"Good point, but not relevant!"

"I don't agree. Is the particle---or the universe for that matter---what we observe, or what we theorize? How do you know that the universe---or the particle---or, for that matter, your poker hand or your suspects aren't impacted by your observations? By *your* actions?"

Jack and Ginger stopped short just inside the entry of the Delano Hotel.

"My God!" Ginger said. "I knew they'd redone the old place, but this is really over the top!"

"Well, it's *supposed to be* over the top, 'out-Decoing' Art Deco." Jack said.

"Do you think they really had yards and yards of creamy silk billowing all over the place in 1930?"

"Who knows, but it *is* dramatic."

"Dramatic?" Ginger said. "I feel I've entered a movie set or at the very least a photo shoot. There are enough beautiful people here lounging on the casting couches and leaning on columns, drinks in hand, to fill *Vogue* and *GQ* in one fell swoop."

"I guess we're not in Kansas any more, Dorothy."

"At least we're dressed for it. I can't remember the last time I saw you in a linen suit."

"It's obviously the scene in which to be seen. Ready to run the fashion gauntlet?" Jack asked.

"What I'm ready for is a great dinner. I hope Bobby was right about the Blue Door."

They made their way through the lobby to a restaurant that was ablaze with candles. Their table was completely bathed in candlelight.

Ginger's eyes widened. "This would sure be a great spot for a special date."

"Yeah, I hate to waste this setting on business," Jack added.

"Nice try, Jack." Ginger looked up at the waiter. "I'll take a Negroni with Ketel One, straight up. My friend here will need your beer list."

"No, I'll have the same as the lady."

"Jack, the plan is to spend a little more than ten minutes on our work tonight."

"OK," he smiled teasingly. "Let's play a game. Let's see who moves off the 'Case of the Missing Robert' first tonight."

"Ha! What are the stakes?"

"Winner chooses where we go after dinner."

"You're on," Ginger answered, holding out her hand to cement the bet. "For starters, what do we make of MacBeth's trio?"

"Who?"

"The three old ladies we just left. Our clients."

"That's a little harsh. I didn't take them to be witches."

Ginger looked annoyed at his break in the mood. "OK. What do we make of our three clients? Are they more upset Robert their shoe salesman or Robert their bridge partner has disappeared?"

"What do we know? They really care about Robert. They're really worried about him. And, they don't have a clue what's happened."

Ginger smiled over the top of her drink. "Well, Dorothy apparently thinks Robert is in the south of France having a hell of a time."

"With any luck she's right, and we get to find him there. But, it's simply not likely someone would pick up and go off on a vacation without telling their employer or their bridge partners that they were going to be gone. It's been three weeks for heaven's sake."

"OK. They're clueless. Where do we go from here?"

"Judging from the look on the guy standing behind you, next we order dinner."

## U.C. Berkeley, Sproul Plaza

Chewing the last of his falafel, Cy observed "I don't see how kids subsist on stuff like this."

"We did. That's one of the things I love about being a Professor. The environment never really changes. Our work takes on such importance to us. Colossal theoretical discoveries. Minute empirical results. But come out here and sit, and it all goes by. Just like when we were students in Charlottesville. The clothing changes of course."

"And the facial jewelry!"

"Oh yeah, the facial jewelry! Sitting here can make you feel so old if you let it. Or it can make you feel such a part of the energy and the optimism. I do really love it."

After a silence while they both just sat and took it all in, Cy reluctantly started up again. "Where does the tiny, quantum world---and, presumably, quantum mechanics---stop being relevant, and where does our observable, classical world and classical physics set in? Where's the dividing line?"

"That's a bit more of a mystery, best answered by 'we may not know.' A number of physicists are working on that, and on reconciling what we know about each world."

"Including, curiously, Tommy, the suspect I told you about earlier."

"Oh. Is there a link between him and Carter?"

"If so, we can't find the slightest hint of it. And he, believably, denies it."

"OK, a cynical view might maintain that it becomes classical when we can observe it. Up until that moment, it is a quantum wave/particle. In its quantum world, it's all pandemonium and random until observed, and then poof, the observation itself orders it into a classical-type existence. We *do* know that the state of the quantum particle---oddly, now that I think of it, called psi.........I never thought of you as a quantum state until now, Cy!"

MB poked him in the ribs. "C'mon Cy. Lighten up!"

Cy just frowned back, so she went on. "Psi, the quantum state, is characterized by, among other things, the nature of its spin. Unfortunately this is a misleading term in theoretical physics. It has nothing to do with revolving around anything. It has to do with angle and momentum of the particle. The spin of each particle determines it....or, more correctly, *characterizes* it. Change the spin, and....poof....you have a different kind of particle. Or, more interestingly, suddenly a *former* particle. This direction and rate of spin accounts for much of the entanglement you mentioned before that Tommy explained to you, and some, if not most, of the strange behavior of particles. But oddly, classical objects--- this bench, that wrapper---don't have a comparable concept of spin. Unlike their quantum cousins, their concept of spin is different and can only be in one direction at once. And before you ask, we don't really know why. And, again, we don't know where the dividing line is, where the quantum world stops, and the classical world begins. It's a mystery."

"OK then. Where do the particles go when they disappear, or when they annihilate each other? And where do they come from when they suddenly appear?"

MB, looking thoughtful, answered. "Well, there are at least two possible answers I suppose. The second one is that the spin changes in a manner that causes the particle to literally change into a particle that isn't there. It disappears.

"And the first, more truthful answer, is *I don't know!* Nobody knows........nobody."

Looking at her watch, MB leaped to her feet. "Yikes. I've got a seminar in ten minutes and I haven't even prepared! My house at seven. See you then."

Cy called out after her retreating figure. "They must be paying Berkeley professors more these days if you can repay a falafel with a dinner!"

He couldn't be sure, but he thought he saw her stick her tongue out at him as she turned before disappearing around the corner. Cy smiled for the first time that day.

"Oh!" Ginger looked up at the waiter. "I'll have the tuna carpaccio to start, and then the sweet breads with the gorgonzola cream. Do I need to order the Grand Marnier soufflé now?"

"It normally takes 20 minutes, madam...and we recommend you order it ahead of time," the waiter replied a bit pompously.

"I'll have the foie gras, the one that's seared with the chutney," Jack started.

"Can it be professional to share, or is that merely social?" Ginger said. "Or do I lose the bet by asking?"

Jack laughed. "I'll have the special veal chop, medium. And, we'll have two spoons with the soufflé." Without missing a beat, he answered triumphantly to Ginger, "professional, of course!"

"Good! Back to business, then. We agree that the clients aren't very helpful so far. What are the next steps?"

Quickly he ticked off a list. "We're meeting with Bobby in the morning. From him we need friends, other romantic involvements, confirmation of his jealousy toward Robert, places to inquire, and places to look. The police told me that there's nothing except the jealous Bobby and that goes nowhere. His employer, also tomorrow or the next day. Then there's the brother in New York. Do you have any idea what a derivatives trader is?"

"No. Should we find out ahead of time or wait to ask him?"

"It doesn't matter. We'll ask him when he gets here tomorrow."

The sommelier interrupted with their wine selection. "Is this the Brunello you ordered, sir?"

Jack checked the label and tasted."Yes. The '97 Brunellos are as good as everyone says they are."

"Yes, but they'll be even better in a few years."

Ginger suppressed a smile until the sommelier left. "Well, he certainly showed us. Do you think he's broken-hearted that we're drinking it tonight?"

Jack shrugged. "Don't care." He held up his glass. "Here's to great wine, great friendships, great loving, anticipation, and....our bet."

Ginger looked at him over a forkful of sweetbreads. "Let's go over what the landlord and the building manager said one more time. He said that there was a guy who came by several times after Robert broke up with Bobby."

"Yeah, you said that he was medium build, probably Cuban. Hey, any chance this is our old Mediterranean friend from the Blind Tiger that befriended Carter?"

"Be serious!"

"I am."

"C'mon. This guy isn't an old Italian hanging around bars with girls."

"OK. Sorry. So back to the Cuban. He never went up to see Robert. He just waited in the lobby each time and then they headed out. Was Robert always waiting for him upstairs, or did he ever have to sit and wait for him to come home?"

Ginger flipped slowly through her notes. "No, both felt Robert was always expecting him."

"Drugs?"

"We'll ask Bobby and some of his other friends if that's possible. At this point, it would be pure speculation on our part. You said the cops don't suspect that."

"Does it seem to you that either of them was holding out on us or had something to hide?"

"No, felt like everybody else---they were only interested in helping to find Robert. They liked him. If they suspected foul play, they would have said something."

"In retrospect, any things in the apartment we need to follow up on?"

"It certainly looked more upscale than you'd expect from a shoe salesman."

"Like what?"

"The Oushak rugs for one. Most Southern women I know would kill to get just *one* of them. Then there was the beautiful damask fabric with expensive fringe on the windows, and crystal and silver all over the place."

"Former boyfriend? Former job? Inherited?"

Ginger shrugged. "We can find out from Bobby tomorrow. Or the brother."

Ginger lifted a forkful of sweetbreads and passed it over to Jack. Never taking his eyes off her, he brushed his thumb along her fingers and accepted the offering.

"Mmmmm," Jack approved.

"Are we getting anything done here?" Ginger asked softly.

"Sort of. Anything in the apartment?"

"Nope. Like I said before, no odd notes, no unusual books, magazines, belongings, nothing suspicious, nothing out of place. But we all agreed it did look like he knew he was going to be gone."

"Yup."

"Review your conversation with the cops."

"Doesn't go anywhere." Jack said. "Everything's a dead end. That's their conclusion, and that's the result of talking to them. They were friendly enough but not very interested in the case. They point out that there's a jealous boyfriend. They agree there may have been a new man in his life, although it doesn't feel very romantic, more like business. There's not much of an estate and it all goes to something called GLSEN, a gay educational organization. There's a depressed, down-in-the-dumps shoe salesman who everyone seemed to like and who had no enemies, no hint of drugs, no other jealous boyfriends, and the one they know about is hardly the killing kind. Or even overly distressed about his disappearance."

"I don't think Cy is going to be very happy with our coming back with another vanished into thin air case."

"Speaking of thin air, here's our soufflé."

Ginger feigned a pout. "Our?" She said as she winked at Jack.

"That wink just cost you our bet."

"No way. It has to be flagrant, kinda like this."

She put a spoonful of soufflé in his mouth, leaned over and softly kissed him.

Jack looked startled. "I never thought a Grand Marnier soufflé this good would be that moment's second choice for something to pass my lips."

Settling in on the couch after dinner, Cy looked out from MB's porch in the Berkeley hills out over the twinkling lights of Berkeley, the dark expanse of San Francisco Bay, and the lights of The City beyond. "OK, so tell me a little about parallel universes."

MB sat at the opposite side of the couch. "You're serious? *Parallel universes*? You need to know that I give no credence to this stuff and I certainly don't want to get involved in some crackpot case where I'm quoted as saying that these things are possible. OK?"

"OK," Cy laughed. "I promise not to quote you or have you subpoenaed."

MB frowned, but went on. "In general terms, there are a number of theories that the universe we observe is just one of the many in existence. And many non-physicists believe this as well. This can take the form of believing there are many existing at this point in time, and/or that there were many before this one, and there will be many after. I assume you're only interested in all the ones that exist today, right?"

Cy nodded.

"Whew, you're in deep! What have you gotten yourself into---what happened to the sensible boy I knew back when? For starters, physicists and astronomers seem to agree that there is more mass in the universe than we can currently account for through our observations. One possible explanation for this is an unobserved, or---at least so far---unobservable alternative universe. Or, I suppose, universes.

"One of the implications of a theory called string theory...."

Cy interrupted. "String theory?"

"Oh, sorry, the theory that strings, one dimensional objects, each with different vibratory characteristics, rather than particles themselves, are the smallest components of the universe. Thus, these strings can be used to explain quantum mechanics and relativity. One of the implications of this theory is that there are eleven dimensions, rather than the four we normally think of......"

"You mean three."

"Time is the fourth. You don't need me to review the space time continuum, too, do you, dear?" Her sarcasm as obvious as it was unexpected.

Cy stammered through his embarrassment. "No, sorry. Stupid mistake. Go on."

"These seven new dimensions implied by string theory are not uninteresting. Most of these would be as tiny as, or even tinier than, the particles we all learned about in high school. But one or more could be large. A universe in dimensions unobservable by us could possibly exist. Physicists are working on testing for two possible versions of this."

Cy sat up and leaned forward. "And they are?"

"One set of theories has been exploring if one of the new dimensions is tiny, and separates us from a shadow universe near ours, so near us we don't have the instruments to measure it. And the second theory is based on the possibility that the new dimensions are huge. And they are---at least so far---unobservable to us. But in this case, since we ourselves perceive things only in four dimensions, we could be blithely ignorant of the larger universe around us in the dimensions we can't perceive."

"Sort of like," Cy said, "if we were two dimensional beings who think, for obvious reasons, that we live in a flat universe, and we only see objects that appear to also be two dimensional whenever they intersect our world? I actually think there was a popular book and movie on this back in the '60's or so."

"Right," she continued, "your universe would then be perceived by you as a, presumably, infinite, plane. One person might be a triangle, and you might be, say, a square"

Cy groaned. "Please!"

"Imagine that a three dimensional globe, say earth, actually passes through your two-dimensional plane/universe. At first, you'll see it as a point, then observe it growing as an ever-increasing circular or oblong object---depending on the angle of intersection---until it reaches a maximum size, then starts shrinking until it becomes a point again and then vanishes."

"I see that. Interestingly, we'd have no explanation for these growing and shrinking objects in our universe."

"You might. Your scientists or theologians or mystics might have theories and explanations that explained what people were seeing, but they wouldn't involve three-dimensional objects. They just wouldn't be able to conceive of such a thing."

"So," Cy asked, "none of the explanations would be correct unless or until we hypothesized or visualized a third dimension?"

"Essentially. Although the definition of "correct" is interesting to work through here. *Your* Einstein would have to see it and then explain it to beings blind to such a third dimension. And then, of course, his theories would explain what was happening, but you'd have a devil of a time proving him right. In a sense, the two dimensional beings would be "correct" in how they interpreted these intersections even without the benefit of perceiving the third dimension. It's just that we, from our, superior, three dimensional point of view, would be more correct."

"But the point is," Cy said, "there *could be* parallel universes. And these universes could be different than we observe them to be, given our limited perceptions beyond four dimensions."

MB shrugged. "Sure. I suppose so, yes."

Jack pulled some pillows from the chairs around them and stacked them comfortably on the love seat facing the Delano's pool. Then he pulled Ginger down on his lap and gently kissed her neck.

She turned toward him and nestled her head on his shoulder. "This is like a dream," she murmured. "I feel like we're in a fancy Italian villa with a roof of stars. We're outside but I feel like we're in a long, beautifully decorated room."

Jack laughed. "A room decorated by a pretty zany decorator....there're actually chairs and a table set up *in* the pool over there. And those shuttered rooms must be private cabanas lining the other side of the pool. Pretty flamboyant."

"But fun," Ginger sighed. She took a sip of her Calvados. "Thank God I lost the bet. This is much nicer than my idea."

"Oh?"

"Maybe I'll tell you later."

Jack reached out, took her hand, and kissed it gently. "Was your place less or more intimate than this?"

"Well, for starters, it wasn't 'my place,' but the potential was the same."

"Am I OK to assume that we are now at the point where we call Cy and tell him? Or do we confront him when he steps off the plane in Charleston?"

"Dammit, Jack. We're going where we're going when we're going there, and we don't know when that is. I feel myself sliding into a good place to deal with it. But talking about our responsibilities can change where this goes."

"Kinda like Tommy's comment on quantum mechanics?"

"Kinda. We can just go with this or we can force ourselves to be observers and change the outcome."

"OK. Forget I brought it up."

Ginger sat up, annoyed. "Too late. Do you always over think everything?"

"Only when it's really, really important to me." He leaned up and kissed her again.

Ginger placed her fingertips along both his cheeks and prolonged the kiss. She sighed. "OK. Great wine, great friendship and bets you can't lose aside, I want you *and* I want my career. *And*, dammit, I want to manage that conflict emotionally, not intellectually. So we need to work through the fact that you're going to be you and you're going to force me to work through it intellectually. Against my will!"

She leaned forward and kissed him deeply and more passionately.

"Well, if it'll help, we can pretend I'm someone else instead of me."

"If you're going to be someone else, then we're not going in this direction."

He bent down and kissed the swell of her breast just above the silk drape of her dress. "OK. I'll be me."

"So. OK Mr. Intellectual. How do we manage our careers?"

"Well, unless Cy has hired a detective to follow us, which seems unlikely, you are currently in the clear."

She playfully pinched him. "We!"

"Well, that's not uninteresting. And when we get where we're going..."

"Let's call it 'there.'"

"Your lair or mine?" Jack laughed.

Then they both laughed.

"As I was saying," Jack continued. "When we get 'there' we'll have two choices—tell Cy, or bring Cy a proposal on how to deal with our new 'there.'"

"The latter feels better than the former."

"OK. So possible proposals are that I go work for someone else, you go work for someone else, we both go work for somebody else; or Cy gives us a shot to prove we can still work together."

"I don't think this will come as a shock to him. He already thinks we're 'there,'" she said.

"Great. Sounds like there's no problem. I'll get the check. Last one to the Tides is a rotten egg."

"Not so fast, Jack. I think even intellectually it is not such a nice, neat solution. And I still have to deal with it emotionally. I'm still sliding to a good place, but I think my sliding is done for the night." She gently took his hand in hers.

"So lemme guess, somewhere out there is one of Tommy's parallel universes, where I didn't mention your career and where we figured it out tonight. And in both universes we ended up in the same room tonight. But in one, you're on top, and in the other, it's me."

Ginger leaned forward to kiss him again. She murmured. "Yeah, something like that, Jack."

"How about if there is a parallel universe to ours with six dimensions?" Cy said. "How would we 'correctly' perceive it?"

"I don't think there is one."

"Humor me."

"I don't know. If five- or six-dimensional objects intersected with us, we'd see them in a four-dimensional intersection. We'd observe them through our own blinders and we physicists would have our four-dimensional-based theories on what was happening."

"Ghosts?"

"What? Oh do you mean, could this explain ghost sightings? UFO sightings? Communicating with spirits? God? God, I suppose so! But it's a pretty fanciful explanation. Not very satisfying to me, anyway."

"Now. How about disappearing and reappearing particles? How about reconciling quantum mechanics with what we observe in our self-limited four-dimensional classical world, existing in an actual six-dimensional universe?"

MB sat up. "That's interesting, Cy. Where'd you come up with that? I'd have to think about it. Where does this all go in the highly practical world of four-dimensional murder and intrigue? I know that some people are comparing physics to Zen Buddhism, and even mysticism, but for all practical purposes, quantum mechanics wouldn't seem particularly helpful to a jury of your typical suspect's peers."

"I have to confess that I don't know. What about the possible shadow universe a teensy tinsy distance away from us?"

"I don't think that exists either, but time will tell, given current research efforts and new, bigger particle accelerators. But I'd have to admit that *that* seems more fun in trying to help explain ghosts, and disappearing and reappearing particles, etc."

"How about disappearing and reappearing relationships?"

MB, startled, didn't answer.

"Sorry," Cy mumbled. "I didn't mean to...........sorry, forget it."

"No," MB said softly, reaching out her hand. "I've been thinking the same thing. But I think it's an illusion, Cy. We're good friends, great friends. We were more once, but I don't think that just 'reappears' for people. You're Cy Fapp. I know who you are, and you know who I am. And we do appear and reappear in each other's lives in a meaningful way. But the original relationship doesn't. It's gone. It's not what you're looking for. Never was. But I'm confident you'll let me know what you were looking for when you've found it."

# *Chapter 18*

*October 23, 2007*

## South Beach

Ginger and Jack, barefoot, hot-footed it across the already burning sand just in front of their hotel.

"How on Earth are we going to recognize him?" Jack said. "We've never seen him in a Speedo."

"I don't think *he'll* have any problem recognizing the only two dorks on the beach dressed for work, with their pant legs rolled up and schlepping coffee and croissants."

Sure enough, a large, lotion-lathered, Speedo- and sunglass-bedecked guy looked up and waved them over.

"Hey, Bobby." Ginger called out. "I see you already got us chairs."

"Yes, Chris the chair boy and I have an arrangement." He gestured to a young teenage boy darting between the umbrellas and lounges.

"Is this typically how you spend your day off?" Jack asked.

"No. This is how I *like* to spend my days off, but it doesn't work out very often. Just when I'm being interrogated by the police or private dicks.....er, sorry. Private eyes."

"Dicks is OK," Ginger said.

"Easy for you to say," Jack dead panned.

Jack and Ginger put the coffee and croissants on a small table and lowered themselves to the edge of their beach lounges.

"How was dinner?" Bobby said. "Did you go to the Blue Door?"

Jack glanced at Ginger. "It was really wonderful---like something out of a movie."

"Sort of a tough place to talk business though," Ginger added. "I'm certainly not used to having to fight off other men to get the attention of my dinner companion."

"Oh?" Bobby said.

"Don't worry." Jack laughed. "It was a great success on all counts. By the way, before we get down to business, I've never known a concierge before. What's generally expected in terms of tipping from clients?"

"Well, it's all over the place. Some people rarely use us but tip really well and some people pester us throughout their stay and tip nothing. One prominent couple comes here every few months and leaves a thousand dollars at the concierge desk every time when they first arrive."

"Do you share tips," he asked, "or do you each keep your own?"

"No, the money is pooled among all of us. What I do when I travel, is introduce myself to the concierge when I register and tip them twenty to fifty dollars at that point, depending on the quality of the hotel, and then leave more at checkout if I feel the service warranted it."

"What sorts of things do people ask for?"

"Anything you can dream up. There was the guy who called and said he needed a toy poodle and a German Shepherd for the week."

"You're kidding! What for?"

"He took them wherever he went. He took them to parties, in his car, all over town. The hard part was finding the dogs for him. The easy part was doing something with them once he had them. It turned out he was just trying to figure out if he wanted to have dogs."

"Any other good ones?" Ginger asked.

"I actually had a guy insist on us finding and renting for him a $500,000 tiara for the evening. And there is the usual number of requests for girls or boys for the evening that we routinely and graciously decline."

"Seriously, people ask you that?" Jack said.

"You wouldn't believe what people ask for. They ask for drugs, companions---hell, I had a woman once ask if I could find her a date who looked like Richard Nixon."

"Shouldn't we be talking about looking for Robert?" Bobby said.

Silence. Jack and Ginger sipped their coffees and peered at the suddenly uncomfortable concierge through their sunglasses.

He finally spoke up. "Are you waiting for me to say something?" Both detectives stared back at him, nodding at Bobby in a friendly way. "Well, what have you found out about Robert? Do you have any idea where he is?"

"That's what we want to know from you," Jack said.

"Oh." He looked thoughtful. "Look, everybody knew that Robert and I split up...OK, I mean that everybody knew that Robert dumped me....three or four months ago."

"When is the last time you saw him?" Ginger asked.

"I saw him three weeks ago at Twist."

"What night?"

"Tuesday night. It was a Martini Night."

"Martini night?" Ginger asked.

"There's an exclusive e-mail list---sort of an 'in crowd' thing. Most of us call it 'martini night,' but it's actually called The Sobe Social Club. A specific bar is identified as a special place to meet each Tuesday night, and the location is e-mailed out. Those of us who can go, go. That night it was at the Short Club."

"I thought you said Twist?"

"Martini Night that night was at the Short Club," Bobby said, clearly annoyed. "I saw Robert briefly across the room, but we didn't have a chance to talk until later that night when we ran into each other at Twist."

"He disappeared that Thursday," Jack said. "Did he give you any indication that anything was wrong? Or that he had plans to leave town?"

"Oh my gosh! Damn. *That's* right, I forgot! He said he was going on a six month sailing trip with his new best friend, Andy. How could I have forgotten?!? I guess I just didn't decide it was important enough to tell the cops or Lillian."

"I think we can dispense with the sarcasm," Jack said evenly. "If you want us to stop asking questions, just tell us what you know."

"Whatever. Look, I had hard feelings after Robert dumped me. But I got over it. I got a little sick of people referring to us as the 'Bobby Twins,' so maybe it's for the best.

"The Bobby Twins?" Ginger asked, startled.

"Yeah, cute, huh? Robert loved it, but I always found it annoying. Look, I don't have any emotional attachment to the guy, but I don't wish him ill. I hope nothing awful has happened to him and as everybody knows, I wasn't hurt enough nor did I care enough to do anything to him. Maybe he fell in a drug hole, maybe he went into a witness protection program, maybe he crossed a new lover, maybe he sold some picky matron a pair of too tight Manolo Blahniks. Hell, I don't know."

"What about your conversation with him that night?" Jack said.

"It was brief. I asked him where his 'new friend' was. He became almost angry. He was offended at my implication that it was a sexual friend. He told me it was none of my business and the guy was merely someone who was helping him with some family matters."

"Were you referring to the Cuban guy who the landlord said met Robert a few times in the lobby of the Portofino on Fifteenth Street?" Ginger asked.

"The Portofino? I'd forgotten that was the name of his apartment building. Robert just loved the historic district and that old Art Deco building. I simply can't stand those sherbet colored places."

Jack rolled his index finger in a circular pattern, trying to get Bobby back on point.

"Oh, sorry. I don't know that the guy *was* Cuban. Robert never would introduce me to him---claimed he was a friend of his mom's and that I was just being jealous. But, those meetings coincided with our breakup, and I couldn't help but think that it was associated. Robert said I was just being silly."

"Was Robert unhappy?" Ginger asked.

"Robert was always unhappy. He talked about trying to find himself, or trying to find, you know, the right place where he could feel more comfortable.He was raised in a small town in Georgia, moved to Atlanta---I think with his mom---went to New York for a while, where the gay scene was a little more accommodating, and then came down here about five or six years ago. But, I wouldn't say he was ever content. Hopefully, he hasn't just disappeared. Hopefully, he's found something better."

"Do you think he would just leave without telling anybody?" Ginger said.

"No, I wouldn't have thought so. But if there was no new boyfriend, and he was just leaving, he would have only told his boss, his landlord, his brother and Lillian's bridge group, and," he paused, "I hope me."

"Tell us about drug holes." Jack interrupted.

Jack and Ginger strolled up Lincoln Road, watching the parade of people and looking in shop windows. Antiques, rundown consignment shops, chic new restaurants, t-shirt shops, contemporary art galleries, all mixed together. A neighborhood in what felt like permanent transition. They each mulled over the implications of starting a search for Robert Flynn in this "Miami Vice" world as they dodged roller-bladers all the way to Pacific Time.

"Want to eat inside or outside?" Jack asked as they reached the restaurant.

"If it were just the two of us, outside would be more fun," she answered. "But this could be dicey with the brother, so let's get a table inside."

They left their name for the hostess, and ordered drinks while they waited for Anthony at the table.

"So, do you think there's any possibility it's drugs?" Ginger started.

"Neither Bobby nor Robert's employer thinks so, but I don't see how we can rule it out." Jack answered.

"It's possible he met someone and got in over his head. The Cuban guy?"

They both looked up as a young man, towering over them, announced, "I'm Anthony Flynn. Are you Jack and Ginger?"

Startled, the two detectives pushed back their chairs and stood up. Robert Flynn's baby brother was imposing. He towered at least half a foot over Jack, had a shock of blond-white hair and a pair of steel grey eyes. Purely from a size point of view, he could have been a tight end for any of a dozen pro football teams. He could obviously have easily intimidated almost anybody, but he peered down at them, smiled engagingly, and held out his hand.

"Sorry, I'm Ginger Grayson and this is my partner, Jack Crisp." She said as she shook his hand and gestured to the open seat.

As they were sitting down, Anthony said, "I couldn't help but overhear. You're not thinking my brother was in to drugs, are you?"

"Do you think it's possible?" Jack said.

"There are a lot of things about my brother we could explore, but he's always avoided drugs and the drug scene. I'd be surprised if he had ever even tried weed. "

"Yeah, that's pretty much the picture we're getting," Ginger said. "But the question is a natural one when someone drops off the face of the earth in Miami."

"Have you found out anything definite yet, or are we still just speculating?"

Jack sipped at his water. "Not much new since you were down here talking to the police two weeks ago. But we just started yesterday."

"We appreciate your coming down," Ginger said. "We do have some questions. First of all, we're dying of curiosity. What exactly *is* a derivatives trader?"

"Are you serious?"

"Yes," she said. "We don't know what they are, except that the press seems to suggest that they may lead to the end of the world some day."

Anthony held up his hands in a helpless gesture, and laughed. "OK. The press also claims that they're so complicated that nobody understands them. But they are actually easy."

"Try us," Jack prodded.

"Let's say that Mr. Crisp here has a stock portfolio..."

"Now *that's* speculation," Ginger interrupted, laughing.

Anthony smiled, and went on "...let's say he's nervous his stocks might go down in value. So he calls his banker at Merrill Lynch, and says 'Hey, I want to protect my stock portfolio in case the stock market goes down.' The banker calls one of my colleagues and we enter into a contract with Jack that requires us to reimburse him for his losses if his stocks fall. More than five percent, or more than 2 percent, whatever he specified. Or he can protect against any one stock falling by a given amount, or whatever. We can protect him against anything he wants."

"For a price, right?" Ginger said.

"Right. Each version he might want has a different price, so we tailor his protection, like insurance, to exactly meet his needs. And we can do the same thing for his bonds or his variable rate mortgage if he's afraid interest rates will go up, or to protect your next vacation in Japan against the yen rising. Whatever you want."

"So if they're this easy," Jack said, "Why do people think they're so complicated? Or so dangerous?"

"Well, if people or companies use them to speculate or to take large positions that could lose them all their money if they're wrong, then they could go bankrupt. They can be abused pretty much like anything else. Say you just bought a contract to sell stocks you didn't have, and they went up in value, for example. But as long as they're used like I described at first, to protect, or hedge your risk, they're safe---pretty much the opposite of risky and dangerous."

"And the infamous complexity?" Ginger said.

"The complications really don't come in at the point of customer contact. That part's really simple---just helping people deal with their financial risks. The complications only arise when you ask me, 'Wait a minute, doesn't Merrill Lynch now have Jack's risk? What do they do with it?'"

"Well, don't they?" asked Ginger.

"That's the really complicated part. We use computerized models based on mathematical financial theory to hedge our risk. That's actually what I do for a living: sit in front of a computer screen all day trading stocks, bonds, futures, and options to make sure Merrill doesn't lose money on Jack's hedge. It's great fun. Highly complex and great pressure, but a lot of fun. Actually, many of my colleagues are Ph.D.'s in physics and math these days."

Jack and Ginger looked at each other. Shook their heads.

Anthony look puzzled. "A problem?"

"No. Probably just a coincidence. So you're saying that we don't have to worry our pretty little heads about Merrill Lynch's risks," Jack said.

Anthony laughed. "No, that's how bank managers and regulators make their money---worrying about whether I'm doing my job right."

"Well, that's settled then," Ginger said. "Now we know enough to be dangerous I suppose.

"Here's where we are with your brother." The two then briefed him on everything they had found out in their two days in Miami.

"I can guess, but what's a drug hole?"

"Apparently," she said, "some people in the underbelly of the gay scene in Miami wind up at after hours clubs, starting with ecstasy and moving to crystal meth. People have been known to disappear for days with a group of friends or even strangers. Some never reappear."

"But that's not Robert," he said, raising his voice.

"Join the crowd," Jack said. "His boss, Bobby, his landlord, even the cops agree that he wasn't into that scene."

"But in our profession, we can't rule out anything," Ginger added. "For example, his apartment is furnished well beyond the means of your average shoe salesman. The Oushak rugs, the porcelain and silver...."

"The rugs are from our mom and the silver pieces have been handed down through the family for generations."

"And the Matisse silhouettes on the walls?"

"I think they were painted by an earlier boyfriend. Robert has always had dependency relationships with his boyfriends and clients. I never had the sense he was only living on his own income. But I never felt there was anything underhanded or dodgy going on."

"That at least explains the rugs. It was bothering me," Ginger said. "Let's go back to Robert. We know he was depressed and unhappy. He might have had a new boyfriend or a one night fling with the wrong person, or people, that went bad."

"Robert has always been unhappy, but I just can't see him avoiding drugs his whole life and turning to them suddenly one night. It wouldn't just be a lark. Something major, something catastrophic would have had to have happened. Does anybody think the Cuban guy was a drug connection?"

"No." Jack answered. "His relationship with the Cuban guy doesn't feel like that to anybody. It seems more like a sudden new friend. Nothing romantic, just a guy he occasionally saw."

"Nobody's been able to identify him and he seems completely harmless," Ginger added. "We were hoping you could give us some leads. Any people from his past he would have gone to if he got in trouble or wanted to get away from it all? Any childhood friends?"

"Well, Robert was an extremely unhappy child. We weren't a close family. Robert was the subject of extreme abuse by our father."

"What kind of abuse?" Ginger asked.

"Frequent, excessive beatings. I wouldn't say that Dad was a drunk exactly, but he had a shorter fuse when he'd been drinking. And, my memory is that he used to beat Robert for the slightest thing."

"How about you?"

"I don't have any memory of being physically abused. I have a lot of memories of being verbally abused. Apparently, I was the prototypical number one son that seemed to always be getting things right and pleasing his parents. I have a clear memory of hiding in my room, feeling guilty that I couldn't help Robert."

"Did your mom get involved? Was there any reason that your dad picked on Robert?"

"I don't know. I was only a kid myself. I suppose it was possible...I know what you're looking for...it was possible he wasn't masculine enough for my dad, but I have no memory or sense of that from the time."

"Where is your dad now?" Jack asked.

"I don't have a clue. One day without warning, he was gone. He didn't say good-bye. He didn't take anything. We never heard a thing from him ever again. And, frankly we never missed him."

"How old were you when he left?" Ginger asked.

"I was thirteen."

"Did your mother ever hear from him again? What did she think happened?"

"No, the police came around for a while. But, as I said, we never heard from him again. We never really cared to. The police felt he just left. And, that was the end of it. Our mom died of a sudden heart attack about six years ago."

"Wait a minute," Jack interrupted. "Is it possible that your dad was in touch with Robert? Any chance he looks like an old Cuban?"

Anthony laughed. "No way. He was a very tall, thin, pale, blond. And besides Robert wouldn't give him the time of day if he showed up on his doorstep."

Ginger slid over the composite sketch of the old Cuban that the police artist had made with the landlord and Bobby. "So this wasn't your father?"

"Nope, not even close."

Jack let out a long sigh and leaned back in his chair. "So what do *you* think has happened to your brother?"

"I think he found a new boyfriend and they went off on a trip together...."

Ginger interrupted. "And didn't tell his boss, his landlord, his friends, his bridge partners, his brother? Anybody?"

"Well, all except the boss, he's done before. In fact, several times I remember when he lived in New York. It drove me crazy."

"But," she asked, "you don't think that happened this time or you wouldn't have hurried down here to meet the police and come down a second time to meet with us, do you?"

"Not telling his boss is new. But Robert is a classic runaway. He always thinks the grass is going to be greener with the next partner, the next gay community, the next whatever. He drove Mom and Dad nuts running away from home several times. And by now I'm an old hand at trying to help find him when he disappears. My meeting with police and friends of Robert's more than once is not abnormal. When you called me, you felt I could be helpful. I could afford to come. So I came. But, I agree that not telling his boss is disturbing. Did the boss indicate that the job wasn't going well? Maybe this was just his way of quitting without being confrontational."

"No, his boss........" Jack started, then looking puzzled over at Ginger

"Fred," she said.

"Right, Fred. Fred said business was slow but that, whereas he admitted Robert was a bit of a brooder, he was happy with Robert, the customers loved him, and Robert seemed to like the job. No reason to believe the job was what he was running away from."

"Then," Ginger asked, "you think Robert will just pop back up one day soon, annoyed that Lillian brought you and us into this?"

"Part of me says 'yes,' part of me says something else has happened this time, but I can't put my finger on it. I think the drugs are a dead end, but I think there's a chance something has happened to him this time. If I were paying you, I would urge you to keep looking."

"Where?" Ginger asked.

"Who's the old Cuban? Does Fred know more than he is saying? I'm not a detective, but those are the only two things I see as different in *this* 'Robert disappearance'."

# Chapter 19

## October 24, 2007

**South Beach, 1:15 a.m.**

Jack entered the Shore Club and spied Ginger waving to him from a corner table. He signaled back and edged his way through the crowd.

"It's happening again," Ginger said as he arrived at the table. "All the eyes in the house are on you. I've been sitting here forty-five minutes and it's the most ignored---and safest---I've ever felt in a bar."

Jack laughed. "Well, now you know how I feel most of the time I'm out with you. Men are always turning to look at the beautiful blonde I'm with. Some days it gets a little wearing."

"I never even knew you noticed! So did you have any luck?"

"If I had been on the make and so inclined, I could have had a lot of luck. But if you mean our work, it was pretty much a dead end." Jack signaled the waiter for another Mojito for Ginger and asked for a Pale Ale for himself.

"Unlike *you*," she responded, "I was relatively free of advances. But I drew a blank at the bars. I went by the gym we discussed, Crunch, then on to the restaurants and bars." Looking down at her notes, "Red Square, China Grill, News Café, The Paradise, Barton G's, Mark's, and, of course," she added winking, "the Delano. A couple of them knew Robert; knew Robert and Bobby had broken up; but no one had seen him in weeks. And, I got nowhere on the Cuban. Not one of them could ID the sketch."

"I had precisely the same results," Jack said. "I checked out Score, Twist, The Paradise, Short Club, Cafeteria, Denim Blue's, Black Stallion, The Dog and Pony."

Ginger interrupted. "You went to Paradise, too?"

"Yeah, my mistake. They were really annoyed, because you had already been there and I came asking the same questions. I really pissed off the bartender. He obviously thought we were calling him a liar."

Ginger shrugged. "Was there any flavor?"

"Showing people the sketch is a total blank. Nudging around about whether Bobby got in with the wrong people or got into drugs met with blank stares. They were cooperative about Robert. They were even cooperative, but ignorant, about the sketch. But all the doors slammed shut whenever I mentioned drugs or possible drug connections."

"Well, what did you expect? You probably came across as a bumbling, rookie drug cop."

"Thanks for your confidence, partner. Did you come up with a better way?"

"Nope," she answered brightly. "I got exactly the same result."

"So where are we?"

"It's 1:30 in the morning and I'm totally exhausted. What do we have tomorrow, er, later today, before we head back to Charleston?"

"We've got the meeting with Fred to try to push him a little, and then we need to brief Lillian before we head back. When do we catch Cy up on where we are?"

"Oh," she said, embarrassed. "I forgot to tell you that he called me. I caught him up on everything we knew before tonight. He wants the three of us to get together the day after tomorrow in Charleston."

"Shall we get a night cap at the Tides?"

"God, no. I'll be lucky just to get to the Tides and into my bed."

"Well, I could help with the last part."

"Jack, come on, I'm too tired to handle your *jokes*, let alone you!"

Jack smiled, paid the bill, and they headed out of the Shore Club into the balmy South Beach night. He put his arm around her shoulder and they strolled down Collins and turned right toward the beach. As they neared the back of the Tides, Jack steered them into the alley and stopped dead in his tracks. A short, well built man stood blocking their way.

"That's far enough," he said. "Why are you interested in Robert?"

Jack stepped back. A voice behind him stopped him in his tracks. "Don't move."

Ginger stepped further away from Jack so she could watch all three men. "Robert who?" Ginger asked.

The first guy, smaller but obviously in charge, glared at her. "I'm talking to *him*, lady."

Jack smiled. "OK. Then, Robert who?" His back was now flat against the wall.

"The Robert you've been asking around town about."

"Robert Flynn," he said. "We're private detectives hired to find him. He disappeared a few weeks ago."

"Friends of ours don't appreciate things you've been asking. Especially the bullshit about Cubans. Very slowly hand me your wallet, and you," pointing to Ginger, "hand me your purse."

Jack reached back to his hip pocket and yelled "Now!" He lunged to his right as the larger of the two men hit him in the side of the head with a blackjack, sending him to his knees.

Ginger pulled her gun and held it, pointing back and forth between the two men. "Drop your weapons, both of you," she yelled. The larger man took a step toward her and she said, "I will shoot you deader than a fucking doornail. Stop right there." The two men exchanged looks, stepped over Jack and disappeared down the alley as Ginger fumbled for her cell phone.

## Miami Beach, 11:00 a.m.

Lt. Waller looked again at Jack propped up in the hospital bed. "You look like something out of a Crimean War documentary."

Jack winced. "They didn't have movies back then, wiseass," propping himself further up on his hospital pillows. "So you still think Robert's disappearance has nothing to do with drugs?"

"We *know* that Robert's disappearance had nothing to do with drugs." Waller answered. "We pulled every street source we have and there simply is no connection. We told you that from the beginning. I think if the two of you keep poking your nose into bars asking about drugs you are going to keep getting attention from people who don't want attention from you. And who *you* definitely don't want any attention *from*. If this has anything to do with drugs, it's now about you and not about Robert. Do you want to try to ID these guys? Press charges?"

"Is there any point?" Ginger asked.

"If you can identify anyone, they're going to claim self defense. They're going to claim you accosted them after harassing them at the bar. Is it worth a couple of days or weeks of your time?"

Jack shrugged. "The guy gives me a bash on the head and I get eight stitches. What about my reputation?"

Ginger waved a hand sarcastically. "Add the sympathy you'll get from your bandages to the looks you've been getting in the bars---not to mention the extra special care I've noticed you get from Nancy Nurse---you'll be OK."

"What about my pride?"

"Well, the lieutenant here and I will keep my saving you under wraps."

Lt. Waller impatiently interrupted."Have you two found anything? Where are we on Robert's disappearance?"

"While Jack has been lovingly nursed back to health here," Ginger answered, "I met again with Robert's boss and Lillian, but we're just at a dead end. We were headed back to Charleston on the noon flight today, but now, doctors willing, we'll still be able to go back tomorrow."

"It may look dramatic," Jack said, "but it is just a minor concussion and they've told me I can leave this afternoon."

"Anything on the old Cuban guy?" Waller persisted. "Anything with Bobby? Or the brother?"

"We've come up with a big zero," Jack answered. "Bobby suspects the Cuban guy. Nobody but the landlord and Bobby admits having seen the Cuban guy. The brother says this is a pattern with Robert. The boss wants to help, but hasn't a clue where his best salesman has gone. Maybe he'll just reappear one day and we'll discover that Lillian has sent us all on a wild goose chase. For now we have a guy missing without a trace."

"OK," Waller said. "Let me know if you change your mind on filing charges. Let's stay in touch if either one of us comes up with anything." Frowning thoughtfully as he started walking out, he cocked his head and looked at Jack again. "You know. Maybe you're right. Maybe you remind me of a refugee from a Russian Revolution film." He disappeared out the doorway.

Ginger crossing over to his bed and gently took his hand. "How are you *really* feeling, Jack? Do you have a headache?"

"Not tonight, dear."

"That's not funny. I'm really worried about you."

"I think another couple of days with my nurse and I'll be fine."

Ginger feigned a backhanded slap. "Are you up for dinner out? I've heard about a great place I'd love to take you to."

"I thought we were due back in Charleston this afternoon."

"Not going to happen! Doctor's orders. I left word on Cy's cell phone about your heroics in the alley and your stay in the hospital. I told him we'd be back tomorrow."

"And who knows? With an extra day, we may yet find Robert."

"All righty then, I'll make reservations for three!" And she turned on her heel and walked out of the room with a wave.


## Coral Gables, Florida, 7:15 p.m.

Jack and Ginger exited the cab on Almera Avenue and hurried across the street into Norman's.

"I promise," Ginger said at the door. "I'll try to stop giggling once we're inside, but you look so dapper in that crazy Panama hat."

"Yes. Less giggling would be appreciated. You're the one that insisted on it."

The Maitre d' ushered them in as they came through the door. "The name of your reservation, sir?"

"Crisp. Two at eight," he said.

As they approached the table, the Maitre d' held out his hand. "May I take your hat?"

Jack reddened with embarrassment. "I just got out of the hospital with 15 stitches in my head and it looks a little unappetizing. I think if we allowed the other diners to vote, they'd vote for 'hats on' in this case."

As Jack reached up to lift the hat, the Maitre d' held up his hands. "No, that won't be necessary. I think we'll dispense with the plebiscite and allow the hat in the dining room in this instance."

Ginger covered her mouth with her hand and looked the other way. She sat down. "I think you are so cute in that hat. I'm not going to be able to contain myself. I feel like I'm out with a *real* private eye. Like Lauren Bacall with Humphrey Bogart."

"If I wasn't worried about bringing my headache back, and annoying the rest of the guests, I could show you 'how to whistle'."

The waiter interrupted and handed them the menus. "You just put your lips together and blow."

They all laughed conspiratorially.

"Can I get you a cocktail?"

"If you have Controy, the Mexican Liquor, I'll take Ketel One straight up with a splash of Controy," Ginger said.

"I'll just have Ketel One, straight up," Jack added

"No way, Jack. That's stupid. You're on medication. You have a concussion."

"Oh, yeah. I forgot." He looked back up at the waiter under the brim of the hat. "I'll have Ketel One, straight up." He looked back over at Ginger. "The next time you get hit in the head, *you* can stop drinking."

The waiter, waiting only a beat, turned and retreated to the bar.

## 40 Bull Street, 7:20 p.m.

At that precise moment six hundred miles up the coast, Ashley was heading up her steps. She was startled to find the front door slightly ajar and all the lights out as she stepped onto the porch. Calling out for Ann, she flipped the light switch and stopped dead in her tracks when the hallway remained dark.

"Ann, where are you? Is everything all right?" She heard a scrabbling noise to her right and was shocked to see Einstein hopping toward the door. "Einstein, what are you doing out...." and she started to scream.

## Charleston Airport, 7:25 p.m.

As the plane was taxiing to the gate, Cy flipped open his phone and checked for messages. He had a message to page Dan at the station. Dan called him back almost immediately.

"I didn't want to bother you until we knew for sure," Dan started, "but some kids found a body in the marshes off St. John's Island a couple of days ago. We've now found three more in the same area, and we're still looking. Late this morning, one of them was positively identified as Cindy Boisseau."

## 40 Bull Street, 7:25 p.m.

A large hand closed over Ashley's mouth and pulled her back, choking off her scream. "Shut up, or I'll kill you *now*," a voice said. The door slammed behind her. An outside light briefly reflected off a steel blade pressing against her throat.

## Charleston Airport, 7:30 p.m.

"Shit! Do you know what happened yet?" Cy said.

"We're not a hundred percent sure, but it looks like she was tied up, strangled, and weighted down in the marshes two months ago. The body's badly decomposed---beyond recognition. We had to use dental records to get the ID."

"Any idea who did it?"

"We've been all over Tommy and Clyde. Back and forth all day. Tommy's being his arrogant self and Clyde is as cool as can be."

"What were their initial reactions?"

"Neither one of them showed any surprise, and only Tommy seemed genuinely upset. If I had to bet money, it would be on Clyde, but we don't have any way to pin it on him yet. The only thing unusual in the remains was a quarter-size silver pendant with enamel blue waves found in an inside pocket of her jeans. Neither Tommy nor Clyde had any knowledge of the pendant. Or so they claim."

"Did you show it to them?"

"No, we're still having it analyzed."

Cy spotted his bag going by on the baggage carrousel. "Any prints?"

"Not likely. Not after ten months."

"Have you asked her roommates?"

"We have calls into them, but haven't been able to reach them. They don't even know we found her yet."

"What about the parents?"

"They're here now. Neither of them has ever seen the pendant before."

"Are you holding Tommy and Clyde?"

"We have nothing on them. We had to let them go."

"I just got my bags and I'm headed into town. Do you have any problem with me going by to see the girls?"

"You sure you want to do that without Ginger?"

"I think I can handle it without her. She's still down in Miami babysitting Jack anyway. He apparently got mugged

205

last night, or at least jumped. I should be at Bull Street in less than 20 minutes. I'll call you when I get there."

"OK. I'm tied up until at least then anyway."

"Always with the jokes," Cy retorted as he flipped his phone closed and headed out to his car.

## Coral Gables, 7:40 p.m.

"In all seriousness, Jack, I'm feeling very maternal. Except for the cute little hat, you look like hell and you're a little slow."

"But with the hat, I'm cute."

"Yeah," giggling, "with the hat, you're utterly adorable. Are you sure the doctor said you were OK?"

"Yes, Mom. I'm going to be fine, I promise."

Ginger reached across the table, as the drinks arrived and took his hand.

"This is getting vaguely Oedipal," Jack murmured.

"Stop it!" She slapped his hand away. "You can make fun of me if you want, but when you went down in that alley, I froze. In this business, we are supposed to be so cool and in control and when I thought that you were badly injured or worse, I was terrified."

"Even in our business, you're allowed to have emotions. Look, let me tell you what my Mom told me. Envision what you are going to do when a problem arises and you'll instinctively do what you had practiced in your mind. As you told the cops, the second the situation got out of hand and I was down, you instantly grabbed your gun and took control. You did the right thing.

"You're a professional. It doesn't mean you can't react emotionally or even be frightened. That time I saved Cy's life, with that kidnapper that we cornered, he and I both admitted to being petrified, but we did what we had to do and learned from it."

"But....," she tried to interrupt.

Jack cut her off. "When you rescued Cy in that warehouse in Charleston, Cy says you handled it perfectly. Better than he would have. You have an instinct for handling tough situations. If it worries you in retrospect, you may need a different line of work."

"You are an idiot, Jack. I'm not talking about professional. With Cy it was professional. In the alley last night, what scared me is that it was personal. You're such an idiot!"

She raised her drink toward Jack, "Here's to bringing the brigands down together."

He touched her glass, and said, "Here's looking at you, kid."

## 40 Bull Street, 7:45 p.m.

Unable to scream, duct tape pulled tight over her mouth, Ashley felt herself being pulled by a rope that bound her wrists together. As she was dragged struggling down the hallway, she became even more frantic when she saw the chaos in Cindy's room. "Don't," snarled a voice from above.

I know that voice, she thought to herself. Mr. Boisseau? And her blood ran cold.

## Coral Gables, 7:50 p.m.

They each took a sip of their martinis. Ginger laughed and said, "OK, Rick. We'll always have that alley in South Beach."

Jack leaned across the table and kissed her. "Can we table the personal part of this conversation until dessert?"

"Keep your hat on, Jack. Dessert in the restaurant, yes. After that, I'm still not so sure I'm ready to fuck an invalid!

And, by a happy coincidence, here comes our waiter to take your dessert order now."

The waiter, feigning puzzlement, "Did I miss a couple of courses?"

After ordering their meal, Jack sat back. "As we've no doubt both noticed, unfortunately Robert does not appear to have joined us for dinner. So, we still have work to do. How did your conversation go with Cy?"

"I caught him up on everything we know.........."

"That shouldn't have taken long."

".........and, more importantly, our dead ends! That knock on the head turned you into a real comedian."

"He and George apparently had a whee of a time at the surveillance conference. There's nothing new on the Johnson disappearance from George's side either. And Cy said there were some interesting aspects of his conversation with Mary Beth about Carter's physics books that can wait until we get home tomorrow.

"But, I've been thinking about the case while you've been consorting with nurses." She looked up and laughed at Jack. "Now that I think of it, thank goodness that nurse hasn't seen you in that Panama."

"Now, there's a thought. Maybe I can wear it to the hospital reunion."

"Hmmmm. Does it strike you as at all odd---or is it purely a coincidence---Carter and Robert each disappeared without a trace while indicating to people that they were searching for a happier place? That each was physically abused as a kid and that their abusive fathers disappeared literally without any trace at all when they were around ten years old?"

Jack looked up. Didn't say anything. Then he finally replied. "I hadn't thought about it. Did Cy suggest this?"

"No. When I told Cy what we knew, he became very quiet. He didn't ask any questions. I sensed he was bothered by something, but I didn't know what. And, as I've thought about his silence, it caused me to wonder if there isn't a link between the two cases."

"Well, it's not uninteresting.But it *is* a little far fetched. As we both know from experience, any missing person who is unhappy, we *assume* from the beginning is a runaway. Any missing person who is generally *happy* we presume to have come to some harm. It's why we focused on whether Tommy or Clyde did something rather than where or if Cindy had run off. It's just a general approach that usually works for us, right?"

"Usually, yes."

"So, *most* cases involving unhappy people have had them, in one sense or another, 'looking for a better place.' It's just a matter of looking for the person until you find them. In that sense, they're *all* linked and coincidental."

"Yeah, I guess," she said thoughtfully. "But, for the unhappy ones---the runaways---there are usually early clues that lead somewhere: a friend is evasive, they've had a fight with the family or a lover, they've taken belongings with them. Something. But in these two cases, there's nothing. And, then there's the coincidence of the identically missing, abusive fathers."

"There's that."

"Too many coincidences, Jack."

"True. But, Carter is what, eight, nine years older than Robert. There is no reason to believe that either one lived in the same place as the other, knew the other, or knew anyone in common. We don't even have the Kevin Bacon 'Six Degrees of Separation' here. Even the fathers disappeared what... eight, nine, ten years apart, and were in totally different geographical locations. Coincidences maybe, but they don't go anywhere."

"Perhaps you're right. Even the physics link between Cindy's boyfriend and Carter's reading materials doesn't seem to have any real connection. Maybe sometimes things just *are* coincidences."

"Like for example, your boyfriend in college was a theoretical physicist. And Tommy's a theoretical physicist. And, Cy's best friend in college, Mary Beth, is a theoretical physicist. Just coincidence? Probably. And Anthony the derivatives guy's colleagues are theoretical physicists."

He shrugged dismissively. "On the other hand, G. K. Chesterton called coincidences 'spiritual puns.' In other words, seemingly unrelated events or facts are, in fact, linked in a larger, less obvious order. Sometimes things *are* just coincidences. But in our line of work, we have to be skeptical. You're right. We have to always be diligent in making sure we haven't dismissed the linked observations, or 'spiritual puns,' as mere coincidences."

"OK. Spiritual mumbo jumbo, quantum mechanics, whatever. All the theory aside, we don't know if these are coincidences or linked. But, what *does* make people happy? What are unhappy people looking for? What are *you* looking for? What am *I* looking for? God knows Cy is unhappy. What is *he* looking for?"

"Well, at least we know what makes Barnum happy." Jack brightened. "Anything to do with food!"

## 40 Bull Street, 7:55 p.m.

The next thing Ashley knew, she had been hurled onto the floor of the TV room next to a sobbing Ann. Strong hands viciously grabbed the two of them and wedged them sharply into the corner. The two terrified girls shrank back from the intense beam of the flashlight that raked over them.

A hoarse, savage voice assaulted them from above. "Don't move, or I'll kill you *now*." They could see the jagged hunting knife pointing down at them from his left hand. It was the second time he'd emphasized "kill you *now*!"

Ashley knew she recognized the voice, but in her panic she couldn't place it.

Setting the flashlight on the table, he began piling electronic equipment on the table.

Ashley noticed with rising horror her own necklaces and rings along with Cindy's and Ann's already in a heap on the table. Trying not to look obvious, and with only sidelong glances at the man, Ashley edged slowly away from Ann and closer to the door.

He yelled. "Stop right there," and hurled an ash tray that just missed her head and shattered on the wall above. Glass rained down on her shoulders and hands.

Her heart stopped as she suddenly realized who he was.

### 40 Bull Street, 8:00 p.m.

Cy drove slowly up Bull Street, past the Bull Street Gourmet trying to remember which house was Cindy's. He was sure he was in the wrong block and did a methodical U-turn so as to not call attention to himself. He headed back east toward the college. Another block and there it was just across the street. Number 40. Now for the true Charleston challenge, a place to park. He drove along the block. There was nothing. He turned left, skirting the college, and then left back onto Calhoun, and then back down Pitt.

Damn! No parking anywhere! He pulled in behind a car, illegally, at the corner of Pitt and Bull, got out and walked back to the house. The house was totally dark. No wonder the cops had not been able to reach the girls. Nobody home.

He trotted back to the car to write them a note. As he opened the car and fumbled for his pen, he suddenly became uneasy. With the inside light on, he made a perfect target on an otherwise dark street. Cy got out, popped the trunk, took out his shoulder holster and jacket, and put them both on. He headed back to the house.

As he walked up the steps, his sense of uneasiness grew. He reached the door and suddenly saw what appeared to be a flicker of light reflected off an inside wall.

He froze.

## Coral Gables, 8:05 p.m.

"You're right, Jack. As far as happiness goes for Barnum, it's food. Have you seen how much weight he's put on," Ginger said. "I'm tempted to put him on a diet when he's with me."

"C'mon, Ging! He's a big boy. He needs his steak and potatoes and donuts."

"Oh no, don't get anthropomorphic on me. He's not you, Jack."

"Hey! Just kidding. You know I wouldn't feed him too much of that stuff. You know how much time I spend at the Golden Retriever Rescue Society. I wouldn't harm an animal with people food. Or at least," wincing at the memory of all Barnum's donuts, "not with too *much* people food!"

"Sorry. Barnum's such a sweetheart. The other day when I was so upset, he sat by me for hours. Kept rubbing up against my knee. It may sound silly, but he cheered me up. Maybe if Cy ever takes Barnum back full time, you can get me a Golden from your Rescue Society?"

"Deal."

"Shucks, what a guy! A tough PI and a dog nursemaid, all in one!"

Jack, now embarrassed, picked up the thread of their former conversation. "But we were talking about happiness for humans. Studies show that our happiness level changes very little from early childhood. Someone who is happy has to be traumatized or abused to be made unhappy. And, nothing seems to make unhappy people happy."

"What about money?"

"That's a 'duh.'"

"What about marrying the one you love?"

"Well, I'm not an expert on this, but from what I've read by those who are, when two people marry, there's a period of about a year in which their happiness spikes higher by a little bit and then they revert back to their original happiness level."

She took a forkful of her rum and pepper-painted grouper, then paused while she chewed. "What about religious faith?"

"We've all met miserably unhappy religious types, and blissfully happy atheists. Look at the kids we've found who've run off to cults. Even if initially they are swept away, ultimately, they haven't found a better place, and are no happier or unhappier in the long run for the experience."

"What about a geographical search for a better place?"

"You mean like Shangri La?"

"No, that's fiction. Is it possible to go to 'a better place?' A real place? On Earth?"

"In a sense," he said, "ever since there've been human beings, people have migrated from one place to another, seeking a better place. Native Americans migrating from Asia. Then continuing to search, sweeping down through both continents. Europeans and Asians migrating away from persecution or toward opportunity. ..."

"There's not much evidence that they became any happier. Kept some of them alive who might have otherwise been killed, I suppose. But happier? Maybe it's just a human condition to feel that it is always better someplace else....hoping to find a Shangri La. I've had friends tell me that Bhutan might be such a place."

"And, as long as the king of Bhutan succeeds in keeping foreigners out, it may have a chance."

"I still think people do work on being happier even where they are," she said.

"No question about that. What we are discussing is does it work? It feels like a person's happiness is a function of how they perceive their experiences."

He leaned forward earnestly. "Look at Christopher Reeves. He had a career ending, life-threatening injury that left him completely paralyzed. And, although he certainly had some bad days, his overall outlook of optimism and being proactive pervaded his spirit. While we're on the subject of physicists, look at Stephen Hawking. His disability would stop most ordinary people. But his humor and his positive outlook ring throughout his brilliant work."

"All you are saying is that some people see the glass half empty and others see it half full."

"That's a useful simplification. I think people's general level of quote, unquote, happiness, is set very early in life. Robert and Carter both had abusive fathers. Not every unhappy person had an abusive father, any more than every happy person had perfect parents. I don't know why Cy is generally unhappy. I don't know why you are happy so much of the time. That's why there are so many analysts and counselors."

"I thought the point of counselors and analysts was to get people to understand the source of their unhappiness and happiness."

Jack paused over a taste of Lobster Tempura. "That may be. But, I don't think we have any definitive proof that that knowledge makes one any happier."

"Well," she said, "I've known people who seem to think that therapy was helpful and made them happier....or at least better able to deal with what they have and where they are in life."

"And, again, that's the whole key---how you perceive everything around you. If you can learn to perceive things in a different way, maybe you can be a happier person."

"And," she said thoughtfully, "maybe that's 'a better place.'"

**Bull Street, 8:15 p.m.**

Seeing nothing through the front window and finding the front door unlocked, Cy stepped quietly into the house. There was silence. His eyes adjusted to the dark interior. He noticed an overturned coffee table and the bunny cowering in the corner. He drew his gun and moved slowly toward the kitchen. Nothing. No light. No sound. Nothing.

He stopped. He heard what sounded like furniture moving from behind a closed door down the hall. Walking stealthily down the hall, his back toward the wall, he approached the closed door. Behind him, a picture he had brushed clattered to the floor.

Damn!

Silence. Cy waited. He heard what sounded like a moan and then a man's terse whisper. "Shut up."

Shit, Cy muttered to himself. Then aloud. "Is anybody home? Ann? Ashley? Are you all right? It's Cy Fapp."

Silence.

Cy took a step forward and hesitated. He heard whispering and then a quivering voice, "Come in, Cy. Please come in."

Cy pulled the door open and was blinded by a flashlight beam in his face. He shielded his eyes and glanced at the floor. Across the room, he quickly took it in: Ashley on the floor, hands bound, eyes bulging and a man's heel crushed into her abdomen; stereo equipment and jewelry stacked on the table in front of him; and Ann being held as a shield at knife point.

There wasn't enough light to make out who the man was. "You won't be needing that gun," the man said, pointing at it with his flashlight.

Cy said, "I'll be the judge of that."

"If you don't drop the gun, I'll slit Ann's throat and we'll negotiate over Ashley."

Ann whimpered and Ashley tried to twist out of the way.

Cy, finally saw who he was dealing with. "If you harm either of these girls, you'll be dead before you have time for the other." He leveled the gun at Clyde's face.

"That just looks like a risk I'll have to take. And, I'm betting that you won't risk Ann's life."

The two men stared at each other.

Cy made a decision. He slowly lowered himself to the couch and placed the gun on the floor behind him.

"No!" Clyde said. "Hand me the gun."

"No," Cy said. "You're in control. That's going to have to be good enough for you for now. You hurt either of these girls and I'm going to kill you anyway."

Clyde looked thoughtful.

Cy interrupted whatever Clyde was thinking. "Actually this is pretty clever: you find out about the pendant on Cindy. You know that Ann and Ashley are the only ones who can tie you to it, so you stage a fake burglary and kill the only ones who can testify against you. It actually would have worked if someone hadn't stumbled on the scene. So what do you think, Clyde? Bad luck or amateur hour?"

"Bad luck for me. And now bad luck for you. Now, after I get rid of the girls, *you're* the only loose end I have to dispose of."

Ann cried out. "I already told Clyde that Ashley and I wouldn't say anything about the pendant."

In the diffused light, Cy could make out that this was news to Ashley, and that she was looking for an opening to make a move.

"Clyde," Cy said. "Why don't you take off Ashley's tape and see what she has to say about the pendant?"

"Nice try, Fapp. But remember, I'm in control here."

"Since you're in charge and we're not going to be around to testify why don't you fill us in on how you killed Cindy?"

"I'm not an idiot. You can go to your grave wondering."

"How about the other girls? Did they piss you off too?"

"None of your fucking business. And you're not going to be around to care anyway."

"What did Cindy's pendant have to do with it?"

"The flirtatious bitch gave me the pendant the first night we slept together and then wanted it back just like I was another notch in her bed post. That night I saw her at Normans with Mr. Fu Man Chu I was carrying it. Later, I waited outside of Big John's for her and showed it to her. I told her I would give it back to her if she let me give her a ride home. Last I saw it, she was holding it in her hand in the car. I never could find it again. I assumed she had thrown it out the window to taunt me."

"Looks like your luck is always bad, Clyde. She found a way to taunt you with it from the grave."

## Coral Gables, 8:15 p.m.

"A better place, maybe," Jack said. "But is it just the same place? With each of us in a universe of our own making?"

"You mean in the sense of control?"

"No," he corrected. "In the sense of perception. We know from our own work that each person perceives the same situation differently. Each witness has their own take on every accident. We each live our own *Rashomon*. There's the delicious scene in *Harold and Maude* where the mother is filling out a dating questionnaire for her morose, suicidal son, and when she comes to the question about his childhood, answers for him. 'You were such a *happy* baby Harold' while he stares malevolently at her over her shoulder"

"So," she concluded, "my seeing the glass half full and you seeing it half empty really is an explanation for how we each experience our own private universe, while we each, in a literal sense, live in the same universe."

"So, are we both perceiving the same headache, or is it just my concussion?"

Ginger made a face at him. "Curious, I never thought about it before, but both Derek and Tommy reminded me that in quantum physics there's a sense in which everything has a probability of being anywhere at once, and only in observing it does it attain a precise location."

"There's a parallel in our larger world: things are going on all around us, but only in observing them do they actually attach themselves to our experience and to our own sense of happiness. And, if by selectively observing, which we all do, then we are controlling our own universe of experiences. And therefore, in effect, what---and, more importantly, *how* we choose what we observe---controls our own happiness."

"So," he pointed out, "if you controlled the impact on you of what you observed, you would in effect be in a different universe of experiences, and, by inference, if you changed how you observed everything going on around you, you could affect your state of happiness."

"Hypothetically, yes. But as a practical reality, probably not by much. As you said, we are each wired at, or maybe even before, birth, with a unique happiness quotient or happiness ability. From the time of birth, this can be changed, and will be changed by environmental effects but changes less and less the older you get. So even small traumas in infants affect their ultimate happiness ability, but adults are pretty much what they are. So, a lottery winner has a fairly brief period of being happier, but then they seem to revert back pretty quickly to their pre-victory happiness level." She looked thoughtful as she sipped her drink.

"And, the same thing with all sorts of adult experiences. You see a movie you like, you have a great conversation with family, you meet new friends. All these things can lead to a short term increase in happiness, but the person, in general, soon slides back to their normal level of happiness."

"And," she added, "the same thing for an increase in income, charitable works, vacations---all things associated with greater happiness don't seem to have a permanent, lasting significant effect."

"And, similarly, an unhappy person can have happy experiences, but it doesn't turn them into a happy person in a permanent, long term way."

"And, they are unhappy because maybe that's the way they were wired or because they had traumatic experiences as infants or children?"

Jack stared at her thoughtfully. "Like Robert and Carter."

"Like Robert and Carter... and Cy." She added with a frown.

## 40 Bull Street, 8:20 p.m.

Ashley tried to squirm away. Clyde kicked her in the head and pointed the knife down at her wordlessly.

Cy distracted him. "There's another piece of bad luck with your plan that you need to know about, Clyde."

"Shut up." He glowered down at Ashley.

"What time is it?" Cy persisted.

Cy looked at his watch and answered his own question. "It's 8:20. The homicide cops knew at 7:30 that I would be here by eight. They expected me to call when I arrived. My guess is you have less than five minutes to dispose of the three of us and your contraband and flee the scene. And, I don't think you're that good."

"That's bullshit, Cy, and you know it. You've been watching way too much TV"

Cy shrugged.

Clyde pulled the knife back up to Ann's neck. "The only time that's ever going to matter to you again is when your time is up. And that time is just about now."

From the living room came a sudden yelling of voices. Dan's voice stood out. "Cy! Ashley, Ann! Cy, are you here?"

All four of them looked to the door.

Cy smiled grimly up at Clyde. "Looks like my estimate was off by three minutes."

Clyde looked panicky. Ashley jerked free of his legs and rolled toward the door. As Clyde reached for Ashley, he sliced the knife down on Ann's neck. Blood spurted over the wall and trickled down to the floor. Cy dove to his right, grabbed his gun and, in one motion, came up firing.

## South Beach, 11:00 p.m.

Jack pushed the button for the fifth floor and the elevator began its assent. As the door opened, they walked slowly hand in hand to Ginger's room. As she opened her door, Jack put his hands on her shoulders, turned her around and kissed her gently. Leaning into him with her right hand tight against the small of his back, she pulled against him, opened her mouth and kissed him back hungrily. He inched the two of them into the room as one and reached back to pull the door closed behind him.

"Yes," she murmured,"Yes….no."

"Yes? No? Here we go again!" he said laughing.

She looked up at him and laughed again.

"What?" he asked.

"That hat. You are so adorable in that hat. You're killing me! 'Yes', I want to and, 'No,' I'm not going to take advantage of a man with a concussion and too much to drink! *And* we both have to get up soon, pack, and head out to the airport. Not tonight, Jack. I'm serious. Plus, I promised Cy I'd call and check in before it was too late."

Jack grinned and reached for his cell phone. "OK. Let's call Cy right now. Together. Let's get this over with!"

"No, Jack. Be serious."

"Well, OK then. As Lauren Bacall said, 'If you knew what you were missing, you would slit your throat.'"

"I *know* what I'm missing super sleuth!" she said, through her laughter. "But not tonight, dear, *you've* got a headache."

# Chapter 20

## *November 14, 2007*

### Charleston

Three weeks later, Jack and Ginger sat distractedly sipping coffee in the office, waiting for their 10 o'clock appointment. At the sound of approaching footsteps, Barnum leapt to his feet and bounded to the door.

Jack called out. "Come in!"

A diminutive man, strangely dressed in an odd combination of work clothes and business casual entered. He was wearing khakis with a work shirt, work boots, and a bright red bow tie.

Jack stood and held out his hand. "Good morning. I'm Jack Crisp and this is my partner, Ginger Grayson."

"Hi," taking Jack's hand, "I'm Daryl Jones. I'm the one who called about my wife."

"Please sit down and tell us about the last time you saw her," Ginger said.

Jones looked puzzled. "Well, at breakfast this morning. She's not missing." He noticed Jack and Ginger's confusion. ".....This is difficult for me....sorry about the confusion...I was expecting something different."

"Than what?" Ginger said.

"Well...than a couple with a lab."

"Well," Jack said, "first of all, we're not a couple. We're both licensed private detectives. And, secondly, we work exclusively on missing persons cases."

"That's what my friend told me. But, I thought you could maybe work on a case *before* it became a missing person's case."

"Actually, we don't work on, I guess you'd say, preventative cases."

"Look," Ginger said. "Mr. Jones, why don't you tell us a little about yourself and what is going on. Maybe we'll know somebody who can help you. "

"I'm an exterminator. I've lived here in Charleston my whole life. My wife and I have been married 20 years and we have four children. Lately she seems distracted and is spending more and more time in Columbia and in meetings between here and Columbia."

"What takes her to Columbia?" Ginger asked, averting his eyes.

"Well, what she tells me is that she is involved with the USC Alumni Association."

"What are the meetings that take place between here and there?"

"Supposedly lunches and committee meetings in Summerville."

"And, what would you like us to do for you?" Jack asked.

"I don't know. See if she is telling the truth. I'm sorry. I've never done this before. I don't know what's involved........"

"Well, that makes us even. Neither do we."

"Sorry that we're not being more sensitive," Ginger added. "This sounds like a difficult situation for you. We don't have any experience with following people and keeping track of their activities. If your wife actually disappears and you're not happy with the police response, then Jack and I would be more than happy to help you." She glanced at Jack. "What about Chief?"

Jones looked back and forth at the two of them. "Chief?"

"That's not a bad idea." Jack answered. "Look, Mr. Jones, we know somebody in Columbia who might be able to help you. Why don't you let us call him and see if he is willing to get involved."

"I hate to bring in more people. Are you sure this Chief person will be discreet?

"We won't even use your name," Jack said. "We'll just check and see if he is willing to help. And then you can call him if you like what you hear."

Jones suddenly stood up, followed immediately by Barnum. "Thank you both. Sorry again for the confusion. I'll think about this and why don't you just call me if Chief wants my case."

Jones and Barnum both scurried to the door, and Barnum supervised his quick exit.

Jack and Ginger were both desperately trying to keep from laughing. Jack tried to say something through suppressed attempts to keep from losing it. When he was sure Jones had left the building, he said, "God......I thought he said 'I'm going to *exterminate her'* rather than 'I'm an exterminator'! I've been dying over here!"

Ginger kept her hand over mouth. "I thought the same thing! It took me practically the whole meeting to figure out where he was *really* coming from."

Later that afternoon, Ginger punched the speaker phone and dialed Chief's number.

"Hello," barked Chief's gruff greeting from the machine.

"Hey Chief, this is Jack, and I'm here with Ginger and Barnum. Sorry we've been trading phone calls all day."

"How are you both doing?"

"Fine," Ginger said.

"Fine," Jack added. "Did you get our message detailing a possible case?"

"Yes, yes, yes. I'm happy to have this guy call me about keeping an eye on his wife. But, seriously, how are you two doing after the fiasco on Bull Street a few weeks ago?"

Ginger looked out the window, then back at the phone. "Well, fine...really. Fine. As fine as can be expected I guess. We're doing what we can on the open cases---mostly Carter here and Robert in Miami. Over the last couple of days we've gone through the agony of briefing both Bailey Lee and Lillian on the lack of progress. And, we're open to taking on any new cases as they arise."

"Speaking of Bailey Lee, what's the news on her?"

"Sorry, Chief," Jack cut in. "Thought we told you. Her lawyer appears close to negotiating a plea bargain for her where she'll get a suspended sentence for a more minor offense in return for turning State's evidence on Antique Jack."

"Not surprising. You white guys always get off."

"Aw shucks, Tonto, how are things on the Columbia Reservation?"

"Boys!" Ginger laughed. "Chief, any news on the Boisseaus?"

"As you'd expect, Mrs. Boisseau is a basket case. And as you know, Mr. Boisseau took a leave of absence after they found Cindy's body.His business is a mess and I jumped at the opportunity to leave. I'd been wanting to do that for a while anyway. I always felt you guys could use a little competition in the PI business. Is there anything new...?"

Ginger cut him off. "We've got a call on the other line. Do we need to call you back or put you on hold?"

"No, we're done for now. I'll let you go."

"We'll have the guy, a Mr. Daryl Jones, call you. Bye for now." Ginger pushed the button for line two and they both said, "Hello" together.

"Hi. It's Anthony Flynn returning your call. Sorry, I was in the middle of pricing a new deal."

"Thanks," Ginger said. "Have you heard anything on your brother?"

"No. When I got your message, I was hoping you had."

"One new development *has* come up. His boss called me and said that he'd forgotten to mention one thing. Apparently when business was slow in the shoe store, the sales staff spent their time in a back room. Turns out that Robert had an entire drawer full of materials that he'd been working through and Fred wanted to know if he should send it to us or to you."

"Did he mention what it is?"

Ginger idly rubbed Barnum behind his ear with her bare foot. "He said it was some books Robert had been reading and a note pad."

"Why don't you have him send it on to you first. Hopefully there will be something in there that will lead you to him. If not, you can send it along to me."

"The police have already looked through it. So, you'll have to call Fred to release the materials from them to us. He's got the address, but tell him that we'll pay the extra to have it overnighted. Here's the number....."

# Chapter 21

## November 15, 2005

Jack returned from lunch and discovered Ginger and Barnum had already beaten him back. "Is there anything we need to go through before he gets here?" Jack asked.

Ginger's shrug was imperceptible, as she handed a dog biscuit to Barnum.

Jack broke the ensuing silence. "Did you ever remember anything else Cy told you about his conversations with Mary Beth in California?"

Ginger looked thoughtful. "No, we already went through all of it. She thought it was odd that Carter had totally ignored the first half of Penrose's book. But she pointed out that Penrose is pretty insistent that a more general theory will eventually capture both quantum and classical physics. Which is not unique to him. She was puzzled by Carter's notes that focused on a missing physicist, but really didn't think she could shed any light there."

"Any chance the missing physicist was her father?"

"Hardly. He disappeared in the thirties."

"Disappearances certainly have a way of popping up in Carter's life."

"Yeah, I s'pose. Coincidences or spiritual puns?" She laughed and tossed Jack one of yesterday's donut holes over Barnum's spinning head.

Even before the sound of approaching footsteps reached Jack and Ginger, Barnum bounded to the door, his entire body quivering as the tail, in fact, wagged the dog.

Barnum bounced up and down as if his hind legs were springs as Cy entered the room. "How's my boy?" He knelt down and rubbed the squirming Barnum. "Look what I got for you." He palmed a donut hole that quickly disappeared into Barnum's mouth.

Ginger hugged Cy as Barnum pushed to get between them. Jack slapped Cy on the back. "Welcome home. You look better."

"I don't think I've ever seen you with a tan before," Ginger added.

"You were both right. Just going and watching a few ballgames and trying to get past it was the right thing to do. It's been awhile since I could just sit and enjoy watching prospects play ball!"

"Well, how are you feeling about everything?" Ginger asked.

"I still feel like crap about it. I'm always going to feel like crap about it. It's never going to go away. But, I'll survive. How is Ashley doing?"

"She's traumatized," Ginger said. "I think she is going to drop out of school for a year....maybe go home. There's a nice bond there between us. I'm going to keep up with her. It might develop into a friendship. We'll see."

"Funny!" Cy said. "I always thought it would be *Jack* and Ashley. The punk rocker and the detective."

Cy didn't notice that both Jack and Ginger winced at this. Breaking the silence, Cy said, "OK! And Dan?"

"Dan's Dan." Jack said. "He's fine. He'll always be fine."

There was a renewed silence. "And Cy is Cy," Cy finally said.

Ginger looked away. No one spoke.

"Anything new in the last three weeks?" Cy asked.

"You're pretty much up to speed on everything," Jack said. "We have a package coming today from Miami from Robert's boss. Some personal stuff of his from a drawer in the shoe store. Chief quit on Boisseau and wants to become a PI. We gave him a referral on a job yesterday---a possible wayward wife situation."

Cy laughed. "Chief will love that." He sat down. "Anything else?"

"George Foster is supposed to be calling us any minute now on the Johnson case." Jack outlined a few other things that had come up in Cy's absence. "We still feel there may be something significant in the parallels between Robert's and Carter's cases. Do you still think it's just bullshit? Just pure coincidence?"

"I don't like coincidences, but sometimes they do happen. I continue to doubt there is a link between Robert's old Cuban and Carter's old foreigner, and, as we all know, people *do* disappear. And many of them *do* have children. It's just too far-fetched for me. I didn't think about it much. I just don't see where it goes. You two don't know this, but my father disappeared when I was nine. Doesn't mean anything."

Ginger looked up sharply. "Why haven't you ever told us?"

"Why would I? We've never talked about our parents. I wasn't keeping it from you. I just didn't think it was important. Frankly, I never thought it would come up."

Ginger just stared at Cy.

Cy shrugged. "That reminds me of a story my mom used to tell. She heard it on a talk show. Always claimed it was a true story. Some celebrity in Florida was running late to her bridge group and opened the front door to leave her house, only to discover a delivery man with a package about to knock on her door. He gave her the package and had her sign for it. When she discovered 'live animals' written on the top of the box, she opened it very carefully. Discovering twin baby alligators, she dumped them in the bathtub with some water, and left for her bridge game, leaving the problem of the alligators to be resolved when she returned home.

"When she got home from her bridge game, she found the following note, signed by her housekeeper taped to the front of the refrigerator: 'Dear Mrs. so and so, I quit! I don't work where there's alligators. I woulda told you before, but I never thought it would come up!'"

Their laughter was interrupted by the ringing of the phone. Cy picked up the receiver, "Hey, George. Yeah, I just got back. I feel better, but not great. Lemme put you on speaker. Jack and Ginger are here too."

"Ginger," George started right in, "did you find anything out at Kiawah about Tim?"

"What's this about?" Cy asked.

"It turns out that Tim Johnson's mom got a postcard from him while he was out here postmarked 'Kiawah.' Since that was new, I went out to the island with his photo and checked around. Turns out they *do* remember him. He had dinner and drinks at one of the clubs. But nobody remembers whose guest he was. And, George," turning back to the phone, "nobody's seen him out there since then. It's as cold as all the other Charleston leads."

"George," Cy said, "I'm assuming these guys caught you up on the Cindy Boisseau case."

"Of course. Just an odd coincidence, I guess, that Tim was in town that particular weekend, and..."

Jack interrupted. "And we think that Clyde's story about Tim seeing Cindy at the bar that night was just bullshit. A pretty flimsy attempt at cover, given what we know now."

"Yes," George continued. "I'm sure Tim had nothing to do with her death. Thanks, Ging, for following up in Kiawah. Unless something very significant happens out your way, I'm going to just confine our search to southern California from here on.

"The other reason I called, Cy, is that Matt, the man with the mini-camcorders that we liked so much at the convention, said he's backordered---"

"Of course," Cy interrupted.

"...and he'll get us each one by the end of the month." George finished.

"OK. Thanks. Anything else?"

"No, that's it from out here."

Cy looked at Jack and Ginger and they both shook their heads. "Thanks again for your hospitality in San Francisco. Good luck with the Johnson case. Let us know if there is anything more we can do."

"Best of luck to you guys. And Cy, hang in there. Your next 'slam-dunk' case is always just a phone call away."

Cy grunted and hung up.

Instantly, the phone rang again.

Cy, seeing it was George again, hit the speaker button and said, "What the hell do *you* want?"

"Sorry!" George called out. "There's one thing I keep forgetting to tell you guys....just an oddity in the Johnson case. I don't think it means anything, but I thought you might want to know. According to his mother, Tim's father disappeared into thin air when Tim was ten years old. They never heard from him again."

Cy opened the Blind Tiger door for Dan. "Let's sit at the big table tonight. The singer's off and it will be quiet enough to talk over there. We've got a lot to catch you up on, Dan. It's been quite a day for my first day back."

After they were seated and ordered their drinks, Jack started. "Here's what we've got. As you know, we've been working on three cases: Robert Flynn in Miami, Tim Johnson in L.A. and Carter here. What you don't know is that they have become spookily similar. In all three cases, not only have they each disappeared, but their abusive fathers disappeared when they were between the ages of nine and eleven."

"All three?" Dan asked, interested.

"All three," Ginger repeated for Jack. "Precisely as in the case of Mr. Ellis. One day there, the next day gone. Without a trace. The kid was suddenly free of an abusive parent."

Jack continued. "Today we received a box of belongings from Robert's boss in Miami....things he was working on when business was slow. It contained exactly the same set of physics books that Carter had sitting on her desk."

"And, the guy in L.A.?" Dan asked.

"We're checking." Jack answered. "The detective on the case says that Tim Johnson had books of all sorts throughout his house. He remembered one of the friends commenting on astronomy being an interest of Johnson's, but so far no confirmation on the specific books."

"Let me guess," Dan said, "there's more?"

"We're not sure of this next part yet," Jack said. "But we could get confirmation in the next few minutes. It's Sean's night off, but he said he would come in to look at this composite sketch," pushing the drawing across to Dan, "of a dark foreigner who had been spending some time with Robert Flynn."

"OK. I'll bite." Dan laughed. "Let me guess. Tim Johnson was last seen with his Mexican gardener out in L.A."

"Here comes Sean," Ginger replied acidly. "Let's see his reaction before we start making fun of this particular shot in the dark."

Dan looked up as Sean approached the table. "Hey, Sean. Thanks for coming in on your day off. We'll buy you a drink if you recognize this picture."

Sean looked. "Where'd you get that? That's the old guy I told you about with the funny accent who used to meet with Carter in the other room. How'd you get his picture?"

The four detectives stared wordlessly at Sean.

Ginger finally broke the silence. "Which one of you two skeptics wants to go first?"

"The plot thickens," Jack added mindlessly.

"What movie is that from?" Ginger asked.

"About a dozen. Take your pick."

Gloomily, Cy looked over at Dan. "How hard will it be to go through Interpol and the FBI to cross check recent missing person cases against fathers who went missing when the kids were, say, eight to twelve-years-old?"

Dan interrupted. "And mothers?"

"Mothers?" Ginger asked.

"Just because your three cases all involve abusive fathers doesn't mean….and, I'm not saying you're right even about that….doesn't mean that whatever this is---if it's about anything at all---can't also be about abusive mothers."

"Good point," Ginger added.

"I think Jack and Ginger and I, working through the department's computers, can get this information pretty easily. Any cases we turn up we can check with the investigating officer to see if a dark foreigner was involved. I think we want to be careful about circulating this picture until we get a feel for how many, if any, other cases we are dealing with. How far back should we check?"

"How far back do the data bases go?" Jack asked.

Dan grabbed a handful of peanuts. "It depends on the country, but I would think that we could get a good feel by looking at open cases for the past ten or twenty years."

"When can we get started?" Ginger said.

"I don't see any reason why we can't go to the station right now," Dan said. "I'll call ahead and we'll pick up some take-out on the way over."

"Go ahead," Cy said. "I'll take care of the bill. Let's meet at the office tomorrow at ten o'clock to see if we have anything further."

As Cy turned to leave the bar with his change after paying, the waitress said, "Cy, there's a gentleman in the other room who just asked me to tell you that he wanted to buy you a drink."

Cy thanked her and walked through the archway into the other bar area. He looked to his left and saw the dark foreigner rising to greet him.

Cy looked at the man. He was much smaller than Cy had expected. But it was obviously him. That was clear from the Miami composite, and from the body language, as this little man waited for Cy to react.

Cy was on his guard. "Can we begin by clearing up why you claimed your name was Cy Fapp?"

The foreigner smiled. "It was just a manner of taking your attention." He spoke with a thick Italian accent.

"Well, it worked," Cy responded. "Where is Carter?"

"She is content."

"No, I said *where* is Carter?"

"She is much content."

"OK, let me try this a different way. Where have you taken Carter?"

"I have not taken Carter nowhere. I have only aided her to reach a place that she wanted to go....of her own will."

"Where are you from?"

"Of the Sicily originally. But now, I am practically from wherever."

"Are you going to tell me your name?"

"When I am more habituated to you."

"Why do you need to be 'habituated,' I suppose you mean 'comfortable,' with me?"

The man laughed confidently. "We have a much to speak about. You are the double of my size and the half my age, armed and justly suspicious. Is true that I intend no damage to you. In fact, is the opposite. To you I can give the possibility to be content for your life, finally."

"Look, buster, for all you know, I'm as happy as the proverbial clam. Give me one reason why I shouldn't drag you over to the police this very minute?"

"First of all, you have seen I have the ability to be---and remain---scarce if it please to me. And, another thing, we have much to speak about your father."

"Those strike me as even better reasons to take you to the police. Not reasons not to."

The stranger shrugged. "Our relation, if they are to function, must be pure voluntary for your part. Just as it was for Carter Ellis and Robert Flynn and others, numberless. If you try to resist or render to me discomfort, I have the possibility to prolong this as much as please to me or I can.... I can let it fall forever."

"Sicily?" Cy said, puzzled, almost to himself. "What was the name of the Italian physicist who disappeared in the late 30's---the one that both Carter and Robert noted in their readings? Wasn't he from Sicily? Wasn't it something like Margarine? Margarino? Majorana! That's it. Does this have something to do with Majorana's disappearance?"

"Molto bene, Cy. This will finish well, for you."

"So, where do we go from here?" Cy asked an hour later.

"I need you to think on what I have said to you," the stranger answered. "You decide if you want to continue to meet me, then we can discuss it more. The conditions are to you equal to your predecessors. If I perceive that you passed a word to someone, or if I perceive that you are indecisive, or if I perceive that you are antagonistic, again I disappear."

"What about my colleagues in the investigation? What can I share with Jack and Ginger?"

"Niente. Absolutely nothing. I am surprised they established the link between Carter and Robert, and, soon no doubt, between all the others, and their fathers. But you must not tell this to them, or I leave. And you will lose all the hope to learn more of *their* cases, or the case of your father, or to benefit from this. Will be a diversion for you. Consider it like a parallel…..a parallel research. 'Noli me tangere.' They cannot touch me. Now you are knowing enough that you can be useful for them. But in the end, it will lead them nowhere. Whereas I can lead you wherever you want to go."

"And your name?"

The stranger smiled. "We will see how you think at our following appointment."

"Which is when?"

He stood up and laughed. "Is mysterious. You do mysteries well, Cy. You can untie *all* these knots."

# Chapter 22

## *November 20, 2007*

Ginger scrolled through the emails at the desk while Jack headed toward Cy's fax machine. She started reading from the screen. "Twenty-eight-year-old female, African American, Portland, Oregon. Disappeared February 6, 1992. Case still open. No clues. Father disappeared in 1973. Case also still open. Girl raised by grandparents."

Jack glanced over. "Put that over on the wall under, "Female, 90's, USA.' My God! I've got four more from Jeff in Dan's office on the fax machine."

"How do they look?"

"Like they all look when he sends them. A perfect fit. The tough part is the next step, getting in touch with someone who can confirm the abuse and the dark stranger part. One each from Germany, Italy, Norway and Wisconsin."

"How about if I call Portland and Wisconsin and you start on the three from Europe? Save Italy for last. We'll see who gets to it first."

"OK. How many is that now?" Jack looked up at the wall, now covered with case summaries.

"It looks like thirty-five confirmed matches and we're still trying to confirm twenty more," she gestured toward the far wall, "with two or three more a day. Cy came up with a pretty good system for staying on top of these. But he seems to be increasingly distancing himself from it."

"Yeah. It doesn't feel as if he has his heart in any of this anymore. Well, at least so far, it's saved us from to talking to him about *us*."

"Hell, we're so busy with these cases that we haven't talked to *us* about us!" Ginger laughed.

The foreigner leaned back with his glass of wine by the fireplace in Cy's living room. "Allora, now you have meditated on these things, how do you think about them, Cy?"

"The hard part for me is what you told me about my dad. On the one hand, I have no positive memories of him. Well, that's not entirely true. He used to bring me souvenirs from the ballgames he went to without me. I always looked forward to getting them. All these years, I've kept the package he dropped in that alley in 1965. The police said a local bartender told them he had forgotten my souvenirs at the bar, and came back for them just before he disappeared.

"But other than baseball, all my memories of him are negative. He was a big rough man and I remember him as being drunk and abusive to my mother and me. Even years later, she couldn't talk about Milwaukee without getting upset. On the other hand, he was the only father I ever had and, whereas, I appreciate your motives and all, I find myself resenting the fact that you took it upon yourself to get rid of him."

"I said not 'I,' I said 'we.' And remind yourself of this: we have not killed him or no other one. We have just, if you want, rendered it possible that he is more content in another place. Remind yourself that the idea was to make an ambience of which you could mature, sanely and more content. We had only good intentions."

"But it didn't work," Cy said. "It didn't work."

"No, in the great majority of cases, the children matured into less content ones than we had previewed." He looked into the fire. Then back at Cy. "In your experience, Cy, what makes the people content?"

"I don't know. You tell me. You're the intergenerational expert. In my line of work, you don't run across very many happy people."

"You have chosen your vocation."

"What's your theory on that?"

"Your father treated you very badly. We arrived too much in delay to change that. I would like to think that now you are more content than you would have been, but I cannot say that you are a content person. You selected clearly your vocation so as to help the persons....the persons up to their necks in traumas that very much have a need of your aid."

"Similar to you. But, aren't you trained as a physicist?"

The stranger smiled. "Si, but let us return to that question later."

Cy insisted. "You're trained as a physicist, yet, you've dedicated *your* life to helping people?"

"Si, a discovery unanticipated from my preparation, permitted me to try and aid the persons. In that sense, I imagine, our vocations are equal."

Cy looked up sharply. "You are the second physicist to compare your profession to mine. The first was my friend, Mary Beth Bracken, at Berkeley...."

"I know of her works."

"....she always joked that she looks for missing particles and I look for missing people."

The stranger had a twinkle in his eye. "Is ironical that it is here our history begins."

Jack looked down at a message coming out of the fax machine. "We just got a fax from Lt. Hollowell in Fairfax,

Virginia, about the Birnbaum case. Remember, this is the only case where it's the mother who disappeared.

"When I spoke to Hollowell a few days ago, he promised to fax us the father's contact information if he was willing to talk to us. Looks from this that Birnbaum is quite a character. Hollowell says he is willing to talk to us, but we should steel ourselves for an eccentric. He has an address on Guinea Road in Annandale."

"Really? Those are my old stomping grounds. It's right near the border of Fairfax and Annandale. Nothing unusual about that location. I wonder what's odd about him? Why don't we give him a call?"

"Wait a sec. Let's review what we know from the materials before we call him."

"Fire away."

"Janet Birnbaum, twenty-eight, court stenographer, Fairfax., Virginia, disappeared seven months ago. There have been no leads. She lived in an apartment by herself on Chain Bridge Road and hasn't been heard from since. Mother vanished when Janet was nine and it says here, according to Hollowell, that she was an alcoholic, both physically and verbally abusive, and that the father traveled a lot back then. Social Services in Fairfax County has a long file on the mother and on several occasions put the girl with the father's family until he returned."

"Is the father a suspect?"

"Not according to Hollowell," he said.

"Career?"

"Well, I was holding back on you so you could discover it directly from him."

"You're so dramatic! What's Mr. Birnbaum do?"

"Did, actually. Something to do with the circus."

"You're kidding!"

"Nope. He was a head hunter for top-of-the-line circus acts. He was on the road all the time."

"And what does he do now?"

"Says here he's a writer."

"OK, let's give the old carnival scribe a ring."

Jack punched in the number. The phone rang twice and a very deep voice growled an answer. "Is this someone with good news or money?"

Jack laughed. "Jason Robards, *A Thousand Clowns*."

"Who's this?" The voice asked.

"I'm Jack Crisp and I'm here with my colleague, Ginger Grayson. We're the private detectives down in Charleston, South Carolina, who Detective Hollowell told you would be calling about your daughter."

"Yes?"

"Are you Mr. Birnbaum? Is this a good time to talk?"

"I am. My friends all call me Carny. If you can help me find my daughter, I'll give you all the time you need."

"Actually," Ginger cut in, "we are working on a whole set of cases that may be similar to your daughter's disappearance." There was a noise at Birnbaum's end and Barnum stood up looking intensely, head cocked to the side, at the phone. Ginger looked curiously at Barnum. "What's that noise, Mr.....uh, Carny," she asked. "Is that something you have to deal with while we wait?"

"You two may be good detectives after all. I've got you on speaker, because I was working on my book when the phone rang. My two labs were just growling at my side."

"Oh?" Ginger said.

"They both believe it is always feeding time and since they both were trained as seeing-eye dogs, they only make polite 'what about me' growling noises when they want attention."

Jack and Ginger laughed. "We'd love to take the credit for figuring it out, but our chocolate lab, Barnum, ID'd your dogs before we did." She said.

"You're kidding! You have a lab named Barnum? My two black labs are named Barnum and Bailey. What a kick!"

Ginger looked thoughtful. "You're not blind are you, Carny?"

"No, just lazy! Too lazy to train my own dogs. So I adopt failed seeing eyes dogs. Already trained."

"What did you used to do for the circus?" Ginger asked.

"I've been on and off with carnivals and circuses since I was a kid. First the usual, odd jobs; then, helping take care of the animals. Then I was a clown for a while; then a terrible magician. Turned out I was really good at sales and with people. I naturally evolved into helping circuses find acts and helping acts find circuses. A sort of unique headhunter specialty."

"But you're not doing that anymore?" Jack asked.

"No, I was really good at it and I liked the work. You meet a lot of bizarre and interesting people in the circus business. But, it left me very little time to be with my family and when my wife started having some....problems, around twenty or so years ago, I sold my book of business to the sword swallower and settled down here to be a writer."

"And, what do you write?" Ginger asked.

"Fiction. Murder mysteries actually."

Both detectives blurted out, "You're kidding."

Carny's reply made it clear they had annoyed him. "Not everybody associated with the circus is an illiterate."

"No," Jack said."We didn't mean that, it's just that if you ever need some material, boy have we got some stuff for you. I've never met a murder mystery writer before. It's always sounded intriguing to me."

"Everybody else's job always sounds fascinating. There are good days and bad days just like any other job. Maybe I'll call you guys the next time I have writer's block. In the meantime, what do you know about my daughter?"

"We wanted to ask you a few questions to see if this fits the profile of our other cases." Ginger said.

"Shoot."

"Around the time of her disappearance did anyone notice that she was with an older, Mediterranean looking man....a foreigner with an accent?" Jack asked.

"Neither of her brothers mentioned anything about that, and I don't remember Lt. Hollowell saying that it came up with her friends. I certainly didn't notice it. The guy I sold the business to is like an uncle to her. He's Spanish and they sometimes had dinners together. But, if you're looking for a stranger, I don't think so."

"Would you characterize Janet as being close to you and her brothers?"

"Yes. We're an extremely close family...certainly from the time her mother left."

"We know that your wife has been characterized as an abusive mother especially with Janet. Would you describe Janet as a happy or unhappy adult in general?"

"Oh, no question about that. She's been the center---the life and spark---for her two brothers and for me her whole life. She was definitely a happy child and a happy adult. Why do you ask?"

Ginger signaled Jack. He pushed 'mute' on the phone and looked over at her. "Sounds like Bailey-Lee's fantasy description of Carter."

"I was thinking the same thing," as he turned mute off. "Had she been talking at all lately about looking for a better place? Somewhere where she might be happier?"

"No. What do you mean? Like a better apartment? Moving away from this place? I'm not sure what you are getting at, but I assure you---and I think Hollowell will support this---Janet is *not* a runaway. She loves her job, loves her family, loves the D.C. area and has many friends. I'm as baffled as the police. I'm certainly frustrated that they don't have any leads. But, whereas I'm sure she didn't just pick up and run off, I'm sure we'll find an explanation when we find Janet. I can only imagine it has something to do with one of the trials she worked on at the courthouse."

"This is a long-shot," Ginger interjected, "but did she show any interest in theoretical physics, especially lately?"

Carny snorted a laugh. "Certainly not to my knowledge."

"Carny, sorry . We're so focused on trying to fit Janet's disappearance into the pattern of what we're working on here that we're not being very helpful to you. What do you and your boys think may have happened here?"

"Well frankly we're bewildered. I initially checked with all my old circus buddies to see if she suddenly got 'the itch,' or to see if anyone was playing a practical joke on me. Then, of course, both the police and we checked in with her mother. But, that turned out to be a waste of time."

"Her mother?" Jack and Ginger both blurted out.

"Yeah, her mother. Sally. She was part of a trapeze act when I married her about thirty years ago. After we had the kids, she began to have problems with drinking. She never was much of mother. Walking a tightrope turned out to be a metaphor for Sally's life rather than just a career. One day I was in Abilene trying to convince a circus owner to buy a trained bear and I got a frantic call from my father that Sally had vanished. The kids must have been....what...nine, six and five at the time. I got back as quick as I could, but the woman had left without a trace. And nobody from her family or old outfit admitted to having heard from her.

"In any case, I didn't care very much. We went through a tough couple of years where the police were all over me and my friends, trying to prove that we'd gotten rid of her. I sold my business and tried writing for a living. It was hard giving up the circus after all those years, but I had to stay around here for the kids. And it was hard being under a cloud of suspicion."

"You said earlier that you and the police checked with Sally," Ginger said. "Has she returned?"

"I'm surprised that's not in the report Hollowell gave you. After twelve years of nothing, Janet got a card from her mother for her twenty-first birthday. Sally had been living in a trailer park outside Las Vegas. We all met with her once about two years later, but the kids didn't feel any connection and I certainly didn't. Suspicion naturally turned on her when Janet disappeared seven months ago. But, the police seem satisfied that she had nothing to do with it."

There was silence at both ends."Is there a problem? Is any of this useful to you?" Carny asked.

"Well," Jack said, "in real life detective work---just like in books and movies---you never know what's important until you've sifted through everything. But from what you've told us, it doesn't feel like there's any link between Janet and our other cases."

"I wish that weren't the situation," Ginger added. "I wish we had some light to shed on your daughter's disappearance. Hopefully she'll turn up safe and there will be some logical explanation for it all. We've seen it happen. In the meantime, it has to be tough on you and the boys."

"That's certainly true. Is there anything I can possibly do to help you?"

"No," Jack said. "We appreciate your willingness to give us so much time today. Feel free to call us if you think of anything else....or if you need a source for some wild ideas."

"Well," Carny said, clearly saddened, "frankly, this has been more than a little discouraging. Feel free to call me if you have any other questions...or if you think of anything that might be helpful in finding Janet. Who knows, maybe we'll have a happy occasion soon to bring the two Barnums together."

The stranger and Cy finished dessert and moved back into Cy's kitchen. "That was quite a story," Cy said. "Let me try to summarize it as we do the dishes, Franco. I want to see if I understand any of this...."

"Before you begin. What thing has happened to your dog? Dov'e Barnum?"

"With the events of the past month, Barnum has taken increasingly to staying with Ginger. And I suppose it's for the best. I'm not much of a companion for anybody, let alone him, these days."

"That could be fortunate. Avanti, tell me your version of my history."

"Your uncle, Ettore Majorana, in the early 30's discovered not only why quantum particles appeared, disappeared and recombined with other particles to appear and disappear, but also how to use the concept of spin to cause it to happen. And, he also discovered, or hypothesized, where they went to and where they came from."

Franco interrupted. "But more to that, in principle, how to apply this quantum concept to grander, classical structures."

"OK. And, you also hypothesized how this could possibly explain what physicists today now know as 'the missing matter in the universe.'"

"Precise."

"Then I have two questions. Number one, why do we only know about your uncle? Why has no one ever heard of Franco Majorana? And, number two, why didn't you publish the results?"

"But, he did. In 1932 he presented his results, and just a handful of fisici believed my Uncle: Heisenberg, Dirac, and I think...it's been long time....perhaps also Niels Bohr. All the others occupied themselves in agreeing with the refuting by Einstein, and would not listen. Nobody was understanding the implications, or if he did, to take it as serious. Veramente, it was a moment of sadness. Therefore, we have tried to demonstrate to them this thing, researching classical objects---ever grander."

"So you went from disappearing electrons and mesons to what? Disappearing plates of lasagna? Did the plate disappear too, or just the lasagna?"

Franco laughed. "We calculated the method to do the plates before the pasta. It was to us a temptation to do them to the cat, perhaps even that damn cat of Schroedinger, but Ettore stopped us at the living things. Until after."

"I thought the puzzle was whether that particular cat could be both alive and dead at the same time."

"Ettore wanted to add a third possibility, but nobody wanted to listen. Then, to finish this phase of the history, perhaps even you know, in the winter of 1938, we made the reservation on the steamship from Palermo, and while we passed L'isola di Capri---you know, the Goat Island---we transformed ourselves and disappeared ourselves for the first time. We disappeared into the...thin air, as the Americans say it."

"Poof! Not drowned, not spirited away. Just, like that," Cy said, and snapped his fingers. "Famous physicist vanishes into thin air, on board a ship."

"Presto! Just like you say. Fisico famoso---and nephew---vanished.

"In respect to why you have never heard no one ever speak of *me*," he laughed, "more importante, why no one has never heard of me, it can be very simple or very complex to explain. It depends on how you want to observe it. Ettore Majorana is a brilliant fisico. But was never given his just credit. Is all more complicated by the political situations of years of the mid 30's. The Germany and the Italy were places to escape from, not places in which the new ideas could flower. The Einstein had America to escape to. Ettore had only his work. Ettore has more than one hundred years this year, but is alive and good and has the aspect of a man who has fifty years."

"As do you."

"Davvero....but I have ninety-five years. To travel ahead and behind seems to function like the travel in time, diminishing the process of aging. In all the cases, I was the young apprentice. He was the brilliant fisico. I tried to understand all of his work so we could continue this work today."

"And where is this place that you transported yourselves and presumably my father?"

"Boh. That is another history, for another day."

# Chapter 23

## *November 21, 2007*

### Berkeley, California

Mary Beth picked up the ringing phone in her office, distracted.

"MB?"

"Yes? Hello. Cy? Cy! Hi! How are you?"

"I've been better. Do you have a minute?"

"Sure. Is this more about your case?"

"Yes, except now it's many more. Dozens. Same physics books. Same highlighting. "

"Really!"

"Yes. But I want to go back to our earlier conversation. If we wanted to get classical sized objects---desks, chairs, people--- to disappear and reappear from our universe into one of these parallel universes, how would we start?"

"'We?' There's no way. This is silly. It was fun for old friends after dinner having drinks, but from here on it gets to be a waste of both of our time. For all practical purposes, this is not an empirical exercise."

"OK, let's try it a different way. If I told you that I knew with 100% certainty that it's been done, that I know by whom, and I know why, and that I need your help in figuring out how, that it's a life or death issue for one of your closest personal friends, would you help?"

"What the hell has happened, Cy?!?"

"And oh yeah, it could lead to untold accolades and riches for the physicist who figures it out."

"Thanks a bunch for thinking of my career, but I'm doin' just fine out here. In the *real* world, I might add, not in the delusional world you've suddenly found yourself inhabiting."

Cy laughed. "We'll note for the record that at least one person thinks quantum mechanics is the *real* world. Not to mention *Berkeley*!"

He went on. "Let's start with my claim that it's been done. Now: how? Let's make the ground rules from here on in that I tell you what I believe can be accomplished, and you work through how, instead of telling me it's impossible, OK?"

MB responded quietly. "OK."

"Then let me take my first nudge at you, Mary Beth." MB started at Cy using her full name. "First, there is not only a parallel universe, but a way to travel between the two. Is there some way to use your concept of 'spin' to achieve this? Appearances and disappearances?"

"Whew! Do you want me to confine these fanciful explorations to spin, or can we go more broadly?"

"Let's take spin, first. If we dead end on it, then we can try to broaden it."

"I'll take a spin at it, but I'm not optimistic."

"Ouch!" Cy said. "I thought you were worried that I was the one who wasn't being serious!"

Ginger studied their wall of cases cross referenced by sex, nationality, and decade of disappearance. She suddenly reached up, remembering to remove the Canadian man whose father had shown up after his son's disappearance.

"Hey, Ging," Jack called out. "I just got a cute e-mail from the inspector in Italy. You remember the case, the one from Florence. He asked for further specificity on "dark foreigner." He points out that what might be a dark foreigner in the United States, could be an average Florentine citizen from where he sits."

"He's got us there. We can't reject any cases from southern Europe, the Middle East or in the Americas south of the United States, on that dimension." She frowned, "How many cases do we have in those areas?"

"We rejected nine that met all the other criteria but failed that one. Let's go back on those nine and ask if there was any older man who approached the victim."

Ginger looked back at the wall. "OK. Why don't you take the ones in Europe and I'll take the Americas. How stupid that we didn't think of this."

"When do you think we should sit down with Dan and Cy and go through these cases?"

"We should have something close to certainty on each of these cases in the next day or so. We've got forty-three matches and five pending. Let's not meet with them, though until we've worked all the way through the list."

"In fact, Cy, I'm in *total* disbelief," MB pointed out. "But let's go with your new ground rule that it's possible, and search for the 'how.' Actually, if we're looking for solutions to a quantum particle mystery, spin is not a bad place to start. We know that there is one theoretical place to look for a whole host of missing particles, namely in the concept of supersymmetry.

"One of the implications of supersymmetry is the discovery that each particle has a superpartner that has less spin than its partner by precisely the same amount. And, I hate to tell you this, but none of the superpartners have ever been discovered empirically."

"Ouch. Let me make sure I understand this. 'Spin' enables this theory to suggest the existence of so far undiscovered partner particles with every particle we actually can see, or detect? Right?"

"More or less."

"OK, I'll bite. Where are they?"

"Maybe they're here, but too heavy to be discovered by any existing accelerators. Or maybe they don't exist and the theory's wrong. Or, of course........let me try to push this alone for awhile. You'd like me to ask if it's possible that the superpartners are of a different dimensionality than our known four and are in a parallel universe, rather than here? If we reduced the spin of a particle by this constant, in effect creating its superpartner, would it disappear? Into the parallel universe? If a superpartner's spin were increased by this constant, would it suddenly appear to us? Could these partners go back and forth between this universe and a shadow universe at our edge?"

"Go on. I'm listening."

She went on. "Well, these circumstances, while I think preposterous, are certainly possible. Certainly as long as we've never discovered a superpartner in our known empirical universe, we can't deny these possibilities. Ironically, one year from now we'll start to find out. I'll be at CERN near Geneva next September when we start up the Large Hydron Collider precisely to look for them. But, could this be applied to classical sized objects like this phone, or you and me? As I told you before, spin is a particle property which has no precise counterpart in our observable classical physics world."

"So what about disappearing particles?" Or, Cy said to himself, fingers crossed, missing people?

Mary Beth went on. "Do you mean that, by affecting the spin, you can change the particles? We know that each particle has a defining spin, so it stands to reason that if you could change it, the particle becomes, inherently, a different particle. But for large, classical sized objects spin is an entirely different concept."

Cy held his hand up and laughed as he caught himself talking with his hands on the phone. "Whoa, MB, you're losing me again."

"I'm asking *your* question, Cy. Could somebody have figured out that there is a comparable concept of spin in classical objects? Granted, it's fun to think about, but I just don't see how there could be superobjects and/or anti-objects for telephones and buildings. Doesn't mean there aren't, of course, but that would mean that your parallel universe is the same as ours, except for one characteristic for each object, whether quantum or classical. I doubt any mathematical construct would support the hypothesis for long. Seems, frankly, like this would require a Creator with a sense of humor rather than a sense of order."

The phone rang. Ginger picked it up. "Hi, Lieutenant Fields. This is Ginger Grayson. Thanks so much for calling back. If you don't mind I'll put you on speaker. My associate, Jack Crisp, is here with me."

"Hello, lieutenant, this is Jack."

"Hello. You're both detectives, right?"

"Yes sir, private detectives. Jack is my colleague here in the agency."

"I understand you are calling in reference to the Haupert case."

"Yes," Ginger said. "We understand that Ralph Haupert disappeared on August 5, 1995. Has he ever been found or has anyone heard from him?"

"No ma'am, not to our knowledge"

"We also understand that his father disappeared twenty-five years earlier. In 1970, I believe. Was that also there in Lovett?"

"You're right on both counts."

"Did anyone ever hear from the father?"

"No. Not that we ever knew."

"What was the relationship between the boy and his father?"

"That was way before my time, ma'am."

"Is there anything in the file about Ralph's disappearance that gives a flavor for their relationship?"

"Several people commented, including several people who worked for the city, that the best thing that ever happened to that kid was when his dad disappeared."

"Was the father abusive to the boy?"

"Things were different down here in the 70's from what I hear. But, I think it's a safe guess, from looking through this file that if it were today, the city would have moved this boy to foster care long before, as it turns out, his father disappeared."

"Thank you, lieutenant. One more thing, is there anything in the file consistent with there being an older stranger, perhaps foreign, in Ralph's life about the time of *his* disappearance?"

"Well, everybody down here in these parts always assumed that Ralph ran off with a boyfriend, or some such. But no one could ever prove it. That's just hearsay. Now that you mention it, there is a note in the file that a couple of his buddies had seen him meeting with an odd man wearing dark clothes. Let me look it up in the file." A rustling of papers followed. "Yes, here it is. Three people, a bartender and two of his friends all claimed seeing him, several times with a quote, dark foreigner, end quote….."

Jack, looking at Ginger, held up four fingers on each hand and mouthed "forty-four" dramatically but silently.

Ginger nodded.

"..... Tell me, Miss, what's this all about. Have you found Ralph or do you know where he might be?"

"No. It's just that we're working a couple of similar cases and we're trying to find a connection. Can we call you if there is anything else that comes up?"

"More'n that, please call us if you turn up anything on Ralph. It would be nice to close the case."

"We promise. Good-bye." She pushed the button and looked over at Jack.

Jack blew a breath toward the ceiling. "Lithe and strong like a tiger."

"What?"

"It's a line from the movie Z about the assassination of a popular politician in Greece in the 60's. The investigators couldn't make any headway until two self-proclaimed innocent bystanders independently used the term that they had seen an assailant attack the victim 'lithe and strong like a tiger.' The repetitive use of the unique term linked the witnesses in an obvious conspiracy and led to the ultimate arrest of the military leaders of Greece who had planned the assassination."

Ginger blew out her breath. "This case gets spookier by the day."

MB paused. Then continued. "Besides Cy, I just don't believe your contention that somebody has done this. All of physics has been trying to integrate these two theories for 80 years. It's an automatic Nobel Prize, if not immortality....your guy would be mentioned in the same breath with Newton and Einstein. Nobody would just sit on it. And you and I sure aren't going to accomplish it through a sequence of casual conversations."

"Let's......"

"I know, I know, let's just start with the premise that they have. If one can observe or find the same kind of spin in the classical world that exists in the quantum world, then there would be well-defined properties of each classical object that was defined by, among other characteristics, its spin. I suppose if you can change the spin, you can change the object. And, as an obvious special case, quite possibly, if you change the spin in a precise way, you could make the object disappear. We, of course, would have no more idea of where it went, though, then we do when we see particles disappear and reappear."

"Where would a sizeable object go if it disappeared in a quantum sense?"

"You got me. Do you have a theory?"

"No. But I've met somebody who says he knows."

# Chapter 24

*November 22, 2007*

**Charleston**

"Am I ever going to get my dog back?" Cy asked, winking at Jack.

Ginger stroked Barnum's velvet ears. "I don't think so. Barnum has transferred his loyalty to Jack and me ever since you went off to all those ballgames without him. Besides, he's figured out that I have more time for him."

"And more dog biscuits, and fewer donut holes," added Jack. "Looks like you'll have to switch to your partners as your best friends."

"Are we expecting Dan?" Cy asked.

As if on cue, the door opened and Dan came in holding a large box from Sweet Julep's. "Pralines anyone? Charleston's best!"

"Ginger and Barnum can have mine," Cy grumbled.

"For you, I got coffee." Looking around he commented, "I love what you've done with the walls, PI."

Jack shot Dan his usual annoyed look. "Each of these sheets represents a case we got from you, the FBI or Interpol."

"And the colors?" Dan asked.

"We color coded them by definitive characteristics."

"So what's the bottom line?" Dan asked, deftly popping an entire praline into his mouth and washing it down with coffee.

"It's interesting," Ginger said. "We were surprised at how many people actually are never found! People actually *do* just go missing! "

"Like Judge Crater," Dan offered hopefully.

"And Amelia Earhart and Jimmy Hoffa," Jack tossed out.

"Let's try to stay on topic, guys," Ginger said. "We started with eighty-six missing person cases spanning the last twenty-five years. Each came from either the Interpol or FBI data file and seemed a possible fit. In twenty-six, the missing parent turned out to be murdered or not missing. In ten there was no sign of any abuse. And, furthermore, in each of those ten cases the missing person was universally viewed as a happy person---content with life and not a runaway candidate. In six of the remaining fifty cases, the police are convinced of foul play and have identified a likely perpetrator.

"That leaves us with our forty-four cases: twenty-three in the United States, eighteen in Europe, two in Canada, one in Mexico. Thirty-one men and thirteen women. Each and every one had a father disappear without a trace when they were between the ages of nine and eleven. Not a single missing mother. The kids all grew up only to then disappear themselves as adults....the youngest at twenty-three, the oldest forty-seven. And, in every case, the father was publicly known to be abusive. And furthermore, in each of the forty-four pairs there has never been a clue...not a trace...no one has ever heard from any of them ever again. Neither the father nor the grown child. In each and every case, the father and, subsequently, the adult child literally vanished into thin air."

"And, lemme guess, there's always a dark stranger," Dan suggested.

"In every single one of the adult children cases, there is a mysterious person who could be interpreted to be something like a dark stranger or foreigner," Jack said. "In many of the cases, witnesses characterize this mystery person precisely as quote, a dark stranger, unquote."

"OK, I'll bite," Dan said. "And the physics books?"

"Only nineteen hits there." Ginger said. "But keep in mind that the majority of the kids went missing before the physics books were even published in the early 90's. Our mystery man would have had to have been a time traveler to get them the books before they were published."

# Chapter 25

*November 27, 2007*

## Charleston

Majorana stood by Cy's window, looking out over the gardens, remembering back to another time, another world. "So therefore, I was at one minute on a ship just by the side of L'isola di Capri and the next minute I find myself to be fished out of the same sea by a stranger speaking a language I had not never heard before."

"And, you expect me to believe this, right?"

Franco shrugged. "The base principles are clear here, Cy. I will present the possibility as I know it. And you will accept my offer or you will refuse it. Is entirely voluntary on your part. There is no need for you to know all the particularities."

So, Cy sat back and let the self-proclaimed Franco Majorana tell him, uninterrupted, of a physicist's dream. Of a noble experiment gone awry. And of an opportunity for Cy. One he had the ability to accept or reject: the ability to seek greater happiness in a way he had never dreamed. To possibly seek 'a better place,' as Majorana laid it out.

*If* he could bring himself to believe it wasn't instead the preposterous hallucinations of a madman.

Two hours later, Cy picked up his ringing cell phone. "Hey!"

"Hi Cy. It's MB. I got your message about your latest thoughts."

"MB, tell me how Ettore Majorana fits in to all this theory we have been discussing. As you'll remember, Carter's highlighting seemed to particularly focus on his accomplishments"

"Majorana. Now *there's* a mystery! If I remember correctly, he was a brilliant Italian physicist back in the '30's......Sicilian, I think. Contemporary of Bohr and Anderson. Wrote a handful of important papers on symmetry, spin, and sub-atomic particles. He kept turning down opportunities and accolades in the early '30's, and, then, tragically he died. Suicide or swept away at sea. Something like that. Nobody ever satisfactorily explained it. There was even some discussion that maybe he was kidnapped to work on atomic bombs by one or another set of countries. I think in fact there was a recent book by an Italian writer claiming that he may have hidden out in a monastery to avoid being involved in the development of the atomic bomb. I think the author believed he died there, in the monastery, not too long ago. In any case, he was, to my knowledge, never seen again."

Cy didn't respond.

She went on. "I know there's a 'Majorana Project' today associated with the Pacific Northwest National Library, named in his honor. And I think there's an 'Ettore Majorana Foundation and Centre for Scientific Culture' somewhere in Italy. They've dedicated a lot of work in his name and memory. I'm sure there's more on the web."

"What work was he best known for?"

"If I remember correctly, it was Majorana who showed that a complex combination of spin directions of a state of a particle could be represented in terms of a single direction."

"Which means, what to me?"

"Which *may* mean that something that has a probability of being in many places at once, at least in the quantum sense of 'spin,' can be represented in one place or momentum or direction. In layman's terms," she laughed, "maybe it can be useful in figuring out whether Schroedinger's cat is dead or alive, not both!"

"And if the spin is changed?" Cy asked quietly.

"Then the particle will be in another momentum, direction, or place."

"Precisely." Cy said.

And then all MB heard was the emptiness of a disconnected line.


Ginger dialed Carny's number as she and Jack pulled their chairs up to the desk.

"Hello," Carny's voice came out of the speaker phone.

"Hey, it's me and Jack. You called us yesterday?"

"Yeah, I thought of something that just might help you find Janet."

"Well, Carny, as we explained to you the other day, Janet's disappearance doesn't fit the other profiles that we're working on. All our other cases involve a missing person whose parent also disappeared mysteriously years earlier. With Sally and you around, we're not working on Janet's case any more. That would have to be something separate, a case you would have to hire us for......actually pay us for."

"You two obviously haven't spent much time around carnies if you believe anything could be for free! Never gave anything for free, never asked for anything for free! I'd appreciate it if you'd consider taking Janet's case as soon as you can....on my nickel."

"Can we get back to you tomorrow on the details and where to start? We're pretty pressed for the rest of the day,"

Ginger asked. "In the meantime, what was the 'something' you thought of?"

"Sure, tomorrow'll be fine. We can discuss how you want to work it then. But here's the deal: when Janet was a little girl, we had a tiger cub that I was trying to place. We secretly had it living with us, and Janet and the tiger became inseparable. Enough so that when I placed the tiger with the Colorado Springs Zoo on Cheyenne Mountain, she was heartbroken. For years, she made me take her to see it on her summer vacations."

"I guess this is obvious, but have you checked in Colorado for her?" Jack asked.

"No. Not relevant. The tiger escaped one winter. Janet was so terrified that it would die in the Rockies or be killed by hunters that she insisted we hire an outfitter to take us into the Rockies to look for it. Long story short, after about ten days of tracking, we found it, thin and weak, but still alive. Damned cat actually recognized Janet and he docilely let us pack him out.

"The zoo wouldn't take it back, and Janet wouldn't let me place it in another zoo or circus. She insisted that 'her' tiger had to go to 'a better place.' Those are the words she used, over and over again. The same words you used about Janet when you first called me. She wasn't going to let me put it back in a zoo. So we lit upon a scheme to send it to a reserve in northwestern India. It was a little tricky, and not entirely legal, but a private pilot I knew from my headhunting days, and Janet and I got him there.

"She was never happier than when she saw her tiger disappear into the jungle that day. He had been so lost and so visible when we found him in the Colorado Rockies, so vulnerable. And he looked so strong, so perfectly invisible, so at home when he casually walked into the jungle. She had always kept the William Blake poem, *The Tiger*, on the wall above her bed. You know the one, 'Tiger, tiger, burning bright?'"

"Yeah, we know it," Jack replied.

"Well, just on a hunch I checked her apartment yesterday, and the poem is gone. I don't know if she went to India or not, but taking the poem with her is a sign of something. I just don't know what. And I was hoping you'd agree to help us."

"Carny," Ginger interrupted, "you're always selling! We'll take it, we'll take the case.....Jack's nodding next to me. Let us get the work on these other cases out of the way and we'll fly up to meet with you and your sons. Maybe we'll drive up just to get the Barnums together," she laughed. "But tell us, did Janet ever give her tiger a name?"

"She was a little girl when I brought him home. When she asked me where I got him, I told her that I found him at the lost and found! So she announced as only an excited little girl can: 'Well, he's not lost any more, so I guess we have to call him Found!'"

"He never seemed more *found* than that day he casually walked into the jungle, into invisibility, into 'a better place.'"

Dan was standing at the window, hands in his pockets, staring out at the river below them. "I think I have to take this up the chain of command here in Charleston. We'll handle turning it over to the FBI. Once we've done that, two things will happen. Number one, the three of you will be besieged by domestic and international law enforcement agencies. And, number two, you will lose total control of this investigation. It will be out of your hands, and you may never know where it goes or what gets resolved."

Jack and Ginger looked thoughtfully at Dan, and then at the quiet, distracted figure of Cy, hunched in a chair looking out the window. Cy broke the silence. "How about those Panthers, huh?"

Dan laughed. "That's right, I owe you five bucks. But it was worth it. First time one of your football predictions ever worked out!"

"Hmmph," Cy responded.

"So, getting back to business, what do the three of you think we have here?" Ginger asked. "What do you really think this is all about?"

"I'll be damned if I know," Dan answered. "On the one hand, it feels like some sort of social experiment and on the other, like some sort of mad scientist. But, literally what we have here, I don't know. Given the time line, I don't see how this could possibly be one serial killer. Or even two, with one oddly following up the work of the other. I just don't know."

Cy looked up and spoke softly. "I'll tell you what you don't have. You don't have a single body. You don't have a single motive. And, you don't have a single crime."

Ginger looked shocked. "Cy, don't you mean, *we*?"

That night, Jack and Ginger walked arm in arm down Bedon's Alley, on their way home from dinner at The Oak Steakhouse.

"It's amazing what a good bottle of wine will do for your courage," Jack mused.

"Maybe he's not home," she added hopefully.

Jack knocked on the door. "Let's get this over with as quickly as possible."

There was noise on the other side of the door and a disgruntled looking Cy opened the door to them.

"I thought we agreed to get together tomorrow."

"We did," Jack said. "But there is something we need to go over with you before that meeting."

"Yes?" Cy asked.

"Can we come in, Cy?" Ginger said. "Is everything all right?"

"Oh, yeah." He opened the door wider. "Sorry. Come on in. What's up?"

Jack peered around the house. "Cy, this is personal, not business."

Ginger looked flustered. "Well, it *relates* to business...sort of," casting a sideways glance at Jack.

"C'mon, you two, spit it out." Cy seemed distracted, but finally came up with a rare smile.

"It's about us," Jack said. "We know you have a strict rule against personal involvement at the agency," looking over at Ginger. "And," he lied, "we both respect you too much to do anything behind your back."

"The truth is, Cy, that Jack and I have fallen in love and we want to be honest with you. I know everybody in town assumes we are lovers. But, because of your standards, there's no way we'd go public without your approval"

Cy looked from one to the other and stifled a laugh. "Are the two of you asking me for permission to have sex?"

Ginger blushed. "Damn it, Cy!" Jack blurted out. "Don't make this harder than it is. Obviously we're both adults."

"More or less," Ginger added under her breath.

Jack continued. "What we're here for is to see if you're going to require one of us to resign from the agency."

Cy smiled at the irony. "Funny you should bring this up. The events of the last month have got me thinking about 'in what direction and when' the agency evolves. The two of you are great together. I have great confidence in how you handle cases. You two are the future of our practice, not me. Our clients would be the worse if we split you up.

"Frankly, I thought the two of you had been sleeping together for months. And, I was well past being bothered by it. Why don't the two of you trot off to....uh...wherever you're going. And let's let things evolve among us as they evolve."

Laughing, he opened the door for them.

Ginger hugged Cy at the front door. "Thanks, Cy, you're a doll. I've been so worried about this." Taking Jack's hand, she walked down the steps.

Cy smiled and looked down at each of them in turn. "Good-bye," he said. And closed the door.

Ginger froze and murmured under her breath. "Good-bye?"

She and Jack walked in silence back to Jack's place.

"I don't like that," Ginger said. "I don't like that at all."

"What do you mean? It couldn't have gone better. He gave us carte blanche to do whatever we want."

"That's part of what's bothering me. It was almost as if he were resigning. Almost as if a door opened and we released him. Instead of vice versa."

"Ging, I think you are reading too much into it," said Jack.

"Didn't you notice there were two wine glasses in the kitchen? And I definitely heard Cy say something before he opened the door for us. I know I heard someone upstairs while you were talking to Cy."

"OK. So what do you think is going on?"

"I don't know for sure. We've both noticed that he's been even more down than usual since his return. And why would Cy say 'good-bye' to us?"

"As opposed to?"

"'Good-night' or 'see you tomorrow,' or 'thanks for dropping by.' No, the more I think about it the less I like it." She reached up to kiss Jack good-night at his door. "I think I'm going to go for a walk, honey."

"I thought you were staying over. We're not celebrating?"

"I'm too worried about Cy. I think it's best if I go now."

"If you're going to go sleuthing, I'll get my South Beach Panama hat and we'll go in disguise. Together."

"That's a good idea. While you're at it, bring me your leather jacket and a baseball cap."

They took up positions in the shadows at either end of Bedon's Alley, Ginger sitting against a fig vine encrusted garage on Tradd Street and Jack hidden in the arched ruins, now a parking lot, at Elliott Street. They each had a clear view of Cy's front door.

At 1:15 AM., lights started going out one by one. The front door opened and two figures emerged. The first was a shorter man in a dark coat. And then Cy himself. They glanced around for a second and headed North, toward Jack's end of the alley.

The two were walking purposefully. They quickly turned left onto Elliot Street and then right on to Church. Ginger quietly followed at a safe distance. She was surprised that Jack was nowhere to be seen. As the two men crossed Broad and glanced around, Ginger's heart caught in her throat. She realized that Cy's companion looked like the descriptions and the sketch of the dark stranger. Reaching back for her gun, she noticed Jack up ahead on Church on the opposite side of the street and she relaxed. She couldn't help but notice that Cy and the smaller man seemed comfortable with each other. It appeared to be an amiable walk between friends. It didn't have the appearance of an abduction.

The two men passed Chalmers and turned right onto Queen Street. The two detectives followed as close as they dared. On opposite sides of the street, hidden in the shadows. As Ginger peered around the corner down Queen, she saw Cy disappear into Philadelphia Alley and she began to run. Jack quickly caught up with her and the two stopped and peered around the corner down the alley together. Cy and the stranger had reached an archway in the Footlight Players' Theater wall. They were talking as the stranger took Cy's arm.

Jack and Ginger each held their breath as they saw the two men step up into the archway.

They looked at each other and began racing down the alley. They reached the archway at the same moment, looked and saw....nothing. There was nothing there. There were no open doors, no windows. There was no evidence of either man. Just a permanently bolted door and a blank wall.

Cy was gone.

# Chapter 26

*December 20, 2007*

**Berkeley, California**

Mary Beth, calmer now, read the letter through for a third time:

> *November 26, 2007*
> *My dear Mary Beth,*
>     *If you are reading this letter, then much of what we have discussed over the past weeks has been very helpful. More importantly, I now know your skepticism to have been unwarranted. And, of course, it shows once and for all that you were always right. We are---or now, more correctly, were---in the same profession all along! Less importantly, you will never see me again.........but let me explain:*
>     *If you are reading this letter, a man claiming to be Franco Majorana, the self-proclaimed nephew/graduate student of Ettore Majorana, claims that he and his Uncle*

*Ettore discovered a way, back in the 1930's, to apply the quantum mechanic concept of spin to classical size objects and transport them to a parallel universe. In fact, to a parallel Earth. I believe he is, in fact, Ettore Majorana himself, but he is so embarrassed by part of what he has done, that he pushed the blame for some of the practical applications on to what I believe to be his mythical nephew. But I can't prove this. Ettore himself, or the nephew, or some combination, it doesn't matter, for the story is fantastic in any case. To be efficient, I will refer to him as "Franco" throughout this letter, even though I believe him actually to be the Sicilian physicist, Ettore Majorana.*

*Hopefully, what I am about to relate to you will be sufficient for you to replicate what I have learned and what they have accomplished and to enable you to make a quantum jump forward in the knowledge of modern physics. "Franco" claims that they used the concept you explained to me, using a single direction representation of spin from Majorana's 1932 paper, to explain the appearance, disappearance, and reappearance of quantum particles and anti-particles. Ettore was very frustrated that the rest of the physics world didn't agree with him on the startling empirical potentials for his discovery. Accordingly, they began experimenting on their own with classical size objects. The key was to change the spin of larger and larger objects by precise, quantum jumps, in direction and momentum, and, if done precisely, they would literally disappear. He* hypothesized, and has discussed with me, that these objects---just like quantum particles, disappear from here and simultaneously reappear in a parallel universe. He claims physicists who have hypothesized a parallel universe a tiny dimension away from ours are correct.

And "Franco's" evidence for this, he claims, is that he---or Ettore---or he and Ettore--- have traveled back and forth between the two universes more or less continuously since then. The first disappearance was the one well-known to the physics world when, in 1938, he disappeared from the deck of the steamship off the coast of Capri. He has described something like an idyllic parallel earth in this parallel universe. And he has been performing an idealistic experiment to make people on "your" earth happier. He started from the hypothesis, born of a childhood experience, that if you took an abusive father away from his abused child around the time they were ten years old, that the child would grow up to be happy. Or at least happier. So he began transporting such fathers to the parallel universe, quite against their will, in the 1950's, and continued for decades. Preposterous as this may sound, he claims that each and every father, within a year, was happier where he was, and that none requested to return to "your" universe.

Unhappily, however, for both Franco and all the children left behind as they grew up, many of the adult children continued, even in the absence of further abuse, to be unhappy. To be continuing to seek something in their lives *that they couldn't find. So Franco claims that he began to transport those grown children, on a purely voluntary basis, to the parallel earth, where he claimed they would be much happier. Where they would reconcile with a now-repentant father, and where they would enjoy a homogenous culture of genuinely, happy people. A people who he claims are uniformly content with their lives and with other people.*

*Among his satisfied "clients" are Carter Ellis and Robert Flynn, the two missing persons cases that put Jack and Ginger and me on to the physics parallels in the first place. Curiously, he claims no knowledge of Tim Johnson, George's L.A. missing person that provided us the parallel about all the fathers. And, of course, as you've no doubt guessed, my own father has been there since he vanished on the way back from a Braves, Cincinnati Reds baseball game that night in Milwaukee back in 1965.*

*He all but describes a Shangri La when he discusses the parallel earth and parallel universe. And the possibility for parental reconciliation is, of course, quite appealing. So appealing, in fact, that yours truly, like many others before me, has agreed to accompany him tomorrow, November 27th. This was not a decision that I took lightly. You know me better than most. You know that I have not been a happy person. You knew that my father had been abusive, and had abandoned me. But even I, until Franco---or Ettore---had me face it, was unaware of how much it colored my ability to enjoy my life. Even my choice of careers clearly was an attempt to help damaged people in a way I have been unable to help myself. The fiasco in Charleston last month was a kind of last straw. I was unable to keep Clyde from stabbing that poor young girl, Ann, the roommate of the girl he had killed earlier. My shots were too late. And I only succeeded in wounding, and permanently disabling the asshole. And for my part, I could only watch helplessly as Ann died in my arms. I'm sure Charleston will do fine with Jack and Ginger running the agency without me.*

*So, MB, if you're reading this letter, good bye and all the best. Our friendship was one of the best things that I had on "your earth." Hopefully, something like it will be the norm where I will now find myself. And hopefully there's something in Franco's claims and in our discussions that will enable you to bring Ettore's work and, hopefully your extensions, to public acceptance. For you, if for nobody else!*

*Yours "forever,"*

*(signed) Cy*

*P.S. Oh, obviously there's nothing in this letter that "proves" that Franco isn't some sort of delusional crackpot who merely made off with me after I wrote this letter. Here's the proof you will need: unbeknownst to anybody but her, I left two letters with Bailey Lee Ellis, Carter's mother. Her instructions were simple and clear. If nobody named Franco came to ask her for a letter addressed to Dan O'Reilly, the Charleston homicide detective, by January 31st, she was to mail that letter to Dan and destroy this letter to you.*

*The letter to Dan details what I know that might help in catching "Franco" if he, in fact, turns out to be nothing more than a persuasive serial killer, and I, his latest victim. If, on the other hand, Franco came to Bailey Lee for the letter to Dan, she was to give it to him, and then secretly drop this letter to you in the mail. If Franco abducted me, or otherwise failed to get me successfully to the "other" earth, Dan would soon be reading his letter from me accusing Franco, and you would never receive this one from me. However, if I am successfully on the parallel earth, I have "confessed" to Franco about my lack of trust and potential indiscretion, and he has hurried back to Charleston, intercepted, and presumably destroyed, my letter to Dan that would have incriminated him in my abduction, and triggered the mailing, instead, of this letter to you. Absent a mistake by Bailey Lee, which you can check on, your receipt of this letter is absolute proof that I no longer inhabit the same earth as you.*

*P.P.S. Can you please send a copy of this letter with the inserted note on to Jack and Ginger? I'd appreciate it. They also deserve to have closure on this.*

# POSTSCRIPT

## *January 11, 2008*

Ginger looked up from her stack of "preparing for your journey to India" books when the phone rang. She looked over at Jack and shrugged. "I got it."

"Hello."

"Ginger?"

"Yeah?"

"It's George, George Foster out in L.A. How are you two guys doing?"

She slipped the phone back in and put it on speaker. "We're fine. It's odd, of course. We're still getting used to its being our agency and still struggling with the circumstances around Cy's disappearance. Never thought we'd see him happy. Certainly didn't think we'd ever be the beneficiaries of his happiness. 'Course, we still haven't actually *seen* him happy," she laughed.

"We're swamped with business after all the publicity. Business *and* crank calls! The FBI is still skeptical and harassing us occasionally, but until they come up with a better explanation than Cy's letter to Mary Beth, we're just staying out of it. For her part, Mary Beth is excited about extending Majorana's theory, but still skeptical. It's fun to watch her chasing her tail about all this. On the one hand, she doesn't believe it's possible; but on the other, like all of us, she doesn't see any other possible explanation either. She's stuck going after the physics part. And she knows it's exactly what Cy wanted to stick her with. Last laugh and all!"

Only silence came out of the phone.

"George? You still there?"

"George?"

"Well guys, that's why I was calling you. Last laughs and all. The FBI may not be quite done with you. Or Mary Beth."

Jack looked up from scratching Barnum's neck, "What's this about, George? What's come up?"

"Tim Johnson's body. The Mexican police just found it down in Baja. He's been dead for months. Drowned. They called me as a courtesy. Said they'd be calling the FBI next. I thought you two would want to know."